STORY STUDIOS PRESENTS:

CHANGING OF THE GUARD

Scott A. Story & Benita G. Story

Books by Scott A. Story & Benita G. Story

Johnny Saturn: Synns of the Father
Johnny Saturn: Homeland Insecurity
Johnny Saturn: Intelligent Redesign

All titles available wherever books and eBooks are sold.

Join our mailing list and keep informed on our publishing schedule and our newsletter!

STORY STUDIOS PRESENTS:
CHANGING OF THE GUARD

Scott A. Story & Benita G. Story

Copyright 2004 and 2019 by Scott A. Story, Benita G. Story, and Story Studios

Cover design and interior illustrations by Scott A. Story

ISBN-13 978-0-9817393-5-9
ISBN-10 0-9817393-5-0

www.johnnysaturn.com, & www.scottastory.com

DEDICATION

Scott and Benita would like to thank the following people arranged in no particular order:

Ian Thomas Healy for publishing advice
Lance Stahlberg for formatting advice
A.P. Fuchs for publishing and formatting advice
Geoff Edwards for proofreading skills
Sandy Ferguson for proofreading skills
All our fans for supporting and encouraging us for over a decade and counting

TABLE OF CONTENTS

PUBLISHING HISTORY AND TIMELINE

The stories collected in this anthology were all written in continuity with the *Johnny Saturn* comics. It is not necessary to have read those comics to enjoy these tales, but if you have you may be interested to know how they all line up chronologically.

First up is the comic short "Time & Johnny Saturn," then the events in the comic *Spire City Noir* #1.

"Death on the Docks," published in *Johnny Saturn Unlimited* no. 11 to 17 follows, occurring before the regular *Johnny Saturn* series (no. 1 to 5) begins.

"Wages of Synn," previously unpublished, happens immediately after the events of *Johnny Saturn* no. 5.

"Halo of Graves," previously unpublished, happens concurrently with *Johnny Saturn* no. 6, and tells the same story.

"Being Johnny Saturn," published in *Johnny Saturn: Homeland Insecurity* (Story Studios 2012) takes place between *Johnny Saturn* no. 6 and 7.

"Johnny Saturn and the Old Wolf," previously published in *Metahumans vs. Werewolves* (Coscom Entertainment, 2013), and published again in *Johnny Saturn: Intelligent Redesign* (Story Studios, 2015), takes place not long after the events of the comic *Spire City Noir* no. 2 and 3, and *Johnny Saturn* no. 8 to 17.

"Skorned" appeared in *The Pen & Cape Society Presents the Good Fight 4: Homefront* (Local Hero Press, 2018).

"I Always Wanted a Giant Robot," originally published in *Metahumans vs. Robots* (Lion's Share Press, 2014) and again in the collected *City of the Broken Gate* (Story Studios, 2016).

"City of the Broken Gate" was published in *City of the Broken Gate* (Story Studios, 2016).

"Le Monde Belle" appeared in *The Pen & Cape Society Presents the Good Fight 5: The Golden Age* (Local Hero Press, 2019)

After these events, the events in the second half of the short comic "Time & Johnny Saturn" happen, published in *Johnny Saturn: Intelligent Redesign* (Story Studios, 2015).

WHO'S WHO

There are a lot of characters who make appearances in this collection, so here is a complete listing of all the people who make appearances.

Note, "m." means member of, and "l." means leader of the group in question.

Abraham Rosenblatt, Esq.: J. William Medal's partner at law

Alaric the Axe: m. Iron Brigade, super-strong brute enforcer, metavillain

Anvil: m. Squadron Premiere, anthropomorphic anvil, metahero

Bacterium Twins: m. Scavengers, metavillains

Boltz: m. Iron Brigade, metavillain

Bombastic aka Nils Zilcher: m. Team Saturn, enforcer, bodyguard, former villain

Candle Man: m. Vigilante Association, Golden Age metahero

Captain Barometer aka Gary Redman: m. Squadron Premiere, retired metahero

Carley: Mayor Medal's personal assistant

Celerity: m. Iron Brigade, speedster, metavillain

Charge: m. Squadron Premiere, electrical metahero

Charles "Doc" Ledmun: l. mole people, street doctor

Coat Man, the: Homeless poet

Crocodile King aka Sobek: Ruler of undercity crocodiles

Deco: m. Squadron Premiere, power armored hero

Decorum aka Patty Angstrom: Cloth telekinesis metahero

Dr. Somnambulism: m. Iron Brigade, sleep inducing metavillain

Drunken Prophet, the: m. Scavengers, metavillain

En Camera: m. Iron Brigade, remote viewing robot

Eris: The goddess of discord and chaos

Eustice Freemantle: British scientist, rebel theorist

Fenris: Ancient werewolf spirit

Fiernor: Ancient werewolf spirit, father of Fenris

Gerhard Synn: Nazi industrialist, Horatio Synn's father

Ghost of Benedetti: m. Squadron Premiere, Manifest ghost of metahero

Harry "Brez" Brezneski: Lt. Det. SCPD 23RD Precinct

Hideous Handmade: m. Scavengers, metavillain

Horatio Synn, Dr.: Terrorist, Industrialist. Persephone's father, John Underhall's father-in-law

Hotfoot: m. Squadron Premiere, speedster metahero

Hyperspace I: m. Squadron Premiere, cosmic powered metahero

Richard Rush: Elderly writer

Rogue Statesman: m. Iron Brigade, multiple personality killer, metavillain

Ronald "Corky" Cork: Bartender, retired police officer

Samantha Rosenblatt: Abraham Rosenblatt's daughter

Sandra Nagachi, Dr.: Medical doctor to the Squadron Premiere

Scary Men: Paranormal thugs

Shadowcowl aka Dennis Fulchres: Metahero with magic cowl

Shiela Rosenblatt: Abraham Rosenblatt's wife

Silverwing: m. Squadron Premiere, 1950's metahero reborn

Skold's Brank: m. Scavengers, metavillain

Skyshark: m. Squadron Premiere, ghost haunted power armor

Staff of Life aka Victoria Shelbourne: m. Squadron Premiere, m. Team Saturn, inventor, technologist, academic, metahero

Stellar II: Cosmic metahero

Subwoofer: m. Iron Brigade, sonic metavillain

Sureshot III: Archery metahero

Tactical aka Nikolai Demetr: l. Iron Brigade, crime boss, war criminal

Tailor, aka Harvey Torres: m. Team Saturn, brilliant costume and armor builder

Tapeworm: m. Scavengers, metavillain

Tara 5.0 aka Tara Wissenschaft: Android created by Dr. Wissenschaft

Terra Rosa: m. Iron Brigade, metavillain

Thomas Buchanan: Greg Buchanan's father, police officer

Tidal Force: Metahero

Tilt: m. Squadron Premiere, Kinetic metahero

Titanium Tom: l. Squadron Premiere, arch-conservative team leader

Topiary: m. Iron Brigade, vegetable metavillain

Triops, aka Denny Chamblis: m. Squadron Premiere, m. Team Saturn, Alien hybrid psychic, metahero

Tripartite: m. Scavengers, metavillain son of Nhorgiel

Utopian aka Brian Farrady: l. Squadron Premiere, supremely powerful metahero

Vamario: Customs official in Monaco

Velvet Cipher: m. Squadron Premiere, meta-spy

Ventilator Angel: m. Scavengers, Vox Malaise's enforcer, beyond horrible, metavillain

Vince: Persephone's driver in Monaco

Vox Malaise: l. Scavengers, demonologist, porn star

Warmonger: m. Iron Brigade, perspective-twisting metavillain

William Miller, Staff Sergeant: U. S. Army, Camp Darby, Pisa, Italy

William Strathmorne, Judge: Spire City Superior Court 3

DEATH ON THE DOCKS

Ramirez "Manny" Calabria limped along I-60 out of Spire City in the breakdown lane, the part of the interstate posted with "No Traffic or Non-Motorized Vehicles" signs. Manny was having the grand whopper of all bad days, and he did not care particularly which laws he was violating. Normally a rakishly handsome fellow, Manny's bellhop uniform was filthy and torn, his face was bruised and swelling, and one of his bicuspids was certainly loose. Manny had to get out of Spire City.

Manny's evening had definitely begun better than it had ended. During the day, Manny was head bellhop at the Northanger Arms, a posh Spire City hotel; at night, Manny ran the Charlie Blockers, an assortment of ne'er-do-wells for hire that all shared the not-so-singular distinction of having served time in Bolden Penitentiary's C Block outside Spire City. Well, all the boys but Lamar, but that was not worth rechristening the Charlie Blockers.

More often than not, the Charlie Blockers were on the payroll of Dr. Horatio Synn. Synn was the Brazilian owner of the multi-national corporation Synn-Tech, and an adventurer; well, Synn was an adventurer, if "adventurer" could be taken to mean world-class smuggler, terrorism financier, black market arms dealer, developer of illegal technology, money launderer, and the high-level partner of many major North American, South American, and European crime cartels. The good doctor had engaged in increasingly darker and more dangerous dealings as the years passed, and his personal actions had become more and more erratic. None of the men could spell or define the term "psychotic," but they knew it when they saw it. For Synn, the Charlie Blockers had gone from moving simple contraband to arson, corpse disposal, extortion, and murder.

Tonight, the Charlie Blockers were working security on the Spire City wharves. They awaited a shipment that was to be delivered in the dead of night by some dark boat that was never entered into the harbor master's logs. Clouds filled the late April sky, their steely underbellies reflecting light from the city beneath. There would be no moon to light this night.

Spire City was perched on Sorrow Bay, on the northeastern shore of Lake

1

Avernus. Avernus was the southernmost and smallest of the Great Lakes, and its connection to Lake Michigan to the north joined Spire City not only to the Great Lakes Watershed and the St. Lawrence Seaway, but to the Mississippi River by way of the Big Opossum River. Spire City was large and metropolitan, yet, like so many Midwestern rust belt cities, it had an air of dilapidation and sadness about it, a hint of brighter days long gone. Wired into the country by Interstate 60, which afforded the city access to both the east and west coasts, and fed by a web of rusting train tracks, Spire City was a city that was easier to describe not by what it was, but by what it was not. Spire City was not quite as tall as Chicago, or as rough as Gary, as poor as Detroit, as dangerous as Los Angeles or Miami, or as sleepy as Indianapolis. Its music scene lacked the character of Indianapolis' Naptown sound, Detroit's rhythm and blues, Chicago's blues, or New Orleans's zydeco and jazz. The Spire City Ferrets never made it to the Super Bowl, and the Spire City Opossums never played in the NBA playoffs.

———

Manny and his twelve men stood at ease but vigilant as the ugly, black, lake freighter docked. This boat, stained with tar and crusted with barnacles, was built to ship dry goods around the Great Lakes, and the vessel had no name and probably had never known the wonders of paint. Newer vessels than this one already had made their final voyages to the docks of Bombay, there decommissioned and scrapped by the acetylene torch. The boat's winch lowered the last of the crates to the docks, and its silent crew pulled in their lines and cast off. The boat's twin diesels had never powered down, nor had its ragged crew disembarked. No manifests were signed, and no words were exchanged.

Manny stationed his men around the three unmarked crates stacked atop a wooden palette and reinforced with iron bars. All the Charlie Blockers had to do now was wait for Synn's men to arrive and collect their goods.

Or, they would have waited, if Johnny Saturn had not shown up.

Manny grimaced. You would think thirteen men, all armed with handguns and assorted brass knuckles, pipes, chains, and truncheons, and easily could have dispatched one vigilante. Most other vigilantes, sure, no problem—but there was nothing ordinary about Johnny Saturn.

The old mystery man appeared as if from nowhere, and he plowed into the Charlie Blockers like a bulldozer through a flower bed. Thugs flew right and left, and none of the Charlie Blockers could get their bearings nor mount a decent defense. City tough guys got tossed here and there, and they littered the ground with head wounds and broken bones. Johnny's massive, gauntleted fists dealt out a lightning array of jabs, cuts, crosses, and uppercuts that would have dazzled most pro boxers, let alone the outmatched Charlie Blockers.

If Manny had been anyone else—preferably someone at a safe distance!—he

2

might have admired Johnny Saturn. Six foot six, as wide as a house and as beefy as a porterhouse, Johnny had spent over a decade dispensing his brand of justice on Spire City's benighted streets. Some people grew feeble as they got older, but some few grew meaner and harder, and Johnny Saturn had decades of grizzled mean and stringy hard saved up and earning compound interest. Dressed in dark blues and blue greens, masked and cowled, the aging mystery man's gauntlets incorporated cruel brass knuckles into their design, and his boots seemed big enough to stomp city blocks.

Manny, not one for fisticuffs, was the first Charlie Blocker with the presence of mind to pull his gun, a .38 special with its serial numbers filed off and its grip wrapped in black electrician's tape. He had wanted to plug Johnny Saturn for years, and Manny owed the old vigilante for a wealth of dental work the thug had undergone. Manny fired, yet the old warhorse had turned sideways against the shot, barely dodging the slug, and Manny's bullet hit Ol' Dickey in the arm.

"Oops!"

"You sonavabitch!" yelped Ol' Dickey, "You shot me!"

Bam! Manny was out of the world, out of his head, and gone to some "other" place. He'd seen a huge fist flying at his jaw, then nothing. Nothing lasted forever, though, and then the world came roaring back—a world of hurt! Manny saw his feet loosely flopping beyond nerveless legs, and he realized that he was being dragged along the docks. He tried to get his bearings, but all he could see were Johnny Saturn's churning legs. No one was coming to Manny's rescue, because all his men were laid out on the dock, unconscious!

Thud—thud—thud! Manny tried to wriggle free as Johnny dragged him by the collar up a flight of iron stairs.

————

At twenty and nineteen, respectively, Shadowcowl and Decorum had been metaheroes for almost a year. Armed with youthful righteousness, endless energy, and tremendous powers, the two young heroes had the world by the tail. Get a mask and codename, and suddenly you were like a rock star, hanging around with Spire City's meta elite, and all doors suddenly were open to you. The two of them had met and teamed up with luminaries such as the Utopian, Tilt, and Musclebound, and they had joined in battles against the likes of Alaric the Axe, Skorn, Bombastic, and Topiary. As far as Shadowcowl was concerned, life above the clouds could not be grander.

It was not all just seeing and being seen. They two had faced real danger, fought people who would happily kill them, and saved scores of hapless civilians from dire threats. When the morning came and the masks came off, but the adrenaline still pumped wildly through their veins, Shadowcowl and Decorum usually fell to wild sex. Truthfully, they did not even like each other all that much, but when their blood was up they tore into each other with savage abandon. They destroyed beds, bedrooms, and whole apartments in their couplings. The sheer joy of being young, alive, and powerful always overcame them. No, they did not like each other much, but they needed each other, and that was enough.

Shadowcowl, also known as Dennis Fulchres, wore a magic hooded cloak, one that made him ghostlike and untouchable. If you wanted to get to him, it was through the cloak or nothing. With the cloak, he could also fly, and the cold touch of his gloved, spectral hand inflicted mind-numbing terror on its victims. Hardened killers cringed before his ethereal touch, and brutal thugs were reduced to whimpering helplessness.

Decorum, aka Patty Angstrom had the hip-swinging swagger of a woman who knew how to move: She was hot in that "bad news" way that made men drool and women sneer. She wore a purple spandex body suit that showed her curves to best advantage, and exposed enough décolletage to distract dead men. As per the current fashion, she wore her brunette hair in that crazy, chopped up style that reminded viewers of an abandoned bird's nest. Her power was over clothing. With a flick of her hand, Decorum had the metahuman ability to blow the clothes off an enemy, or turn his own clothing against him. High school vengeance had turned into a thriving crime-fighting career for young Patty.

Soaring above the city under Shadowcowl's power, the two metaheroes settled into the shadows atop one of the giant cranes that towered over the wharves. There had been a battle below, and Charlie Blockers were laid out like bowling pins. From the metas' vantage on high, the two young heroes watched an imposing old vigilante man drag a thug up wrought iron stairs and onto a warehouse's roof. The thug struggled uselessly as he was pulled across the filthy, tar-papered roof. A billboard towered above the mystery man and his prisoner, one that proclaimed "Spend a special evening with Persephone Helios, Nobel laureate, art collector, and philanthropist, May 11, hosted by Spire City Public Radio." Persephone's well-known visage looked out from its placard, unmoved by the scene below.

Shadowcowl and Decorum were intrigued—the situation unfolding below was so hardcore that they had to watch!

Shadowcowl watched as the giant effortlessly lifted the thug skyward, as if to toss him off the roof. The young hero was sure he knew the big guy's name—it was "Johnny" something, something, something … it was a planet ... *Johnny Saturn!* That was it! The young vigilante remembered now — Johnny Saturn was a non-powered, old-style, street-level avenger; nothing like the modern metaheroes, with their powers and flight and wild battles above the city. No, Johnny Saturn was more like the cowboys in old Westerns, fascinating in a Sergio Leone, "The Good, The Bad, and the Ugly," sort of way.

"What are you going to do?" demanded Manny dismissively, "Dangle me over the street and try to scare me into talking? Metaheroes don't kill, everyone knows that!

I've got nothing to say to you, Saturn!"

Johnny Saturn did not crack a smile, and Shadowcowl figured that Saturn's face would break and fall off if he ever attempted a grin.

"We're about two stories up, Manny," replied Johnny Saturn. "I'm going to throw you off the roof, and then drag you back up here, again and again, until you talk. Or," Saturn added as an afterthought, "until you die. I'm pretty sure you'll talk by the second time you hit the street."

"But … but … metaheroes don't kill!?" cried the thug.

"Manny, I'm not a metahero," said Johnny as he carried Manny to the roof's edge. "I'm a mystery man. Mystery men, unfortunately, sometimes have to kill in the pursuit of justice. I figure if I give you a good toss I can get you past all the stuff that might break your fall."

Johnny reared back for the toss while Manny squirmed overhead.

"Wait! Wait, you bastard," shrieked Manny. "You're crazy! I'll talk! I'll talk!"

"Are you sure?" asked Johnny. "It would be a lot more fun to send you sailing a few times."

Manny babbled like a broken bully who had just gotten his comeuppance. He was working for Dr. Synn. No, he did not know what Synn was up to. Yes, Synn should be here soon, or else his men. No, Manny did not know what was in the crates below. Before Johnny let him down, Manny was a snotting, sniveling, weeping mess. Manny had tossed his fair share of victims off roofs in his time, but he doubted he would ever have the balls to do it again! Turnabout was not fair play!

Johnny listened to Manny's monologue, barely having to supply any prompts. "Okay, Manny, enough. The cops will be here to collect your boys and whatever is in those crates anytime now. You can go to jail with them, if you want, but, if I were you, I'd get out of town for a while. Spire City is about to get very hot."

Manny did not have to be told twice. He was off that roof, down the stairs, and out of there. Johnny stayed behind, watching the scene below. His guess was correct, and police cars began rolling in, surrounding the crates and the ring of unconscious Charlie Blockers that circled them.

Shadowcowl could not stand it any longer. He and Decorum leaped from their hiding place on the crane above and glided down to join Johnny Saturn.

"Dude! That was so old-school! Wow!" exclaimed Shadowcowl.

"Yeah, gramps, you got all medieval on their butts!" added Decorum.

Johnny Saturn did not turn to look at the newcomers, nor did he flinch in surprise at their arrival. Shadowcowl was impressed. The old mystery man had known they were there the entire time.

———

The Spire City Police Department arrived on the scene with all the pomp and circumstance of a circus coming to town, their strobing lights painting the night with red and blue, and their sirens wailing an ear-splitting cacophony. Six patrol cars skidded to a halt, effectively enveloping the prone Charlie Blockers. Many of the twelve thugs were already regaining their senses as the police, shielded behind their cruisers with their guns raised, took position around them.

Detective Greg Buchanan, or "Pretty Boy Buchanan" as his fellow cops called him, stepped forward. He was a homicide detective with the 23rd Precinct. At 27, Buchanan was handsome, but not that he would have known it. Some would say that he resembled a young Brad Pitt, but only if Pitt walked around enveloped in a dark cloud of gloom, hid his face from the world behind dark sunglasses that he never took off, and wore his facial hair in a trendy goatee and moustache combo. No matter where the sun shone, this Buchanan moved as a dark, trench-coated ghost in a world of eternal night.

"Move in, officers," he commanded. "The suspects are already down. Restrain them and read them their rights. Someone call in a paddy wagon, and an ambulance too."

Buchanan pushed over one of the Charlie Blockers with his foot. Lamar rolled onto his back and groaned.

"Who did this to you?" asked Detective Buchanan.

"Shatunn … Sjonny Shatunn…" Lamar helpfully offered up, despite a swollen lip, a mouthful of blood, and the loss of his front teeth.

"Figures," said Buchanan with the air of a man who almost was bored into somnambulance. While the cops secured the Charlie Blockers, the detective broke open one of the crates and looked within. (He felt confident in doing this, because he knew a judge who was always willing to hand out search warrants retroactively.) Buchanan knew what to expect inside the crate, and he was not disappointed: bizarre weaponry, circuitry, and assorted rare and expensive raw materials. The sort of supplies that an illegal cybernetics lab would need. There were also freezers that Greg knew would contain a mixed collection of black market human tissues: eyes, hearts, livers, and much, much more.

"Wissenschaft…" muttered Buchanan.

————

"That was so cool," said Decorum, "the way you shook that guy down. He really thought you were going to throw him off the roof!" Decorum momentarily had forgotten her affected swagger, and now she was all admiring fan-girl.

Johnny Saturn showed no interest in talking to the young metaheroes, and he walked away without acknowledging them, heading for the stairs down. It was not his style to jump from rooftop to rooftop, as modern metaheroes did, and he preferred elevators, stairs, or ladders - in that order - when he could find them.

"Wait," cried Shadowcowl, heading Johnny off. "We never get to meet real old-timers like you! Shouldn't we join forces or something? I want to see you kick some ass like they did back in the day!"

"Yeah," added Decorum. "All we ever fight is metavillains, and those guys fold or run all the time. Let's do a team up!"

Johnny Saturn stopped and surveyed the two. He frowned deeply, and, even though this was his default expression, his eyes conveyed the impression that he was not pleased. Truly, admired Shadowcowl, no one had ever worn a sour disposition with more dignity or arrogance than did Johnny Saturn.

Johnny stepped around Shadowcowl, and the old vigilante pulled a white plastic bottle from under his belt. He upended the container, spilling a half-dozen or so white pills into his mouth, chewing them without the benefit of anything to wash them down. His actions were not self-conscious; it was as if he did this multiple times a day without giving it thought.

"Dude, what are you poppin' there?" asked Shadowcowl.

"Yeah, like, that can't be healthy," added Decorum abashedly.

Johnny grunted. "Pain pills. If you kids live as long as I have, then you'll probably be as full of pins, sutures, plates, and staples as I am." Johnny then said, "Out of my way, metaheroes. Go do whatever it is you do. There's a truck coming to pick these crates up, and I am going to intercept it before it gets here."

Shadowcowl grabbed Decorum around the waist, saying "Not if we get to it first!" Into the sky they shot, leaving Johnny Saturn on the roof.

"Dammit," swore the big mystery man. "Damn, damn, damn…"

———

If you were to ask him, Dr. Horatio Synn could not have told you why he liked Spire City. He had business holdings here, but then he had holdings all over the world. His daughter kept a condominium here, but then she also had homes in Buenos Aires, Monaco, and numerous other cities. Dr. Synn's son-in-law called Spire City home, but that certainly was no recommendation for this Midwestern town. Dr. Synn's father's mentor, Dr. Wissenschaft, called Spire City home, and Wissenschaft Inc. was a division of Synn Tech, so perhaps that was it.

In truth, Dr. Synn had no sentimental feelings for Spire City. It just seemed that fate (or synchronicity) brought him here again and again. The doctor could not remember when he had last visited his estate in Buenos Aires, let alone the homes he kept in Cornwall, Madrid, Hong Kong, Manhattan, Havana, and Mexico City. Spire City simply had a pull that kept bringing him back.

Dr. Synn tossed aside his last newspaper for the day (he read at least eight), and refilled his tea. Horatio Synn was a dashing figure, with a Roman nose and black, swept back hair. Slender and handsome in his early fifties, Dr. Synn was dressed impeccably in his standard white linen suit, black tie, and white fedora with a black hat band. His cane, polished ebony with a spherical silver grip, was near at hand.

Bombastic, Dr. Synn's bodyguard and enforcer, knocked politely. Dr. Synn acknowledged the hulking brute with a polite "Yes?"

"We have a problem, Dr. Synn," said the newcomer. "Your shipment has been intercepted. Apparently, Johnny Saturn took out the Charlie Blockers, and the police have surrounded the crates. They'll impound your goods once they secure the scene."

Bombastic, born Nils Zilcher, had more genetically-transposed metafuels pumping through his veins than blood, and he was so over muscled that his wrists were bigger than most men's necks. At six-feet seven inches, he was a monstrous slab of interlocking muscles from head to foot, a walking anatomy lesson, a freak of no known Nature, produced in the horror labs of Wissenschaft Inc. When wicked old Dr. Wissenschaft delivered this one back in 1992, he had gone all out, and Bombastic came with a reinforced skeletal structure, armored epidermis, and backup internal organs. Add to this a black leather bondage harness, "painted on," tight-fitting clothing with all the straps, buckles, pouches, and reinforced boots one frame could carry, and everything about Bombastic screamed "1990's." Include an arsenal of knives, spikes, throwing stars, guns, grenades, and bandoliers, and you had the man. Bombastic had long, flowing hair because he believed it made him look like a famous movie barbarian.

"This will not do, Mr. Bombastic," said Synn matter-of-factly. In Dr. Synn's world, those crates were his property, and if the police had taken them, then he would simply take them back; it was that simple. The only laws he had ever respected were the laws of physics and chaos, and other rules simply did not rank.

"Borrow six or so of Dr. Wissenschaft's mercenaries, would you, and warm up the diesel," said Dr. Synn. "We are going to collect my property."

———

From their vantage on a shadowed warehouse roof two stories above the docks, Decorum and Shadowcowl watched the police secure the scene. The Charlie Blockers were cuffed and crammed into a paddy wagon, except for two of them loaded into ambulances. More people arrived, apparently crime scene investigators, and they taped off the wharf as men and women in yellow jackets milled about, took photos, made measurements, and dictated into handheld recorders. Decorum and Shadowcowl could see Detective Buchanan biding his time, his dark glasses failing to hide his impatience. No matter where the detective was, he appeared to want to be somewhere else.

"He looks sad," commented Decorum.

"I hear he's got issues," said Shadowcowl.

"Hmm," purred Decorum. She was sure Buchanan just needed the right woman to fix his problems. Perhaps she should volunteer?

Johnny Saturn had left an hour ago. The crabby old vigilante had retrieved his motorcycle, an old Harley-Davidson Tour Glide, and he had ridden off. Maybe he had headed off the truck and its driver, maybe not; Decorum didn't know, and right now she didn't care.

"Why are we waiting here?" Decorum asked for the third time. "Nothing is happening! I want to go!"

"Something is going to happen, and soon," replied Shadowcowl. "Don't ask me how I know—maybe it's because of my magic cowl. But something is going to happen here, and it won't be long now."

Decorum did not like it when Shadowcowl got all creepy, but she bit back her comments and waited. The two metaheroes sat exposed to the cold wind and shivered in relative quiet. Sure, there was sound; the lapping of the waters beneath the docks, an occasional car horn from nearby streets, the growl of a big truck gearing down. But, these were just part of the local soundscape, or what passed for "quiet" in a major metropolitan area at night. Somewhere, a car's bass turned too loud thumped an urgent rhythm.

"Why are we ...?" began Decorum again, but she trailed off.

That big truck gearing down in the distance? It was here. A long-nosed eighteen-wheeler raced onto the dock. The police, seeing its lights, saw the big vehicle appear well down the wharf in the distance. The officers stood frozen in tense expectation for a moment until they heard the big diesel's engine rev up—the truck was accelerating!

Even the old or portly cops discovered new speed. They jumped this way and that as the 119 foot long tractor trailer crushed four police cars before it skidded to a stop that left burned rubber in its wake. The police fell back without being commanded, taking up positions behind the two remaining police cruisers, or behind the crates they had come here to confiscate. Crime scene investigators ran and kept running; they were unarmed and untrained for this type of emergency. The remaining police fired a few warning shots, shouting futile commands for the intruders to "get out of the truck and lie down!" but to no effect. The police, usually so good at keeping situations under control, were not running this operation.

Eight men leaped from the semi-trailer. These soldiers were armored from head to foot in heavy, beige armor cast from some synthetic material. Wissenschaft's mercenaries were trained killers culled from assorted hotspots around the world, and they each carried m16a4 assault rifles. The cops immediately recognized that their small arms were all but useless here, and their standard police-issue bulletproof vests were badly outclassed.

High caliber bullets ripped through the night, chopping the last two police cars to shreds. Several SCPD men were killed or lay dying, and the survivors were pinned down behind the crates. The mercenaries took care not to shoot the containers, so the police hunkered behind them fared better. Detective Buchanan, trapped behind the crates as well, screamed into his walkie-talkie for backup, a S.W.A.T. team, the National Guard, the Navy Seals—he would take whatever help he could get!

"This is it," cried Shadowcowl—"let's go!"

Shadowcowl wrapped an arm around Decorum, and they dove from their secluded roof. Wind roared past them as they shot straight for the melee, taking the mercenaries by storm.

Shadowcowl laid into the soldiers ferociously—wrapped in his mystic cloak, he was immune to all the bullets, knives, and fists that came his way. The mercenaries could not touch him, but he could definitely touch them! With a mix of karate, savatte, and Krav Maga, he punched, kicked, held, twisted, and took down everyone in his path.

Decorum was just as effective. Her power was garment control—if someone wore it, she could control it! To call her power telekinesis was like calling a blue whale "sort of big." She blew the armor off a mercenary; she pistol-whipped a fighter with his own rifle; and she turned a merc's helmet backwards, blinding him. Chaos followed in her wake, leaving bound and near naked men in her path!

———

Dr. Horatio Synn climbed down from the semi tractor's cab, surveyed the scene, and clucked in disapproval—these meddlesome metaheroes had made a real mess of things! It had taken a mere forty-five seconds for the mercenaries, who had dominated the police, to fall before the two vigilantes. This would not do.

"Bombastic," said Dr. Synn. "I believe it is time for you to earn your pay. Remove the interlopers, if you would."

Bombastic climbed down from the truck and grunted his acknowledgement. He did not bother to unholster his guns, knives, or various bladed projectiles, because he had nursed a grudge against Shadowcowl for quite a while now.

"My pleasure, boss," said the brute, popping his knuckles in anticipation.

"Ha, Bombastard!" challenged Shadowcowl, meeting the huge brute's uncannily swift charge. "You got away last time, but—"

Bombastic was not unintelligent. His previous encounter with Shadowcowl had taught him that the way to hurt the hero was through his magic garment. Bombastic grabbed Shadowcowl by the cloak, and then swung him to and fro, smashing the young hero again and again against the docks.

Shadowcowl was tougher than his age suggested, and he twisted each time to absorb and disperse much of the impact's energy. He flew at Bombastic, and then Shadowcowl turned his gloved hand astral and thrust it repeatedly into the hulking villain's chest, the icy ghost hand inflicting terrible agony with each penetrating strike.

That spectral grip had been sufficient to reduce the mercenaries to helplessness, but not Bombastic. The monstrous villain was no stranger to pain—he had never met a torture he could not tame! The two combatants struggled back and forth, neither gaining the upper hand or decisive blow.

Dr. Synn grew increasingly displeased. This retrieval operation had turned sour, and he realized that he was not going to be able to collect his goods. Furthermore, it was only a matter of time before the irritating Decorum noticed him and attempted to use the doctor's own clothing against him. Horatio considered pulling his pistol, a beautifully-restored WWII-era 9-mm Luger, and simply shooting her in the back; the semi-automatic gun was not particularly powerful in its own right, but the custom ammunition he had created for it was usually more than adequate for punching holes in meta-humans.

Instead, Synn decided retreat would be more advantageous, and proceeded to cover his exit. Calmly removing the top of his ebony walking stick, he armed the silver sphere by pressing a hidden button, and gently rolled it toward Shadowcowl and Bombastic, the powerful bomb nearly unnoticed by the embattled warriors.

Dr. Synn did not stay to watch. He was confident in his aim and his custom munitions, so there was no reason to hang around and gloat; leave that for silly, attention-starved metavillains, not brilliant scientists and businessmen such as himself. Bombastic had ably served Dr. Synn for eleven years, yet Nils Zilcher had now exceeded his usefulness, and Horatio Synn would never think of him again. As with gloating, he had no use for sentimentality. Dr. Synn was already exiting the scene at a comfortable pace when the explosion ripped apart the night. He felt the heat on the back of his neck, and he held his fedora in place so that it would not get blown away.

Dr. Synn would hail a cab, and then maybe he would dine in tonight. He had a taste for fresh seafood. He had no trouble flagging a cab down, because he did not look dangerous. The sign on the cab's side read "Spend a special evening with Persephone Helios, Nobel laureate, art collector, and philanthropist, May 11, hosted by Spire City Public Radio." This pleased the doctor, and then he thought of it no more.

————

Decorum did not see the bomb coming. Rather, she saw Detective Buchanan and his remaining two men leap from their cover behind the crates and run, hell-bent for leather. When she turned to see what had spurred them to flight, the silver ball that had so recently mounted Dr. Synn's cane rolled under Bombastic and Shadowcowl.

The shining sphere, an incredibly powerful explosive that made Semtex seem like a firecracker in comparison, blew a huge chunk of concrete out of the dock, exposing the wooden pilings and waters below. At nearly a thousand pounds per square inch of overpressure, the tiny bomb had the equivalent force of the U.S. military's so-called "Daisy Cutter." Bombastic was blown twenty feet into the air, a flaming missile that crashed nearby. Shadowcowl's cloak was blown to shreds.

Later, Decorum could not be sure how she survived the blast. As best as she could figure, Bombastic had absorbed much of the energy that would have ripped the flesh from her bones. She quickly came to, bleeding from her eyes, mouth, nose, and ears, and where the blast hit her she was bruised uniformly blue-black, even through her clothing. She did not feel the pain, yet, but she knew that when it came she would feel as if a truck had hit her, again, and again, and...

"Dennis!" She called after Shadowcowl—at least she thought she cried out, but, having been struck stone deaf by the blast, she could not be sure.

Decorum found Shadowcowl nearby. Where the magic cowl was still whole, his body was apparent. Where the garment was ripped, he was transparent. The cowl was shredded, and so was Dennis. Decorum saw Shadowcowl shudder, expelling a wheezing breath, and then what was left of Dennis Fulchres was gone. All that was left to mark his passing were blackened rags.

"No," whispered Decorum, "no..."

Greg Buchanan felt the bomb blast hit him square in the back. The force of the explosion was such that it lifted him and his fellow officers and threw them face first to the blacktop. There was no fighting it, no preparing, and no resistance that he could offer. He hit the decking, skinning his nose and forehead, as he tumbled along the blacktop for a good dozen feet. Greg saw stars, and he felt blood geisering from his nose. The wind had been knocked out of him, as if someone had viciously kicked him in the crotch, and he could not draw a breath. His fellow police officers were in no better shape.

Greg pushed himself to his hands and knees, pausing only to adjust his sunglasses. He could not believe how badly tonight's operation had gotten out of control, and he wondered if it would cost him his badge.

Bombastic rose, and he was not much worse for wear, all things considered. The over-muscled metahuman had taken the explosion square on, and he was already back on his feet. His clothes were singed, and some of the cartridges in his bandoleer fired off randomly, but the giant brute was definitely ready to finish the fight! Decorum, bent over her fallen comrade, did not even know the danger she was in.

A thundering growl filled the night, the call of an 88 cubic inch V-Twin engine. Johnny Saturn, bent forward on his Harley-Davidson, reappeared through the smoke and haze as though he were the fourth horseman himself. Saturn ramped the huge Tour Glide bike off a smashed police cruiser, using the ruined car as a launch pad, and the mystery man and his motorcycle vaulted high into the night sky.

The big bike hit Bombastic in the chest, knocking him to the tarmac again, and Johnny Saturn gunned the engine, grinding the Harley's back wheel into Bombastic's groin. The wheel whirled in place, smoke rose, and Bombastic screamed. It only ended when the huge metahuman swung a right cross, smashing the motorcycle away from him, sending its twisted wreckage flying across the docks and off, into the slip between the piers. The bike's engine still roared as it flew, and a blast of steam rose from where it sank into the depths.

Johnny Saturn had already leaped clear—he had no intention of following his transport to a watery grave! He grabbed a huge, iron pipe, apparently a reinforcement blasted free from the palette that Synn's crates had arrived on, and Johnny turned to meet Bombastic.

"That hurt, you little—" bellowed Bombastic.

Nils never finished his challenge, because Johnny smashed his improvised weapon into Bombastic's head. Johnny was no metahuman: he had no metahuman strength, but prodigious steroid use and cruel workouts had pumped his muscles to excessive size, and years of hard-bitten struggles had pared him down to the steely core. Add to that his U.S. Ranger training, his martial arts know-how, and his beloved boxing experience, and this was a fighter who could hit you with the conviction of a careening locomotive!

Bombastic smiled evilly—the blow had left no more than a faint welt above his eye.

Undeterred, Johnny Saturn laid into Bombastic, striking blow after punishing blow, pounding the huge brute until the thick metal bar began to warp. Saturn was maniacal, a berserker. Buchanan had never seen anything like it.

Bombastic had had enough. He knocked Johnny's weapon away, and grabbed for the vigilante. "I am going to snap you to bloody bits, Saturn! I am—*urkh*!"

Everyone—Bombastic, Johnny Saturn, Greg Buchanan—was surprised by what came next. Bombastic's clothes—especially his bandolier—had suddenly rolled up his body and tightened around his neck. The possessed gear and garments squeezed tighter and tighter, and Bombastic could not get a grip on them. First Nils Zilcher turned dark red, and then he turned purple, as his bloodshot eyes bulged grotesquely.

Decorum stood defiant, her will controlling the giant brute's gear and clothing, choking him to death. "That's for killing Shadowcowl, you piece of shit." She did not say it loudly. She did not have too. Her words rang out clearly in the shocked silence.

Bombastic turned to flee, perhaps hoping to get out of range of Decorum's power. He only made it a few steps before he stumbled and pitched forward, unconscious. Only then did Decorum release Bombastic from her suffocating death grip.

"I would have killed him," said Johnny Saturn to her. He was not joking, Buchanan was sure of that. He also saw that the mystery man's eyes looked sad. Typically, the old fighter had no use for metaheroes, but this girl had just learned a hard lesson. Clearly,

Johnny Saturn could appreciate her pain.

She did not hear his words, of course. She was deaf, perhaps forever, and the grief for her partner was beginning to overtake her. Sirens wailed into the night, and the lights of a dozen more police cars flickered into view in the distance.

Greg, battered, bloody, and probably a little concussed, staggered over to Johnny Saturn. Buchanan did not really know Johnny—who did, actually?—but he respected the old mystery man.

"You'd better leave, Saturn, if you don't want to answer a lot of questions," offered the detective.

Johnny nodded a silent recognition that seemed to say, *I figured you for an all right cop, Buchanan.* At that, Johnny Saturn strode off into the night and soon was swallowed by shadows.

Buchanan looked around as a small army of police descended on the site. This operation was a complete washout. The contraband was destroyed by Synn's bomb, reduced to a smear on the tarmac that would offer few clues in a court of law. There was the crying girl, the dead and injured officers, and the unconscious metahuman. A total washout.

This is not over, thought Buchanan. *It's never over...*

———

Manny Calabria wondered just how far he would have to hike along the interstate before someone gave him a ride. *Probably all the way to Indianapolis,* he thought wryly. Dirty, tattered and bloody as he was, everyone probably assumed he was dangerous and passed him by. Normally, he was dangerous, but not tonight.

A white limousine pulled onto the curb, and its rear door opened. There, in the back seat, sat Dr. Horatio Synn, as meticulous and proper as ever. Manny felt his stomach turn—there was no way this could turn out well for him.

"Hello, Manny," said Dr. Synn cheerfully. "You and I need to talk. Get in."

DR. HORATIO SYNN

THE WAGES OF SYNN

When Dr. Horatio Synn began his day, he was naked, caked with demonic blood, bile, and gore, and quite lost. In the last few days, he had been killed, unjustly carted off to hell, consumed a wholly disgusting demon named Nhorgiel, and returned to Earth as a demonic terrorist of sorts. However you looked at it, this week's plans had gone pear-shaped.

All this was now behind him, and it was time to get on with life. Sure, he was lost deep beneath Spire City, defenseless and without allies, but Dr. Horatio Synn had not become the successful and admired man he was today by complaining. He was of good German stock, the son of prominent Nazi industrialist Gerhard Synn, and had long ago learned to take the bad with the good!

Normally, Horatio was noted for his polite, gentlemanly nature and his vanity. On a good day, he was a dapper, very fit middle-aged man with jet black hair swept back from his prominent widow's peak and he wore his trademark white linen suits and fedoras. He had a genius for creating special munitions and extraordinarily powerful bombs, but that genius also left him with a history of severe psychosis.

As he stumbled through the pitch blackness, lost, disoriented, and reeking of demon viscera, Dr. Synn made a point of finding a suitable light source. He liberated this from the first few, hapless mole people he encountered. A pressure point jab here, a throat punch there, and these poor unfortunates were quite amenable to turning over their flashlight and store of batteries. Synn would have taken their clothes too, but they fled, and he did not know the lay of the underworld the way they did.

Maybe it was the hunger, or all the vomiting that he had been doing since being separated from the demon Nhorgiel, but Dr. Horatio Synn realized he had made an error in judgement—before he robbed the mole people, he should have asked them how to climb out of this endless subterranean maze!

"Well, live and learn, I always say," said Dr. Synn to himself. Next time, though, he would not be so hasty.

The depths beneath Spire City were a vast maze of subway tunnels, cisterns, access-ways, steam pipes, sewage channels, and enough open areas to house a sizeable population of the surface world's unwanted people. The homeless, the so-called mole people, built whole shanty towns down here in the dark and lived in a barter-based cooperative system that did not place much value on the United States of America dollar.

Dr. Synn was not overly concerned by his current predicament—he had already called for help. Horatio Synn owned and operated the multinational corporation Synn-Tech, and one of its subsidiary companies was Wissenschaft Inc. Dr. Wissenschaft, an old-school Nazi, and one of the original Operation Paperclip scientists relocated from Germany to America after the fall of the Third Reich, was an old friend of Dr. Synn's father. Dr. Wissenschaft also was one of Dr. Synn's occasional "allies of convenience."

A few years back, Dr. Synn and Dr. Wissenschaft had devised the ultimate fallback plan. Dr. Wissenschaft worked in cybernetics, so he took three psychics, preserved their living brains in a psionic resonance device, wired them in parallel, and programmed them continually to scan the aether for the phrase now dominating Synn's conscious mind. Distance was a non-issue for psychic abilities, so this system was able to cover the entire planet.

The blood banner is risen—Welcome, Fourth Reich, Welcome, thought Dr. Synn, wording his thoughts in a succinct, clear way that was only to be expected of a powerful, disciplined mind like his. *The blood banner...*

Even now, alarms would be ringing in Wissenschaft Inc.'s offices, emails would be dispatched, and private lines would be ringing. The cyber-psychic machine would have already detected these thoughts, pinpointed Dr. Synn's location, and a rescue team would have been dispatched.

Dr. Synn felt self-conscious with the silly "blood banner" stuff. Not only did he not care about the future of the Nazi party and its unlikely Fourth Reich, but he did not believe that the fascists ever really went away. Still, he had to make good-natured allowances for old Wissenschaft and his antiquated goose-stepping beliefs. It was the only polite thing to do.

Dr. Horatio Synn wandered among the depths, avoiding the ersatz mole people towns, always climbing up whenever ladders, stairs, or ramps allowed. Even were he not rescued, he must eventually find his way up and out of this labyrinth!

Light flickered ahead, down a long, arched tunnel, and Dr. Synn followed the illumination, finally turning off his "borrowed" flashlight. The tunnel opened up into a large sewage tunnel, an old junction chamber with a wide cistern and dozens of other tunnels branching off and away. From what he could see, this was the old waste disposal network, long abandoned for the more efficient, modern complex. Now, rather than sludge, the old ceramic-lined tunnels were full of a foul mix of sluggish ground water and old bacteria.

A large, stone access platform sat at the center of the cistern, connected to the outer walls and walkways by rusting, iron bridges. There, on that subterranean island, on a makeshift throne built of weeping stone, sat the Crocodile King. His subjects, the crocodiles, filled the water around him like so much flotsam, and their dull black eyes followed Synn.

———

The Crocodile King was no mere myth, it seemed. The stories of these huge, aquatic reptiles inhabiting the sewers of large cities throughout the world had become the stuff of folk tales, jokes, and clichés. Yet, here they were.

The Crocodile King turned his great head to Dr. Synn. This thing was shaped like a crocodile, but he was whiter than an albino and was bloated and obese. He sat on his throne as a human would, his short arms resting on his huge, distended gut. Some of his teeth were missing or broken, and he bore the scars of innumerable battles. Dr. Synn estimated that from snout to tail this royal reptile must have been at least twenty-five feet long.

"Who are you, Man, that you enter this place willingly," grumbled the giant, white crocodile. "How did you come to smell of Hell?"

"I am Dr. Horatio Synn," he declared, as if that were sufficient explanation for anyone in the world. "Who am I addressing if I may ask?"

"I am Sobek, the White Crocodile King, but my true name is no business of yours. Approach me, human—neither I nor my people will harm you because you reek of brimstone, demons, and Hell. You are a man who has returned from the worlds behind the world, and you would be quite toxic to us."

Dr. Synn proudly approached the Crocodile King by stepping from one crocodile's back to the next as if they were stepping stones. The crocodiles remained still and made no move against him. It was warmer in here because Sobek had illuminated his little island with numerous torches. Next to the Crocodile King was a pile of moldy, well-used books, and a pair of huge spectacles.

"You are clearly no mere, overgrown crocodile, at least not in the traditional sense," said Dr. Synn. "Are you some sort of self-aware meme, or perhaps an ancient, but otherwise forgotten, primordial god? Perhaps you are the avatar of the Egyptian god Sobek, as your name implies?"

"That is none of your concern," said Sobek.

Dr. Synn and Sobek spoke of many things, but what those subjects were was never recorded. Perhaps those two dark minds conferred on the state of the world, of the coming age, or things that no sane beings beneath the sunlight could ever discuss. Neither Dr. Synn nor Sobek have since spoken of it.

"So," asked Sobek, "you survived the destruction of your demonic form because your daughter intervened? Am I understanding this correctly?"

"Indeed you are," replied Synn. "As the vigilantes blasted my demonic body to shreds, my daughter Persephone lent her immense magical strength and restored my true body. I cannot claim to understand how she accomplished this, but I can report that her allies Johnny Saturn, the Utopian, Staff of Life, Captain Barometer, and Hyperspace, knew nothing of her true actions. They believed Persephone was aiding them in my destruction! I'm a man of science, so magic makes little sense to me."

Sobek considered this for a moment. "As I have mentioned, you have been to the dark realms hidden behind the world and you have returned. Your life will be different now. You have been dead, so things that are hidden from living men will no longer be veiled to you. You will be something of a mystic. Mark my words."

"Mystic?" said Dr. Synn with a wry grin. "No thanks, your majesty, but I bear no interest in mysticism."

When Dr. Synn made his exit of the Crocodile King's lair, he was a much-changed man. He had been given clean water so that he could wash, and given clothing. He was told these garments were left over from mole people who had been trapped and eaten here. To the crocodiles, the clothes were little more than packaging, like candy wrappers, to be disposed of or tossed aside.

Now armed with instructions for escaping this underworld maze, Dr. Synn set out on his way. He crossed forgotten subway tunnels, great chambers with ruined generators, steam vents, and mysterious, rotting causeways across deep, terrible places. Hours passed in this way, but the indefatigable scientist pushed on. He knew he truly was alive again when his stomach began to growl with hunger.

Horatio found his way into an open area that the purloined flashlight barely illuminated. It appeared he had stumbled onto an old street, one that had been paved over, leaving a forgotten tableau of earlier times. Here was a dry fountain, there a crumbling storefront. Parking meters lined the forgotten street, and an empty tavern gaped wide with its front window smashed. Dr. Synn had heard about forgotten city streets like this—they existed beneath cities such as nearby Chicago, or Seattle, or distant Edinburgh in Scotland.

Horatio registered no surprise when he realized that he was not alone, because a woman had appeared in between the blinks of his newly-aware eyes. The Crocodile King had warned him that he would see things formerly hidden to him, and now he understood what the giant reptile had meant by this.

She was seated on the fountain's edge, silent and seemingly waiting for him. It was impossible to tell where her clothing ended and her skin began, and her outline was a window of sorts into a space of swirling chaos and an eternal maelstrom of boiling randomness. Her hair rose from her head like a fountain of pulsating energy, and he could not see where it ended—it was as if she were bound to the unseen sky by a writhing tether. This was obviously no typical, mortal woman, but someone far more mythological in nature.

The woman, or whatever she was, was as awesome as she was unsettling. Her beauty was maddening, truly awful and terrible in the classical sense. *She's a living obsession wrapped in a woman-shaped package,* thought Dr. Synn. Her perfect form was in flux, and her contours faded in and out in some areas but remained tantalizingly solid in others. She was the quantum wave that was lost in superposition, a wave which for some observers would never collapse.

Dr. Horatio Synn was not most observers.

Horatio Synn was no stranger to classical goddesses. His dalliance with Circe Helios had produced a daughter, Persephone Synn Helios Underhall; and his brief romance with Artemis Magne had left its mark on both of them.

This woman was different from the others. Horatio Synn had seen this person before, glimpsed her in passing again and again throughout his life. Always she had eluded him, yet he remained deeply enchanted by everything she represented. She was none other than Eris, the personification of chaos, strife, and discord, and Horatio Synn had spent a lifetime pursuing her.

"Milady," said Dr. Synn, sketching a quick bow.

"Do you know me, my servant?" said Eris.

Dr. Synn was momentarily dazzled—her eyes were black holes, her skin like quantum foam, her voice the echo of the Big Bang. She had the air of danger, luck, doom, success, and probability unbounded.

"My Lady Eris, Mistress of Discord—you do me great honor!"

In his more than five decades of life Dr. Horatio Synn had spent all his days, his every waking hour, serving the call of chaos. Now she was here, the anthropomorphic embodiment of this fundamental principle of his science and life. Dr. Synn took her hand in his own, and politely kissed it. It was an electric moment.

"You take great liberties," said Eris, yet she did not pull her hand back.

"Yes," said Horatio, "I do. You are my guiding light. I'm no longer just a man—I am your avatar, the knight who does your bidding on the earth above."

"I should punish you for your excessive familiarity," Eris chided.

Dr. Synn said nothing. Rather, he pulled Eris's into his arms. "You dare too much, mortal," Eris said, but she did not stop him as he gently pressed her back into a laying position with his hands. She complained no more, and she became compliant in his arms.

Alone, in the oppressive dark beneath Spire City, the terrorist and the goddess became one flesh. This was nothing new, for Dr. Synn already had been a literal incarnation of terror in the truest sense for a long time. In the flickering light of the flashlight, amid the dust and rubble, Dr. Synn was made whole again.

They lingered together for a long while, then the goddess spoke secrets to the mad industrialist.

"Soon," Eris said, "a man will come for you. Dr. Wissenschaft would prefer you to be dead, so, the thing that comes for you is no rescuer, but an assassin meant to make sure the old fool's wish comes true."

"I expected as much," replied Dr. Synn, rising, putting his ill-fitting clothes back on. "Management is a cutthroat business in the best of times. Perhaps I would have done the same to him if our roles had been reversed. But, no worries."

"Yet, you have not asked for my assistance," noted the goddess.

"Of course not," he said. "You would not love me if I were that sort of avatar. I don't pray for chaos! I make it!"

"You have no weapons," said Eris.

"Weapons are nothing but an extension of the will. Watch, milady."

The ceiling above began to crack, splitting apart under the brutal force of hydraulic powered steel fists. A portion of the roof gave way, and a cyborg dropped down through the new-made hole and onto the forgotten street amid a rain of stone, rubble, and dust.

At eight feet tall, the cyborg now was more machine than man. Once he had been a mercenary, but military service for Wissenschaft Inc. had cost him most of his body. Now he was an abomination of pistons, pulleys, circuits, and gear boxes where once there had been muscles, tendons, and bone. A human brain still functioned in that steel-clad cranium, making the cyborg all the more dangerous for the human brain's superior processing power, pattern recognition, and instincts.

The cyborg's targeting system locked onto Dr. Synn and its guns rose. They never fired.

Dr. Synn had not bothered to move from his seat.

"So, you've come to kill me yourself," said Dr. Synn evenly.

The cyborg paused, seemingly unsure of itself. Dr. Synn stood and then approached the man-machine conglomeration, and he took the cyborg's still human hand in his own.

"So, you've come to kill me yourself," said Dr. Synn again, this time squeezing the cyborg's hand when he said certain words.

What specifically Synn said to the cyborg was not all that important, but the cadence of his voice and the words he chose to emphasize were critical. Shocked and amazed at what he heard, the cyborg slowly turned his gun on himself. He blew his head off, and the eight-foot mechanical warrior was suddenly just seven feet tall. His mindless body slumped to the ground with a loud, metallic rattling. It shuddered once, and then it settled into a pile of scrap as its tension drained away.

Eris, perhaps as amazed as the cyborg had been, turned to Dr. Synn. "What did you do?"

"Neuro-Linguistic Programming, or NLP, my dear," said the doctor in a matter-of-fact tone. "I tapped into his subconscious mind with my words, and I reprogrammed it. Then, I told him to kill himself. It was down and dirty work, as NLP goes, but still quite effective."

"Impressive," said Eris. "Now I see why Circe wanted to keep you for herself."

"Oh, I did not invent NLP, but it can be very handy. It is just one of the many skills I have at my command. Now, shall we follow this poor fellow's tracks back to the surface?" Dr. Synn liberated the cyborg of his water, energy bars, knife, and machine gun.

Later, the lovers arrived at Wissenschaft Inc.'s private subway terminal.

"Horatio, my boy," Dr. Wissenschaft greeted them. "Welcome back to the land of the living! I was concerned that rumors of your death were justified this time."

The old Nazi butcher made no reference to the assassin cyborg he had dispatched to make sure Dr. Horatio Synn was dead, nor did Horatio himself raise the issue. What was past was past, and what was a little attempted murder between old partners?

"Karl, my old friend," replied Dr. Synn, "it is good to see you. I've had quite a journey. Indeed, it's fair to say that I've been to Hell and back."

"Ah, the less said the better," Dr. Wissenschaft noted.

"Allow me to introduce my lady, the goddess Eris," said Dr. Synn.

Dr. Wissenschaft looked where indicated, his good eye darting about, and his mechanical eye sifting through the electromagnetic spectrum. The elderly Nazi saw no one. *If Dr. Synn is making invisible friends, now, then so be it,* thought the elderly man.

"Let's get you cleaned up, my boy," said Wissenschaft. "I'm sure you are ready for a filling meal, a shower, and one of your fine, linen suits."

"True," replied Dr. Synn. "I'm ready to get back to work. Chaos waits for no man," and then Dr. Synn shot a wink at his invisible friend.

Chaos beamed a smile back at Dr. Synn.

TACTICAL

HALO OF GRAVES

A ngels wept for Spire City, for demons had come to town. Specifically, an actual demon who wore the visage of international terrorist, Dr. Horatio Synn, had come, and he had wounded the city with all the subtlety of a blunt machete.

At two-hundred feet tall, with the power of seven on the Richtor Scale, and the subtlety of an F5 tornado, this horrendous demonic entity had scored a trail of destruction over sixteen blocks long and three blocks wide through downtown Spire City. Skyscrapers were flattened, collapsed into a rubble strewn rift between great mountains of steel, stone, and broken glass. Seven days had passed, and the huge cloud of angry gray particulates had yet to settle, smearing the city with ugly streaks.

Where were Spire City's famous metahuman defenders during this invasion? Those that could fly had risen in a righteous flock, and they had battled in the sky above the city with the terrible invader that had been belched from the Netherworld. In what had come to be called the War in Heaven, the metaheroes paid a terrible price, dozens were killed, and dozens more were critically injured or crippled. It later was reported that a small band of heroes finally brought the demonic terrorist down in the subterranean vaults deep beneath the city, but little was known of that conflict.

The aftermath was biblical in scope and furor. Mayor Jeremy Newstead, having fled the town during the conflict, wasted no time in calling for the Governor to deploy the National Guard. (The National Guard's response was minimal, because most had been long employed overseas in another conflict.) The President of the United States, in a characteristic show of paternal care and patriotic brotherhood, carefully inspected the carnage from the window seat of Air Force One at 30,000 feet while en route to somewhere else. Spire City was declared a disaster area, and help began to flow in from across the country. FEMA set up shop, the few available National Guard rolled in driving all-terrain vehicles, and the media arrived by the thousands. Congress reaffirmed troubling elements of the Patriot Act, giving the President and the Department of Homeland Security sweeping powers to restore America's broken peace and safety. Resident aliens were rounded up and sent to foreign lands to be tortured in a wave of Extraordinary Renditions; roving wiretaps were placed by the tens of thousands on unsuspecting citizens; and everyone had to remove their shoes to board flights. If demons from hell attacked again, they would not be able to use their phones with impunity, enter the country without proper passports, or check out a library book without the Federal Bureau of Investigation knowing what they read.

Within the destruction zone, Spire City's own Ground Zero, skyscrapers burned, or collapsed from weakened foundations, or had been knocked down by the demonic terrorist. As the days rolled by, there was no help for survivors, no collection of the slain, and no demolition crews to implode unsafe buildings. One might have assumed that it was a bottleneck of poorly coordinated federal workers that kept the aid out, but that was not it. Rather, a gang war that had broken out in the destruction zone.

The residents of Spire City, looking out from the windows of the nearby skyscrapers that were not condemned, watched the violent skirmishes play out, yet they had no idea who was fighting or why. The police knew, of course, but they had been gagged by the Federal Bureau of Investigation, so they had issued no statements. The few remaining metahumans knew, but they were too busy containing the conflict, keeping it from spilling out into the city proper. If they were not vigilant, Spire City could be engulfed in a civil war. The National Guard knew, because they had made repeated forays into Ground Zero and they had been rebuffed each time by one side or another in battle. In Washington D.C., the President knew, and he used this as the justification for attacking another "Axis of Evil" member in the Middle East. The problems in Spire City, contended the President of the United States, could only be corrected by a major troop surge abroad.

Johnny Saturn, aka Greg Buchanan, knew what this nasty little war was about.

The mystery man had been fighting without sleep for days. He had not yet picked sides in the Dirty War, and he had engaged all takers. In the last twenty-four hours alone, he had captured Terra Rosa, Mr. Ambiguous, and the Hypodermic Man. Johnny had lost count of how many costumed lunatics he had battled in the last week. Most of these had been looters of opportunity, not soldiers in the Dirty War.

The stakes in this war were simple—control of Spire City's criminal underworld. On one side, there was the Iron Brigade, a large team of metahuman criminals led by Tactical, a Balkan war criminal wanted for innumerable crimes against humanity. On the other side, there was the mercenary army of Dr. Karl Wissenschaft, Johnny Saturn's most bitter enemy.

These opposing armies did not care that the city bled. They did not care that stock markets had dipped dangerously while they fought, that gasoline prices soared, and that FEMA trailer home camps swelled in cramped, muddy fields with displaced people. All the Iron Brigade and Dr. Wissenschaft cared about was who held the reins of the Midwest's criminal underworld.

Johnny Saturn bound the Hypodermic Man with plastic restraints and hauled the unconscious villain to the edge of Ground Zero. The police officers that met him there asked no questions—by now, they understood Johnny Saturn was on their side, and they took Hypodermic Man into custody. Much like a bounty hunter, Johnny Saturn was a licensed vigilante, and he had become a relatively well-regarded member of the local crime-fighting community.

"Another looter," Johnny Saturn said. "It's my guess that whatever he loads those syringes with is a controlled substance, too." Johnny Saturn accepted a couple bottles of water and a few energy bars with a nod of thanks. Without further comment, he turned and marched back into the smoky, dusty maze of broken masonry and twisted girders. Fires smoldered under huge heaps of rubble, and the place had begun to smell horribly.

Few knew or suspected, but this Johnny Saturn was not the one they had known over the years. For the new man, Ground Zero had been his baptism of fire as the new hero behind the Johnny Saturn mask. There had been another man in the costume, a giant brawler named John Underhall. He was gone. John Underhall had died fighting, and Greg Buchanan, a homicide detective with the 23rd Precinct, had taken up the old fighter's mantle. This town needed a Johnny Saturn, and the young detective was determined to live up to the name. As a detective, Buchanan had been burned out, alienated, and clinically depressed; as a mystery man, he was useful again, reborn as a man with a mission. He still suffered from depression, but that only made him edgier, more of an extreme risk taker. In fact, he was growing manic as the days went on, a tell-tale sign that his mental illness had moved into a new stage. This was not a job for a happy-go-lucky soul with a sunny disposition.

As a good detective, Greg had not confined his efforts to capturing looters—all that did was treat the symptoms of the Dirty War while the root cause went untreated. Rather, as Johnny Saturn, he had been surveying the whole of Ground Zero. By now, he knew where the rival forces' camps were located, the Iron Brigade and those of Wissenschaft Inc. He had an idea of their movements, and he had a plan. Johnny Saturn was going to do what the National Guard, the Spire City Police Department, the Federal Bureau of Investigation, and the Federal Emergency Management Agency could not. Johnny Saturn was going to end the Dirty War.

———

Tactical, also known as Nikolai Demetr, sat naked on the edge of his camp bed smoking an unfiltered cigarette. Behind him, his two sex partners, Alaric the Axe and Skorn, slept entangled in a knot of pale, tattooed flesh. Nikolai was glad for this time alone, because his mood had turned sour. His war with Dr. Wissenschaft for the mastery of Spire City's crime scene was not going well. As Demetr's code name suggested, he was very experienced at war and combat tactics. His opponent, Dr. Wissenschaft, was old and canny, however, and he had proven no easy adversary.

Tactical exhaled slowly, and long tendrils of blue-gray smoke snaked up his face. The left half of his head was heavily scarred, with all the whorls and twists of one who had been burned. His left eye was gone, the eye socket covered with scar tissue, so he usually kept it covered. Much of the left half of Tactical's body was the same, burned and enfeebled. Without his armor, he was a cripple, and this very much galled the soldier.

Once, Colonel Nikolai Demetr had been an important man, and much feared. He had been called the Wolf of the Balkans, and he had set up rape factories, ethnic cleansing camps, and well organized death squads that had filled scores of unmarked graveyards with enemy corpses. Nikolai had pursued his terror campaign with glee, and he had not shied away from pulling the trigger when his turn came. His gore-soaked crusade had brought him estates, honors, and wealth. To his own people, he had been a hero, destined for a high post, and perhaps one day the presidency.

Nikolai Demetr had lost it all. Indicted by The Hague for war crimes, Nikolai's own government was going to surrender him to the World Court in order to avoid economic sanctions. Betrayed by his own country, Nikolai Demetr charted his own course of action. He raided his nation's secret cache of metaweapons, and he fled into exile. He paid dearly in his flight, however, because he was caught in a blast and burned terribly.

Most people would have counted themselves lucky to have died quickly from such injuries. There were days that, if Nikolai could have reached a gun, he would have blown his brains all over the walls. But, he could not reach a gun, and he did not die. The gods seemed determined that he suffer for what he had done. He had not been a patriot—everything he had done, he had done because he wanted to.

Tactical would have done almost anything to have won his old life back. He had been feared, rich, and whole in body. Now, he was a criminal and would-be crime boss in the Midwest region of the United States. The irony that he had ended up in one of the countries that brought about his downfall did not escape him. He found it funny, in a paradoxical, non-humorous way, that his bank accounts grew fat off the United States of America.

Alaric, Demetr's bodyguard and lover, woke up and mumbled, "Nik, come back to bed." Tactical ignored the huge metahuman, and Alaric drifted back to sleep. Tactical valued the big man. Alaric was not only his lover and bodyguard, but his primary enforcer and lieutenant. Skorn, the woman who lay next to Alaric, was similarly useful and quite powerful in her own right. Tactical was not as sure of her loyalties, but she could bench-press a bus and withstand a grenade, so he allowed her into his bed as well. Really, Nikolai kept her around to entertain Alaric's gigantic lusts.

Tactical's army, such as it was, was a metavillain group called the Iron Brigade. They were the most dangerous squad of criminals in the Midwest, and one of the most dangerous in the country. Since Tactical had taken charge of them, he had made them rich, filling their individual off-shore accounts with untold millions of dollars as they cut their way into every racket in town. Drugs, prostitution, media piracy, gambling, porn, the unions, radio—Tactical had sunk the Iron Brigade's hooks into every one. He had bought his own bank, the Capital Union, to launder their money and store their wealth; and he had acquired the law firm of Holt and Hargrove to represent all their legitimate holdings. If there was a new, emerging market for illicit gain, Nikolai Demetr had his eye on it.

What he had not seen coming, however, was the ascendance of Dr. Wissenschaft. The ancient Nazi war criminal had planned nothing less than the complete domination of Spire City. The old monster owned nearly every judge, councilman, and cop in the city. Wissenschaft had wide interests, some legal, some not, in this region's medical establishment. All that was not enough, apparently, and now the elderly demon coveted the city's underworld as well. Greedy monster.

For a week now, the Iron Brigade had battled Wissenschaft's mercenary forces up and down Spire City's Ground Zero. Both sides had taken casualties, but neither could win the upper hand. Wissenschaft Inc.'s mercenaries, heartless thugs drawn from every chronic conflict the world over, may not have been metas, but they were well armed, armored, and trained, and if they were injured they were quickly recycled into cyborgs by Wissenschaft Inc.'s illegal cybernetic labs. Some of them were even recycled after death as sort of cyber-zombies known as "zomborgs." These mindless horrors were very difficult to put down for good.

Tactical's reverie was cut short. Outside the half-ruined parking garage where they had established their camp, he heard yelling, a zapping energy discharge, and the clatter of combat. They were under attack!

"Quickly, Alaric, Skorn, help me into my armor!"

————

Johnny Saturn had not intended to take on the whole Iron Brigade, but, here he was, and here they were—it was time to party, and his dance card was full.

Again and again, Johnny Saturn had disproved the myth that metapowered opponents were too tough for non-augmented humans to defeat. Lacerater, with his huge projected claw, was the equivalent of an enemy armed with a sword—problem solved, and Lacerater was knocked unconscious. Johnny Saturn treated Warmonger, the assassin who could twist the laws of space and perspective by going around one corner and coming out from another, as fighting multiple opponents. Problem solved, and Warmonger was out. Johnny Saturn broke the concentration of Dr. Somnambulism, who made her victims pass out from sleepiness, with a standard off-the-shelf taser. And so it went; metavillain after metavillain.

It was not that the villains were weak, or inexperienced it was just that Johnny Saturn had become that good. The mystery man had become a modern day Jack the

Giant Killer, and the metavillains knew his reputation and were more than a little frightened of him. Greg Buchanan, the man beneath the Johnny Saturn mask, knew that much of this reputation was inherited from the former Johnny Saturn, but the villains did not know that Greg was not John Underhall, and Greg was not going to enlighten them.

Johnny Saturn had come here to make contact with the Iron Brigade and meet their leader, Tactical. The metavillains he approached were not in the listening mood, however, and now he was in for a fight. Everyone played to their roles and did what was expected of them, establishing their bona fides and alpha dog status's in the process. Even more sociable meta's often had friendly "misunderstandings" when they crossed paths, all for the joy of a good rough and tumble. The Iron Brigade knew nothing of "friendly" or "joy," but at least they were polite enough to wait their turns and fight the new Johnny Saturn one at a time. To them, it was a game.

Johnny Saturn took Manic Max out with a savage elbow to the face, smashing the man's nose, making it into a bloody geyser. When Johnny Saturn turned to his next opponent, none came. Tactical had made his appearance, and he quietly motioned his soldiers back. The Balkan warlord, arrayed in his black and yellow armor that made him look like an anorexic bumblebee, stood on slab of broken concrete above the conflict, staring down at Johnny Saturn. He was flanked by his lieutenants, Alaric the Axe and Skorn.

Greg did not relish the idea of fighting Alaric. A good martial artist knows how to use an opponent's strength and mass against him, manipulating the other's center of gravity. This was an excellent tactic... up to a point. Beyond a certain level of mass, however, physics made this less and less likely. A speeding city bus had a center of gravity, for example, but you were not going to use the bus's strength and mass against it with your shoulder. Alaric was something like a bus—a bloodthirsty, vindictive bus with a huge battleaxe.

"So," declared Tactical, "it is the man who would be Johnny Saturn. I've faced John Underhall in battle, and you are about four inches too short and sixty pounds too light to be him. Why are you here, pretender?" Tactical's English was good, but it still had that Eastern bloc cadence.

"I came to talk," replied Johnny Saturn. "Are you in a listening mood, or do I keep kicking ass?" He was still breathing hard from his exertion. His armor was well ventilated, but fighting was hot, dirty work.

Tactical snorted, and the good side of his face, that part not covered with a mask, twisted in amusement.

"Let us talk, mystery man. Perhaps you will amuse me."

The scene that followed was surreal. The two men sat on camp stools amid the rubble and chatted as if they were having coffee at a local diner. The air above and around them was filled with a low hanging cloud of particulate matter, dimming out the night sky and the lights of the skyscrapers that surrounded them. Fires burned, most smoldering beneath great mounds of rubble as they had now for a week. In the distance, car horns and alarms, the usual sounds of a city at night, ghosted in from another world, the world beyond Ground Zero and the Dirty War.

The Iron Brigade metahumans extended their cordon around them, circling Johnny Saturn in, but he appeared unconcerned. He did not make the mistake of thinking that Tactical was honorable, or that some sort of protection as a guest had been extended to him. These were cold-hearted killers, predators, and they would snuff him out without hesitation or remorse. At least Johnny Saturn hoped they would kill him, if it came to that, because he knew that Tactical was a sadist of the first order.

"So," began Tactical, "Talk. You've earned it."

Johnny Saturn considered his words for a moment, and then he came right to the point. Tactical was not the type of man you could "play" or manipulate with cunning words, so Johnny Saturn did not even try. "I know where Wissenschaft's base camp is. I also know where the subway tunnels that access his base are, and I have good intel on the tunnels he uses to re-supply his mercenaries from outside Ground Zero."

"Ground Zero? That is what your American press is calling this? How unimaginative you Westerners are." Tactical paused, waiting for a response, but there was none. "What is the source of this information?"

"I have friends among the mole people. There is not much that happens under Spire City that they do not know about." The mole people were a population of homeless and disenfranchised people that lived in the sewers, steam tunnels, open reservoirs, and access tunnels under the city. They lived there in the thousands, forgotten by the world above, shunned as vagrants and drifters. In the deeps, they had formed communities, but Dr. Wissenschaft's mercenaries often preyed on them.

"Why should I believe you, my ersatz Johnny Saturn? Better yet, why would you give me this information?"

"That's simple," replied Johnny. "I would do anything to destroy Dr. Wissenschaft. Anything." This last word, spoken quietly, almost a whisper, carried great weight, and Tactical nodded. He understood raw hatred.

"Here is what I propose," said Johnny Saturn. "I can't break through Wissenschaft Inc.'s defenses alone and get a clear shot at the old monster. But, the Iron Brigade could break through, and I could take out Wissenschaft in the chaos that followed."

"You would kill him?" asked Tactical. The villain's lips made the words, but his good eye showed that he already knew the forthcoming answer.

"I will bring him to justice. As my predecessor was so fond of explaining to people, I'm a mystery man, not a metahero. I don't take killing lightly, and I've only ever killed in self-defense. But…"

"But?" asked Tactical.

"But, nothing. I will bring him to justice." Johnny Saturn's hands squeezed closed, as if subconsciously strangling someone, and the space-age materials that gloved those hands made popping, plastic on plastic sounds as he did.

The two men sat in silence for a moment. Johnny Saturn knew this meeting could still go wrong. He had information that Tactical needed, and there was a chance that the villain might prefer to have his men torture the knowledge out of him.

"I believe you," said Tactical. "Whatever your personal reason for hating Wissenschaft, your needs run parallel to mine. I do not believe that you were sent here by Wissenschaft to lure us into a trap. Yet, I can but wonder, you speak of justice for Wissenschaft?"

"Yes?" asked Johnny Saturn.

"I was the "Wolf of the Balkans." My crimes are well known. How do I know that you will not come for me one day?"

Johnny Saturn smiled for a moment. "One villain at a time, Tactical. Justice can be patient."

"Ha! Johnny Saturn, you do amuse me. Now, we must make plans…"

———

Dr. Karl Victor Wissenschaft was ninety years old, and he looked every year of his age.

His skull and skeleton were prominent, barely concealed beneath crumpled, papery skin. He had shriveled gums and yellowed teeth, a wispy wreath white hair, and over time his ears and nose had grown to outsize his features. All this was belied by the spring in his step, and the vast intelligence that lighted his left eye. (His right eye was hidden behind an oculus, shielded from further damage after his recent injury at the hands of John Underhall, the man who previously had answered to the name Johnny Saturn.)

Dr. Wissenschaft looked almost grandfatherly. He was, in truth, the most evil man in the world. During his seven decades of research, he had visited the most horrible, disgusting, dehumanizing medical procedures imaginable upon countless innocent victims. The doctor had not done this out of sadistic glee, or high-minded pursuits such as advancing science or improving the human condition. He was no psychopath, or sociopath, nor was he afflicted with any type of textbook mental illness. Dr. Wissenschaft did what he did because he wanted to. It pleased him to carry on his work. He was a monster, and had earned top honors at monster school, and hung the monster school diploma proudly in his office. It was for this reason that he had come to be known as the "Father of Atrocities."

Karl Wissenschaft had a near stranglehold on Spire City. He owned every judge, councilman, and police officer of note. Most of the city's medical establishment was his, and most of its media outlets, including the *Spire City Gazette*. As one of the Nazi

DR. KARL WISSENSCHAFT

scientists smuggled into the country in Project Paperclip by the Central Intelligence Agency after World War II, he was officially untouchable by any law enforcement body in the United States of America, and he enjoyed perpetual immunity as a consequence. Dr. Wissenschaft owned Spire City in a very real way. But, he did not own its black market. For Karl Wissenschaft to expand his illegal cybernetics operations as he saw fit, he needed to control the black market medical economy, the one that trafficked in illegal drugs and human tissue. To control this market sector, the doctor had to annex the Spire City criminal underworld. Thus, the Dirty War.

Dr. Wissenschaft watched critically as his cyborg assistants unloaded a large, metal container from his private subway car. The cyborgs hauled the box up onto a metal platform above, part of a series of metal catwalks throughout the complex. They were located in a more or less intact warehouse in Ground Zero: The warehouse's exterior had been obscured by debris, but its subterranean access ways were intact. Dr. Wissenschaft used his private subway train to move about town, and his private subway tunnels connected all his research facilities. A new batch of mercenary soldiers was disembarking from the train as well, stone-cold killers drawn from all the globe's hot spots.

Wissenschaft watched as the cyborgs settled the container onto its new platform. This was the doctor's secret weapon, the metaphorical sword with which he would overthrow his enemies and end the Dirty War. The container looked like some sort of steampunk-inspired deepfreeze, and it gave no hint what it held, but Wissenschaft knew that it enclosed nothing less than the new, long arm of his evil, twisted will.

An explosion rocked the warehouse, and Dr. Wissenschaft steadied himself against a metal railing. That was close! Their location had been discovered, and the enemy was near at hand!

Unperturbed, the Father of Atrocities climbed the metal steps to the platform where his new weapon had just been installed. Below him, mercenaries rushed about, forming up firing lines, loading rocket propelled grenades, and readying guns. Cyborgs, those poor souls that Dr. Wissenschaft had reconstituted from a variety of mechanical limbs, weapons, and devices, likewise readied for the assault that was sure to come. Wissenschaft did not know how Tactical had located this lair, but it would not help the Balkan crime lord.

The Iron Brigade breached the warehouse, smashing through walls, dropping through the ceiling, and bursting up through the concrete floor. Many of the metavillains had come in behind the mercenaries' lines, surrounding them. There was no clear field of fire, no territory that was the Iron Brigade's or Wissenschaft's mercenaries. Sheets of armor piercing bullets filled the air in burst after burst, and the warehouse floor became a hotbed of hellacious death, a bubbling mass of armor piercing munitions and metahuman fury. Bellicose roars and agonized screams drowned out all other noise.

Dr. Wissenschaft knew he should board his private train and flee—no matter how he worked the math, this conflict was not worth dying for. He took a long view of things, and he decided losing a battle to win a war was an acceptable loss. But, he was not going to leave without his masterpiece. He stroked the boxy container with a bony, spotted hand, finding its control pad.

"Wake up, Tara," he said, smiling smugly, deftly punching in codes as he spoke. "It is time for your coming out party…"

———

Johnny Saturn couldn't believe his luck—Dr. Wissenschaft was on location—he was here! This operation had always been a gamble, because Johnny Saturn had not been able to pin down the wily old vulture's location with any certainty.

"I've got you now, you monster… " growled Johnny Saturn.

The mystery man threw himself into the melee of blood, bullets, and butchery that the warehouse had become. He had to cross a wide open space to get to the elderly Nazi, and there were a lot of mercenaries, cyborgs, zomborgs, and metavillains between here and there. He knew that the metavillains were just as likely to kill him, because now that he had gotten them here, his usefulness to them was over.

Dr. Wissenschaft stood above on the metal platform beside a metal machine that looked like a cross between an industrial air-conditioning unit and a meat locker. He seemed to barely notice as Johnny Saturn closed on him.

Johnny Saturn ducked beneath a mercenary's swing, shoving his shoulder into the fighter's hip, upending him. Johnny Saturn diverted a bowie knife thrust from another, dislocating the attacker's arm. Johnny Saturn was not quick enough to avoid a short blast from a laser rifle, but the crystal polymer emulsion that the Tailor had sprayed on the vigilante's suit was sufficient to refract small arms laser fire. Foot by foot, foe by foe, he closed on Dr. Wissenschaft. Johnny Saturn climbed over stacks of bodies—the carnage was so furious that he could not tell which side the corpses belonged to.

Dr. Karl Victor Wissenschaft, that horrible relic of the SS and Project Paperclip, turned from his machine and regarded the mystery man.

"You are not the Johnny Saturn I know. You are not the man who injured my eye, yet I feel sure we have met before. Do I know you, man beneath the mask? I think so."

Johnny dropped his last foe, and he stepped forward, onto the stairs that climbed to Wissenschaft's platform above. Behind the saturnine vigilante lay almost a score of armed mercenaries, all broken, unconscious, and incapacitated. Johnny Saturn no longer seemed a man, but a force of nature, an impending doom, an awful judgment approaching step by gory step

Gripped by fate, powered by destiny, Johnny Saturn saw something beyond what was visible to the naked eye…

Wissenschaft, like Johnny Saturn himself, was a tool of destiny, touched by the gods, wrapped in fate. In a brief glimpse, Johnny Saturn had a symbolic vision of what he really faced. The hyper-realism of combat, that altered state of consciousness where time slows to a crawl and everything is more real than real, loaned Johnny Saturn new eyes to finally behold the truth behind the shriveled old man.

Radiating from Dr. Wissenschaft was an awful aura, a thing of horror. This aura was not made up of light, but thousands upon thousands of victims restrained in iron beds, their screams welling up through the years, the horrors they endured beyond comprehension. Where those terrible, blood-soaked beds ended, long ditch-like mass graves radiated out. Untold legions of victims filled these unmarked, forgotten trenches, but their cries of horror and anguish were just as loud, albeit muffled by the dirt. It was a screaming halo of graves and misery, and it was the worst thing Johnny Saturn had ever seen by many magnitudes. He would take this hellish vision whole and undiminished to his grave. Once seen, such things could not be unseen.

"Have you come to kill me, mystery man?" asked Wissenschaft. The aura was gone, and he appeared as a frail, geriatric man again.

"Oh, yes," said Johnny Saturn, climbing the stairs inexorably.

"I thought as much. Allow me to introduce my latest innovation."

Dr. Wissenschaft punched a final button on the boxy machine's keypad. Power arced and filled the air with cinders and the smell of ozone. White smoke billowed forth with a hiss and a smell of turpentine, the box split open, and the cabinet revealed its contents.

It was a girl.

"What? What are ..." queried Johnny.

"Behold," cried Dr. Wissenschaft, "The Tara 5.0, built for spying and wet-work. She's a prototype, and much too expensive to mass produce, but I think you'll find her engaging."

Energy still crackled around Tara, and she blinked, apparently waking up for the first time. Whatever Wissenschaft said she was, she appeared to be a young girl, maybe sixteen or seventeen years old, with a cherubic face and spiky, blond hair. Incongruously, she wore a sheer evening gown and high heels. She stepped from her metallic womb, and her grace bespoke a mix of finely tuned machine and stalking lioness. She interposed herself between Johnny Saturn and Dr. Wissenschaft, and then she smiled sweetly.

Johnny Saturn pushed forward, as he intended to sweep Tara out of his way and throttle the old man. His whole career, as a cop and then a mystery man, had been about stopping the ancient Nazi forever, and Johnny Saturn was going to snap Wissenschaft's neck. Greg Buchanan had finally overcome his uneasiness with killing, and he was ready to get on with it.

With blurring speed, Tara twisted and pivoted, tossing Johnny Saturn overhead and across the warehouse.

He never saw it coming, although he might have if he had been paying proper attention to her and not to the doctor. Tara's strength was such that Johnny Saturn bounced on the concrete floor like a rock skipping across a lake. He hit the far wall with sufficient force to cave the bricks in, which momentarily buried him in a pile of rubble and dust. Beyond this new, Johnny Saturn-shaped hole in the wall lay another large warehouse space that was free of fighting.

Johnny Saturn blanked for a moment, his head rattled. The shearing fluid that impregnated his armor had hardened and protected him as it was intended to, and the impact absorbing gel had soaked up most of the strike's force. Still, the blow had been the equivalent of riding a rollercoaster while trapped in a cycling washing machine, and it had been sufficient to black him out for a moment. He rose wobbly in a rain of bricks as Tara 5.0 approached.

Johnny Saturn shook his head.

At five foot two, her hips swayed like a real girl's, and her lips twisted at the corners in a sardonic smile. Was she really an android? Could Wissenschaft's command of robotics be this impossibly advanced? Or, was she merely a metahuman girl or augmented human? Johnny Saturn could see the feral expectation in her half-lidded eyes as she reveled in her grand premiere.

Programmed with a wide range of martial arts, Tara closed and struck, leading with an uppercut followed by a scissor kick. Johnny Saturn was a talented martial artist and an award winning Krav Maga practitioner, but it was going to take all his wits to last long with this opponent. When it came to "cunning," Johnny Saturn was lucky to have plenty.

Johnny Saturn gave ground before the deadly kicks and jabs, and he lost his footing on a loading ramp, rolling away, tumbling to the bottom of the incline. Tara did not know it, but this was a ruse. She leaped impossibly high, descending with a deadly axe kick intended to cave in Johnny's helmet. He rolled aside, and her foot shattered the pavement, sending a shock wave through the floor. They were alone now, beyond the hole in the wall she had made using Johnny Saturn's body.

Johnny Saturn twisted where he lay, like a break dancer twirling on his back, and used his legs to sweep Tara off her feet. Then, using his feet to pivot her on her center of gravity, he sent her flying face-first into a steel post. She connected with the force and sound of a bad automobile accident, and she appeared stunned or confused.

Johnny Saturn got to his feet and backed off. If this ploy did not work, he was out of tricks. He could only hope Tara's processors were in her head, or perhaps all her sensory systems.

Tara rose and turned to face him. It had not worked. A spider web of cracked "flesh" radiated from where she had hit the pole, and her left eyeball had fallen into her chassis, revealing the camera lens beneath. She was otherwise unharmed.

Tara leaped, and this time there was little Johnny Saturn could do. He tried to turn the force of the blow to his advantage, but she was too strong. The original Johnny Saturn, John Underhall, had once used such tricks to deal the Utopian a beating, but Greg Buchanan was no John Underhall, and he knew it.

Tara pinned Johnny Saturn to the ground, her hands and knees immobilizing his limbs. She did not look like she weighed more than a hundred pounds, tops, but her strength, mass, and metal frame rendered him momentarily helpless.

"You think I'm just a robot, don't you?" Tara asked, her voice teasing. "I'm not, not really. I was patterned after a real, metahuman girl. Grandfather downloaded her mind into my hard drive."

"Um… That's nice…" said Johnny, desperately trying to think of a way to turn all this to his advantage. A little help now would be appreciated, or even a nice distraction.

None came.

"I'm supposed to kill you now," she said.

With a sweep of her hand, she ripped off Johnny Saturn's helmet, and then she re-secured his arm. Greg Buchanan's face was now exposed to her. Greg knew the end had come, and he had failed. He had not killed Dr. Wissenschaft. Now the Tara 5.0 would crush him, and he could not think of any way to escape.

Greg Buchanan did not expect what happened next.

Tara dipped down, and she tenderly kissed him. To Buchanan's surprise, her flesh was supple, like that of a human being, but cooler. Even the shattered spider-web of skin around her missing left eye looked like human skin.

"I am not going to kill you," said Tara coyly. "Grandfather does not know it, but I do not have to do everything he tells me to. He shouldn't have based me on a real girl, should he?"

Tara kissed him again, then she rolled off Johnny Saturn, letting him go. She backed away.

"I'll never kill you. Ever. You're the first man I've ever seen, and I…" She struggled for the right words, and failed. "I need this little bit of rebellion. I'll need it in the days to come. Goodbye."

Tara turned and fled back into the warehouse with inhuman speed.

Greg passed out for a while, and he lay unmoving in the dark of the warehouse. When he came to, he shook his head in simultaneous confusion and relief, and then he retrieved his helmet with its straps broken. Some things were just too incredible.

"This is the weirdest job in the world," he said, heading up the ramp and back into the warehouse.

Dr. Wissenschaft and Tara were gone. Greg knew they would be.

Johnny Saturn had come this far, fought this hard, and he had lost. There was no doubt about it. His mission was to put Dr. Wissenschaft's terror to an end, and he had failed.

Johnny Saturn stood on the catwalk above the warehouse floor and surveyed the carnage. Soon, he would leave Ground Zero. He had not slept in days and days, and his mind was beginning to play tricks on him.

He had achieved one of his goals, at least: the Dirty War effectively was over, and Spire City could begin to heal. Fallen towers would be rebuilt, and federal money would wash in like the tide. He took no pleasure in this victory, because the blood the Iron Brigade would spill in the future would be on his hands too, not just theirs. He had made a monstrous compromise to make this happen, one that Greg Buchanan knew that John Underhall would not have made. Buchanan had thrown in his lot with one devil to fight another, and had thereby proven he was no angel.

A worse temptation had been denied him. If he had cornered Dr. Wissenschaft, would he have killed him? Put him down? Greg did not want to dwell on that. The only justice that could harm Dr. Wissenschaft now was vigilante justice, for the ancient monster was insulated from warrants, prosecution, or the judgment of his peers.

Johnny Saturn pulled his helmet back on over his head, and turned to leave Ground Zero, but in his heart he knew even that was pointless. No matter where he went, the bitter ruin of Spire City's Ground Zero would stay with him forever.

BEING JOHNNY SATURN

BY BENITA G. STORY

G reg unlocked the door to his apartment. It had been over three days since he was last home. It felt like three years.

Greg stumbled across his threshold, pushed the door closed and began pulling off pieces of his uniform as he tripped, bounced off the walls of his hallway and finally fell onto the mattress on his bedroom floor. He was asleep before he had the chance to cover himself with the single blanket on his bed.

Sniff.

"What?" Greg slowly fought his way to consciousness. As he did, he realized that his bladder was screaming in agony. Awkwardly, he groped his way into a standing position and headed toward the bathroom. As his body began to awaken, the screeches, pops, and cracks from his muscles and joints joined his bladder in a symphony of pain. He had never felt more like giving up and dying than at that moment. After what felt like an hour, his bladder finally emptied and his brain began its journey back toward reality.

Sniff.

"Is that bacon I smell?" Greg's head came up from being slumped against his chest, which caused a series of pops and cracks to issue from his upper vertebrae.

Greg slowly washed his hands. Then he splashed cold water onto his face and gasped as it hit his skin. All of a sudden, Greg was fully awake, and he opened his eyes to the face in the mirror. "Holy shit! Is that face mine?" What peered back at him was a series of bruises and swellings that barely resembled anything human. He glanced at his watch. 10:30. "Morning or night?" Without waiting for an answer, Greg left the bathroom.

Sniff.

"Coffee? I smell bacon and coffee." Greg stumbled down the hallway toward what would have been a living room in a normally furnished apartment. As he walked the short distance, the smells became stronger. And when he finally reached his kitchen he stopped in awe at what he saw.

There, standing at the stove, was a man with shoulders as wide as a bull-dozer. The man had his back to Greg and was taking something out of the skillet.

"It's about time you woke up!" came a gruff voice. Greg just stood there with his mouth open. The man turned around, a plate in one hand and a steaming mug in the other. He was about 6'6", had short, gray hair, and was dressed casually in a polo shirt and neatly creased slacks.

"You've been asleep for over two days," the man said.

Greg watched the giant man set the plate and mug down on the counter in front of Greg. "I'd put this on a table and offer you a chair," the man said as he looked around at the bare living space, "but it seems as if we are short on those this morning."

GREG BUCHANAN & JOHN UNDERHALL

Greg swallowed hard. "Y-you're John Underhall."

John smiled and said, "So, you aren't a total imbecile this morning, Mr. Buchanan.

Good. We have a lot to talk about." Greg took the fork he was offered and began shoveling food into his mouth. For several minutes the only sound to be heard was munching and slurping as Greg gulped down the hot food and liquid. As he ate, John turned back to the stove.

"Did you know I knew your dad? He, Brezneski, and I entered the force at the same time. Your hair style is different, but otherwise you look like Tom."

Greg had not known this, but he said nothing. He had known that Thomas Buchanan and Bruce Brezneski had been partners, but not about their association with John Underhall.

When John finished cooking his own breakfast, he leaned against the counter next to the stove and slowly ate. As he did so, he watched Greg closely. When Greg finished his meal, John reached into the pocket of his pants and tossed something at Greg. Greg barely caught it. It was a medicine bottle.

"Vicoden." Greg stared at the bottle.

"It'll help with the pain," John said as he paused from eating.

Greg continued to stare at the bottle, then, slowly, he placed it on the counter in front of him. "No, thank you."

John shrugged his shoulders. "Suit yourself. But, if you keep treating your body like you have in the past several days, you are going to need it."

Greg looked up. "And be like you? I heard you were a painkiller junkie."

John continued eating. "Used to be. Not anymore."

John Underhall, also once known as Johnny Saturn, took his now empty plate over to the sink and rinsed it, and then he did the same thing with Greg's. Greg kept a tight hold on the mug. John glanced at him, grinned and asked, "You want some more coffee?"

Greg's face muscles contorted into the closest semblance of a smile he could make at this time. "Sure!"

John chuckled and poured both of them another cup from a coffee maker that Greg didn't recognize – he didn't own one. Then John picked up his cane and led the way over to a wall next to a window. Greg watched as John slowly eased himself down into sitting position on the floor. Once John had settled, Greg slowly, and achingly, joined him.

Greg looked at John Underhall.

"What do we need to talk about? Not to be rude, but aren't you supposed to be dead? I was at your funeral."

John took a sip of the coffee and leaned his head back against the wall. "You. You and your future as Johnny Saturn."

Greg looked surprised. "My future as Johnny Saturn? You mean you aren't here to tell me to cease and desist?"

John shook his head. "Do I look like I'm in the position to take the job back?"

"Well… No. I'm here to help you become Johnny Saturn in more than just name."

Greg sat silently for a minute.

"How?"

———

JOHN UNDERHALL, GREG BUCHANAN, PERSEPHONE SYNN UNDERHALL

The Monaco International Airport terminal was crowded as John and Greg climbed down from the plane. Greg's face was still a multi-colored patchwork of bruises, but the swelling had gone down, thanks to ice packs applied regularly while John made their travel arrangements. Greg, once again, was wearing sunglasses.

From their right came a voice of welcome. "There you are!" A tall, beautiful woman with dark flowing hair came over to them and reached up to kiss John.

John turned to Greg. "Greg, this is my wife, Persephone. Persephone, this is Detective Greg Buchanan."

"Ahhh… Our own Boy Wonder!" Persephone laughed. Then she took John's arm in hers and motioned them to walk with her. "The limo is parked at our private entrance waiting for us. I'll have Vince retrieve your luggage." She looked back at Greg, and asked, "How many bags do you have?"

Greg coughed. "None," he muttered.

Persephone chuckled and looked up at her husband. "Oh! So that is how we are doing things!"

The three walked on silently. Airport employees went out of their way to keep other passengers and visitors out of their path and the trio was waived through every check point. Persephone motioned one of the employees over to her.

"Vince, be a good boy and bring John's bag to the limo. The other gentleman doesn't have any," she said as she smiled sweetly at the man.

"Very well, Ms. Helios." The man bowed slightly and walked away.

Greg watched this with a sense of moroseness. *I am making a mistake. I shouldn't be here,* he thought. John Underhall had made a convincing argument the previous night in his apartment, but the past 12 hours had shown Greg a world he had failed to remember. He had forgotten what money could do for a person, and he wasn't sure he wanted to be reminded.

Persephone and John turned down a hallway and, suddenly, there were no more passengers surrounding them. A guard saluted as the trio passed by, and then hesitated when he saw Greg. John turned toward the guard. "He's with us, Mr. Vamario." The guard nodded and saluted Greg, too. Greg nodded at the man as he walked by, unsure how to answer the salute.

The limo was a gleaming black Mercedes, and Greg squinted at the brilliant shards of sunlight that glinted off the chrome trim despite the sunglasses he was wearing. John opened one of the doors and motioned Greg to get in. Persephone followed him and John got in last. Vince appeared and loaded the one piece of luggage John had into the trunk and the driver pulled away from the curb as soon as the trunk lid was shut.

"Shouldn't we tip the man?" Greg asked before he could stop himself. Persephone's laugh rang out. "I don't have to, Mr. Buchanan. He is on my payroll."

"Don't let my wife tease you, Greg. She is the majority shareholder of this airport, as well as several other things around here," John said with a smile at Persephone.

"And don't let John fool you, Mr. Buchanan," Persephone purred as she looked lovingly at her husband. "He isn't the poor member of this family and he owns several things, too. Like the Baumgarten building in Spire City, for example."

"You own my apartment building?" Greg asked in astonishment.

"Well, yes, I do. As of last week, that is. I also own several buildings in the less… prosperous parts of the city," John said. "I own real estate all over Spire City."

"Such as?" Greg asked.

"Like the Kane Building at 3rd and Clinton that the Tailor lives and works in," John answered. "You ever wonder that you never see anyone else in the hallways when you visit?"

Greg gave him a blank look. "I just assumed it was because I am a cop."

John just smiled at him.

"Oh…," Greg muttered. "I guess we do have a lot to discuss, don't we?"

"Yes, but tomorrow. You're still recovering from battle, and what we have to talk about isn't going to be pleasant in some ways." John suddenly frowned at Greg, and

Greg wisely dropped the subject.

The house that John and Persephone owned wasn't as large or as fancy as Greg thought it would be, although it was large and fancy enough. *The truly rich don't need show homes,* thought Greg. *They aren't like the typical Nuevo riche, and John and Persephone didn't need to prove anything.*

The view over the bay was magnificent and the furnishings were tastefully expensive. His room boasted a balcony jutting over a sheer rock cliff, and the breezes coming in from the waters of the Ligurian Sea carried the taste of salt and the sound of the gulls as they hunted for fish below him. He could have stood there drinking this sight in for the rest of eternity and never tire of it.

Dinner that night was quiet and informal. Servants silently catered to their every need, with a butler in attendance to make sure all was done correctly, and then the domestics all disappeared entirely once Greg and the Underhalls had settled into a comfortable room with a wall of windows that framed a glorious sea-scape that was similar to the view from his bedroom.

Together the trio discussed recent happenings in Spire City, and Greg was very surprised to hear how well-informed John and Persephone were on the smallest details of everything on all fronts. *Their network of informants and spies must be enormous,* considered Greg. Several times, Greg found John looking at him with a frown on his face and Greg, much to his consternation, found himself almost physically flinching under its influence, the intensity of John's gaze beating down on him like a hammer. Somehow, he knew tomorrow was not going to be fun.

At 11:00 PM, a very sleepy Greg Buchanan crawled into bed. His entire being was relaxed and his blood was warm with the effects of the wonderful port he had drunk that evening. He was asleep before he knew it.

———

Bewilderment was the first feeling Greg had when he opened his eyes the next morning, and he stared around the room. The sun pouring in through the wall of glass next to him was very bright and the luxurious furnishings of the room surprised him. Then he remembered he was not in Spire City, but somewhere in Monaco at John and Persephone Underhall's home. Suddenly the so-called Dirty War that Greg Buchanan, acting as Johnny Saturn, had helped end seemed like a lifetime ago.

There was a light knock on the door and a young man walked in. "Ahh…. Mr. Buchanan is awake I see. Shall I prepare Mr. Buchanan's bath and set out all things at readiness for him?"

Greg stared at the man. "Ummm… sure."

The man bowed slightly and disappeared into the next room. Greg could hear water running and other sounds as the man did whatever it was he was doing. Curiosity overtook Greg and he got out of bed. His muscles were still very sore, and the long plane flight yesterday had done nothing to help. He found himself limping across the room as he walked toward what must be the bathroom.

The sight amazed him. The room itself was about the size of his apartment in the Baumgarten building. It contained, among the familiar tub, toilet, bidet, and sink, a raised table with padding on it and several sheets neatly folded on top. A huge glassed-in shower, as well as cabinets, chairs, paintings, china containers, and many other items were also there. It was a cross between a bathroom and an expensive spa.

The young man at the tub added some oils to the water. When he finished, he turned to Greg. "There you are, Mr. Buchanan! Please get undressed. Your bath is ready for you."

Greg slowly did as he was bidden. When he eased himself down into the scented water, he found his muscles relaxing. "What did you add to the water?" he asked.

The young man's face lit up. "That was some oils I had mixed especially for you, sir. Ms. Helios said you had been through some physically demanding times and asked me to help your body heal from them. I mixed together some helichrysum, Roman chamomile, rosemary and lavender. They will ease your muscles, clear your mind and help you feel rested."

"Oh." Greg said as he looked down at the liquid surrounding him.

"And now," the young man continued, "We must make you ready for your day. Mr. Underhall has given your schedule to me, and we must make sure you are prepared for it." The young man would have bathed Greg, had not Greg decided to do so himself.

After the bath, hair washing, and shave, Greg was placed face up and naked on the table. He closed his eyes and felt heated sheets being draped over different areas of his body. Gently and carefully at first, then roughly and hard, Greg got the massage of his life. He was soon told to turn over, and he fell asleep less than half way through the massage on his back, but when he was awakened and helped into standing position, his body was no longer in pain.

Greg smiled at the young man. "Damn! You are good! I don't hurt anywhere!"

The young man beamed. "Thank you, Mr. Buchanan. You could not pay me a greater compliment. Mr. Underhall hired me himself when he came back from your country and had surgery on his back. He says I am the reason he can walk today as easily as he does. Before long, I hope to get him to the point where he is able to move freely enough to no longer need his cane. But we have a ways to go before that happens. Now make sure you drink a lot of water today or the toxins I released from your muscles will make you very ill." The young man handed him a full water bottle to emphasize his words.

Greg nodded as he followed the young man back into the bedroom. The man went over to a wardrobe and pulled a pair of slacks, shirt and blazer from it and laid them across the bed. Then he went to a cabinet and took from it underwear, socks, and a belt. Lastly, he opened another cabinet and took a pair of shoes out and brought them over to the bed.

"You may get dressed now. I will return in 10 minutes and take you to where you will be having breakfast with Ms. Helios and Mr. Underhall." The young man bowed again, and left the room.

Greg fingered the clothes he had been given and shook his head. He got dressed and smiled at himself in the mirror. He had to hand it to the man; Greg looked and felt more human today than he had in a long time.

————

After a delicious breakfast, Persephone got up, kissed her husband on his forehead and left the room. Greg's relaxed state fled as soon as the door closed behind her.

John sat and continued eating and drinking his coffee, not paying any attention to his guest.

"Well?" Greg asked.

"Why did you partner yourself with Tactical?"

Greg winced at the question. "I couldn't think of any other way to stop the war between him and Wissenschaft. The conflict had to end so the city could begin rebuilding. I figured Tactical was the lesser of the two evils."

"You thought wrong." John sat his coffee cup down with a bang. "And that's why you are here."

Greg said nothing.

"What do you know about Nikolai Demetr?"

"Who?"

The look on John's face was grim. "That much, huh?"

John stood up and walked over to the window and looked out. "If you are going to use my old title, you have to do a better job than you have so far. I will not let you take the Saturn tradition and destroy it."

Greg sat silent. Here it comes, he thought.

"But, since you have done what you have, then it's time to do some research and figure out how to undo it." John turned and looked at Greg. "It won't be easy. Tactical, whose real name is Nikolai Demetr, isn't a man to give up what he has gained without a bitter fight."

"But Wissenschaft... I couldn't let that old Nazi butcher win!"

"Yes, I know how you feel about Wissenschaft. I know how, every time you have had him arrested, you lost, even when you had enough evidence against him to send him to the electric chair half a million times over. I know who and what he owns and how he has corrupted the system."

Greg banged his hand on the table. "Then you understand why I had to beat him!"

"At the cost of the entire city?" John's voice had a dangerous undertone in it that made Greg sweat in spite of himself. "Wissenschaft still owns the city's government, but now you have given the other half to a man who will stop at nothing, not even at destroying the very thing he seeks to rule, in order to remain on top! Where Wissenschaft is well aware of whom he hurts and doesn't care, Tactical wants to hurt everyone. Wissenschaft has some order to his life, even though we don't agree with it. Tactical is anarchy incarnate. Wissenschaft is somewhat sane. Tactical is not even close."

Greg glowered back at his host. "Then what would you have done?"

"I would have beat them both and be rid of them."

"How?"

John smiled and it was not a pretty expression. "That's what you are here to learn."

The two men glared at each other. Then Greg looked away and sighed. "I screwed up that badly?"

John crossed his arms and looked at his guest composedly for a time. "Let's just say you rushed things along too quickly. If you had done your research more thoroughly and had done some strategic planning, you could have found a way to use both of them to your purposes. They would have destroyed each other leaving you to sweep up the pieces and throw them in the trash."

Then John leaned over and planted both his hands on the table, bringing his face within inches of Greg's. "What you did, instead, was defeat neither and prolong the inevitable. You think Tactical has won and that Wissenschaft has been beaten? Wrong! Wissenschaft is just catching his breath and working out his next move. And, we now know nothing of his plans or whereabouts. You, essentially, have taken months' worth of work and set it back to zero. We have to start all over again. And Tactical and Wissenschaft will both be stronger for it. You wait and see."

Greg's head swam! Had he really done that? Had his actions been misguided by his personal vengeance against Wissenschaft? "Damn!" Greg muttered and he gritted his teeth in anger and frustration.

"You allowed yourself to become Tactical's pawn. He used you and you let him." John straightened up and recrossed his arms. "In fact, you gave yourself gift-wrapped to him."

"Damn!" Greg said, again. After regaining control of his own emotions, he looked up at his mentor. "Okay, then help me fix my mistakes."

John nodded, picked up his cane from where it leaned against his breakfast chair, and turned away. "Follow me." (John's "cane" began life as a long-handled sledge hammer, its wicked steel head gripped in his oversized hands.)

The garage facility beneath John and Persephone's house was a collector's dream made real. There had to be close to 50 vintage Indian and Harley-Davidson motorcycles in various stages of being rebuilt along with those in working order. Then there were the cars. Greg's jaw dropped as he stared at the mint condition DeLoreans, Lamborghinis, Jaguars, Bentleys, Rolls Royces, Mercedes, Porsches, Aston Martins, and Ferraris, to name just a few. There were a couple dozen mechanics working on various vehicles in several areas of the huge complex.

John looked around the place, pride showing clearly on his face. "Like my play room?"

"It's overwhelming!"

John laughed. "I can see that." Then he walked over to a group of motorcycles with Greg on his heels. "Which one do you want to use while you are here?"

Greg swallowed. There were so many to choose from that his eyes couldn't stop at any one in particular. John glanced at him. "How about that Harley?" he pointed to a gleaming navy blue bike to his left.

"Sure!" Greg found himself grinning like a little kid at Christmas. If he didn't hurry up and get out of there, he'd find himself giggling like one, too.

"Keys are in the ignition. Just follow me."

John walked over to another Harley-Davidson. On it was a special sheath for his cane.

Greg joyfully threw his leg over and sat astride the machine. He admiringly rubbed the gas tank and looked at the gauges in front of him.

"Before you decide to make love to it, we have someplace to go to," John said as he started up his bike.

Greg felt his cheeks flush. He started up his bike and heard the chugging rhythm so distinctive to Harleys. Yes, he definitely could get used to this!

The streets of the city and the roads beyond were crowded at this time of day, and it took John and Greg nearly an hour before they reached their destination in the adjoining French province of Cote D'Azur. There was a building there with a fenced-in and gated parking lot, and the parking area was about half full of vehicles that looked like junkers in comparison with what Greg had seen in John's "play room."

The interior of the building seemed stuffy and warm compared with the fresh air outdoors. John led Greg past several desks and the most notice they got were a grin or a nod. Then they arrived.

The room was large, well-lighted gym containing modern weight-lifting equipment and boxing rings. On the room's sides there were several areas of padded floor mats in different colors of blue, gray, green and black. Men were sparring with one another on many of the matted areas.

John led Greg over to a side door and knocked. The door opened to reveal a short, thickset, heavily muscled man.

"You're late, Mr. Underhall."

"Yeah, so. You have nothing better to do."

"So you say."

Greg was surprised by the man's definite Brooklyn accent amongst all of the French, Italian and German voices around him in the training room. Also, he was surprised by the two men's look of comradery as they playfully groused at one another.

John turned toward Greg. "This is Pete Andrews. Pete, this is Greg Buchanan."

Pete looked at Greg and grunted, ignoring the hand that Greg offered.

"So, he's the one?" Pete said to John.

"He's the one."

Pete pointed his thumb to a locker. "Suit up, Mr. Buchanan, and meet me over by those bags when you're ready." Pete then walked away.

"Nice manners," Greg muttered.

"He was being nice to you, Greg. You should see him when he's being rude." John laughed.

Greg's next two hours were grueling, and that morning's massage seemed like a sweet dream. Pete assigned Greg a trainer who tested what Greg already knew, then the fighter nodded and let lose. The trainer made contact several times and Greg stumbled back in pain. Greg surprised the trainer a couple of times and nailed him. Instead of getting angry, however, the trainer would nod his approval and get back up to face him.

Finally, Pete came over and threw a towel to each of them. Pete turned to the trainer. "What do you think, Jean-Claude?"

The trainer toweled off his face and vigorously rubbed his head. "Not too bad, Monsieur Andrews. He relies too much on the one technique he is good at, but he is weak in other areas."

Greg felt himself bristling in spite of himself, but remained quiet.

"Then, again," the trainer continued, "I understand that he has recently faced many opponents and that he is standing here, alive, to fight again. That shows courage! He has much potential."

Pete grunted and turned to Greg and pointed off to their right. "The shower room is over there. Meet me and John in my office when you are ready." Pete then walked away. Greg looked at Jean-Claude who was chuckling. "That Monsieur Andrews, he is droll, but he likes you."

"Really?"

"Oh yes! If he didn't, he wouldn't have asked my opinion. He would have just shown you the showers and then the exit."

"Joy!" thought Greg as he thanked the amiable trainer and headed to his locker to retrieve his clothes before heading to the shower room.

What is John setting me up for? Greg wondered.

By the time Greg was clean and dressed, he had begun to hurt all over. He hoped and prayed the massage of that morning would be repeated the next day…or that evening before going to bed. John and Pete were sitting, relaxed with coffee cups in hand when Greg walked into the office.

John handed Greg a cup and indicated a chair. Greg sat with a groan.

"Well, Mr. Buchanan, here's what we are going to do," Pete said. He pointed to a sheet of paper in front of him with what looked like a list written on it. "You are good at the Krav Maga style, but any fighter worth his salt is going to figure that out pretty quick and use it to his advantage."

"Okay…"

"So, we are going to teach you boxing, judo, and some down and dirty street fighting techniques I learned growing up in Brooklyn. That way you can use whatever works from each of them and keep your opponents off-guard." Pete handed the list to Greg.

Greg looked it over. It was a schedule of workouts and training sessions. Greg's eyes widened and he looked at John. "How long will all of this take? I thought we had work to do in Spire City?"

"Two months," said John. "I should have a bead on our friends by then."

Greg looked back down at the schedule. "All of this in two months?"

John looked at him with a grimace that passed for smile on him. "That's only the start of it."

———

Dinner that night was just the two men.

"Where's Ms. Helios?" Greg asked.

John looked concerned. "She's not feeling very well. She thinks she ate something while out today that isn't sitting with her very well."

"Oh. I hope she's okay."

"The doctor says she will be."

The two ate in silence. At the end of the meal, John led Greg to his study, and old-world affair that hinted at Gothic. John's chair was a huge, wooden seat with a Saturn symbol carved high into its back. John opened a file cabinet and handed Greg a couple of thick files. "Your bedtime reading material," John explained.

The first file was labeled Nikolai Demetr and the second was labeled Dr. Karl Wissenschaft. Greg nodded.

John then handed Greg a tablet of paper, a pen and a highlighter. "Those are your copies of what we have on file to date on these individuals. We'll discuss what you have learned tomorrow after breakfast."

"And then?" Greg asked.

"And then we'll begin working out how to defeat both of them without destroying the rest of the city in the process."

Greg nodded again and bit his bottom lip.

Once in his room, he got undressed and climbed into bed. Next to his nightstand he discovered a lap desk and a tablet computer and he put them to use.

The following morning, the young man who had assisted him yesterday morning woke him up by shaking him gently. Greg had fallen to sleep over his research and the bed was covered with paper.

"It is time to get up, Mr. Buchanan. I have brought Marco with me. Beginning today, he will help you as I did yesterday. He is my apprentice!"

Greg then noticed the man standing behind the masseuse. If Greg had been called "Pretty Boy" it was only because the rest of the Spire City Police Department hadn't seen this young man.

Marco helped Greg with his bath and worked Greg's muscles into order that morning. Marco was a quiet man, whereas his supervisor had been talkative. But Marco's hands had worked the same miracles and, when Greg praised him, Marco's smile was just as bright. It was obvious that he enjoyed his work.

Greg continued to study the files until called for breakfast. Again, it was only he and John eating together.

"Is Persephone still sick?" Greg asked.

"I think she is better. She said she didn't feel very hungry so left us to it," John answered. But his face still showed signs of worry.

Over the meal, they discussed what Greg had read, or, rather, Greg talked and John listened with a frown on his face. When they left the table and headed to the garage to retrieve their bikes, Greg felt like a school boy who had not studied the right subject for a test the following morning. He frowned in consternation as he followed John through the city and out into the country east along the coast. Their destination that day was not the same as it had been the day before. This time, John took Greg to the nearby U.S. Army base, Camp Darby, near Pisa, Italy. Even though John was no longer a member of the military, he still had powerful contacts and security clearance to certain areas.

After signing Greg in as a guest, John took Greg to the office of one Staff Sgt. William Miller.

"Staff Sgt. Miller, this is Detective Greg Buchanan," John said by way of introduction.

After shaking hands with Greg and John, Staff Sgt. Miller indicated chairs for them to sit in and returned to his seat behind the desk. "And how can I be of service to you today Captain Underhall?"

"I need Greg to learn some important strategy techniques and how to implement them in combat, and I need him to learn quickly."

Sgt. Miller's eyebrows rose. "What do you have going on?"

John briefly outlined the recent events in Spire City. "Since I am no longer able to take an active part in this, I am training Detective Buchanan to take my place and continue what I began."

The staff sergeant frowned. "Under whose authority is this being done?"

"Mine."

Staff Sgt. Miller and John Underhall stared at each other for several moments. "This will have to be off the record, of course," John added.

"Of course." Staff Sgt. Miller rose from his desk. "If you will follow me, Detective Buchanan." Greg wondered what favor Staff Sgt. Miller owed John for this to be happening.

———

The next month was a blur to Greg. He spent every other day at the training center getting beaten to a pulp, and the alternate day at the Army base being drilled on tactical and strategic techniques. At the end of each day, he fell to sleep over his "homework" and each morning he was tended to by Marco. He lost all track of time and place as he worked.

By the beginning of the second month, Greg noticed that his workouts were becoming easier. He no longer found himself kissing the mat several times during each session and, in fact, more often than not, had Jean-Claude groaning on the floor in front of him. At this time, the training facility began a rotation of other trainers working with Greg. He found himself looking forward to the workouts and each new challenge thrown at him.

His work at Camp Darby, too, became, if not easier, more interesting. He had graduated from studying books and manuals to field work. Greg found himself a member of different teams, all working on different assignments. He screwed up sometimes, but the situations he dealt with were becoming more and more difficult. Soon, he graduated from teammate to squad leader. This didn't fill him with pride, but it terrified him that he might make a wrong decision and lose his entire team. More and more, he found that his gut reactions were the correct choices and gained confidence by this discovery. He was learning to trust his abilities and himself.

Each morning, after breakfast, John and Greg worked on the Tactical-Wissenschaft problem. The main issue was that no one had been able to discover where Wissenschaft was hiding. To make the situation more dire, Tactical had surrounded himself with a band of mercenaries, all metavillains, which made the original Iron Brigade look like a bunch of kindergarteners.

One morning, when Greg entered the breakfast room, he was surprised to find that there was an additional guest at the table. She was a tall woman, nearly Persephone's height, with long blond hair, piercing green eyes and a straight, inflexible posture.

"Good morning, Greg. This is Victoria Shelbourne. Victoria, this is Greg Buchanan," Persephone said.

Greg and Victoria shook hands, and then Persephone smiled and added, "Better known as Johnny Saturn and Staff of Life."

Greg's face lit up. "You're Staff of Life? With the Squadron Premiere?"

"What's left of the Squadron Premiere, yes," Victoria answered. "And you? You are taking over John's old job?"

"Trying to continue the tradition, but John has left some pretty big shoes to fill, Ms. Shelbourne," Greg said.

Victoria looked from Greg to John. "Actually," said John, "once his training is complete, he will be well on his way to becoming the "real" Johnny Saturn."

"I've heard you handled yourself really well during the Dirty War," said Victoria.

Greg was horrified to find himself blushing. It was the first compliment that John Underhall had paid him since his arrival five weeks earlier.

That night, after dinner, the four of them retired to the library to talk. Greg could sense that Victoria was uncomfortable. He was tired and quiet, so he let John and Persephone lead most of the conversation. Finally, Greg stood up and said he was off to bed.

"Please stay, Mr. Buchanan," Victoria said. "Since you are part of this whole mess, you might as well be a part of this as well." Greg sat back down.

Victoria got up from the couch and walked over to the window overlooking the bay. The sun had set and the lights from the royal palace next to them and the hotels and other businesses along the coast made a picturesque setting. Greg watched her and waited with John and Persephone to see what Victoria had to say.

"I failed." Victoria spit the words out like venom. "I failed, and look how many people were killed because of it."

Greg's face registered the shock he felt, but both John and Persephone's faces remained relaxed and calm.

Victoria turned around. "Who do I think I am? I am a physicist, not a metahuman. I am a college professor with absolutely no metapowers trying to be a hero in a world of metaheroes."

"I have no metapowers, either, but I don't consider myself a failure," John said quietly.

"You didn't watch a team member who was like a little sister to you get fried to a crisp in front of your eyes, either!" Victoria then broke down to tears and sobbed. Persephone quietly rose from her place next to her husband and went over to Victoria. After some soothing words from Persephone, the two women left the room together.

"Well…" Greg said.

"Hmmm…" John answered. "My father-in-law has a lot to answer for, doesn't he?"

"Father-in-law?"

John looked up at Greg. "Something else you didn't know, eh?"

Greg looked embarrassed.

John smiled. "Well, I'm not surprised. It's not something I've advertised much." John then rose from his seat. "Let's call it a night. I think we are all tired."

The next morning, after a quiet breakfast with no Victoria Shelbourne or Persephone in attendance, John and Greg rode out, but not to the Army base, but to a place several hours outside of the country and high up in the French Alps. The house they arrived at was isolated, with no other soul present. The wind hurtling itself down the mountainside made dust devils near one corner of the building and threatened to send everything back to the valley via the short route.

John took a bag out of his motorcycle's trunk and led Greg into the house. It was cold, barren and dusty. John tossed the bag onto the only piece of furniture in the one-room building, an army cot in the corner next to an empty fireplace.

"Wood is out back. Why don't you bring in some while I bring in your bike," John suggested. Then he walked out the front door.

Greg stood still for a moment, and then did as he was told. He no longer questioned the man he looked up to as his mentor. There was a large stack of split firewood just outside the back door. Greg could also see the stone base and roof of a well, the rope from the wench disappearing down through a hole in its lid. He gathered up as big an armload of kindling as he could carry and took it back inside. John was just parking Greg's bike against the room's back wall.

"You have some matches in that bag, Army rations, a flashlight, a notebook and pen, a blanket and a small, blow-up pillow," John said indicating the bag on the cot. "I'll be back in a few days. You stay here until I return."

"And do what?"

John gave Greg a hard look. "Think."

With that John walked out, and Greg heard the big Harley-Davidson start up. Before he could get to the front door, John was gone.

Greg took a deep breath and then let it go, his cheeks puffing out as he did so. He looked around him slowly, taking it in. He looked at his motorcycle, tempted to just get on it and follow John back to his house. Then Greg shook his head. This was part of his training. Something here was supposed to teach Greg how to be stronger. Shivering in the wind that was whistling through the two open doors, his first move was to close the doors and build a fire.

The house never got warm enough for Greg to not to see his breath. His one blanket was hardly worth the trouble of unfolding it and he slept in his clothes and coat that night, hands tucked in his armpits and teeth chattering. By morning, he had gone from inwardly cursing to creating new and elaborate curses just for John.

When he went outside at daybreak to relieve himself and gather more wood, the view stopped him in his tracks. The wind had softened into a breeze and a hard frost had fallen overnight making the trees bare branches hoary white. There was a mist rising up from the valley below and the early morning sun turned the clouds at the eastern horizon into soft pinks, lavenders and peaches. Everything sparkled with the freshness of the dawn. He had not realized how high into the mountains John had taken him.

After washing his face and trying to clean his teeth (John could have at least packed him a toothbrush!) with the icy water from the well, Greg sat down and looked at his choices for breakfast. It wasn't a cheery sight and he pushed it all back into the bag until he finally got hungry enough to face it.

That day, he alternately tended the fire and brooded. By sundown, the rations allotted to him finally began to look appealing and he was surprised to find that they tasted better than expected. With the rising wind as his company, he carried in as much wood as would fit between the back wall of the house and the back door, the activity helping to warm him. He stoked the fire and watched it roar. Later, he banked the fire as best as he could and lay down on the cot.

That night he actually slept.

That next morning was a repeat of the previous one. After washing down breakfast with the icy well water (John could have provided a coffee pot and some coffee!), Greg decided to take a look at his surroundings. He quickly discovered a path at the back of the house and followed it. The view around him caused him to pause and stare every few hundred feet, and it was mid-afternoon before he thought of turning back toward "home."

John had left him there to think. Fine. What was he supposed to think about? Tactical? Wissenschaft? What he was going to do once he got back to Spire City? Greg frowned and sat down on a stump. Fine. So, he would think.

The silence finally pierced his awareness. There were no birds here, high in the late autumn mountains. In a couple of weeks, it would be Thanksgiving. What had he to be thankful for this year? What had he to be thankful for in any year?

For the first time since he had decided to become Johnny Saturn, Greg felt his old constant companion, depression, settle over him. Since his first visit with the Tailor who built his armor, Greg wanted something harder to drink than the expensive port wine John and Persephone had poured for him each night after dinner.

For the first time since he had gone out and bullied Manny and his crew into giving him information on Wissenschaft's whereabouts, Greg remembered that he was Greg Buchanan, Pretty Boy Detective, hated throughout the entire police force, and not Johnny Saturn, vigilante/hero.

He suddenly understood Victoria Shelbourne's frustration at being a non-powered person in a metapowered world. Who did he think he was, trying to play in a game much bigger than himself? What made him think he could take over and make things better just by wearing a stupid costume and punching people? What gave him the right to take other people's lives into his own hands and manipulate them in accordance with his own vision?

For that matter, what gave Wissenschaft and Tactical that right?

Greg stood up and began walking back toward his little hide-a-way in the mountains. The more he thought, the quicker his steps became and soon he was almost running.

Then he stopped. Why was he running? Was he running toward or away from something? That made him think harder. What was behind his intention of being Johnny Saturn? Was he really trying to make the world a better place, or was he just trying to destroy one man? And, what made that one man worse than any of the others in the first place? Was it because of what he saw as a child while with his father?

It was gone. His memory almost produced something that had set him on his self-imposed path of self-destruction and the destruction of Dr. Karl Wissenschaft. But it was gone. Greg sat down where he was and wept silently.

Three days later, while Greg was gathering his evening firewood before sitting down to the next to last ration package, he heard something. His head came up. Was it the wind in the chimney or had some animal gotten onto the roof?

It was getting louder. It was the familiar rumble of a Harley-Davidson motorcycle. Greg Buchanan's exile was over.

That night, sitting next to a roaring fire in a mountain lodge, his stomach full of hot, simple, filling food, Greg turned to face John Underhall. Apparently, John had been waiting for this.

When John had arrived to take Greg away from the house on the mountain side, there had been very little conversation between them. Even over the hearty supper placed before them, nothing was said. Only now, here in the mountain darkness, the only light coming from the dancing fire before them, did words come.

"You told me to think, so I did," Greg said.

"And?"

Greg frowned and looked into his wine glass. "Why did you become Johnny Saturn?"

John's eyebrows rose. "Because I wanted to make a difference on a level that the metas and the police couldn't touch. Besides, this last time, I watched my father-in-law, Dr. Synn, sink deeper into his psychosis, and I knew I was the only one who knew what he was capable of doing. I had no intention of it lasting beyond stopping him."

"No overwhelming urge to save the world?"

"No, only my community, my city. The rest of the world could be saved by their own local people, but not by me."

"Oh." Greg looked into the fire.

"And what did you think about?" John asked.

Greg took a long sip of the mulled wine and waited until the warmth of it spread throughout his body to his toes and fingers.

"I thought about why I decided to follow in your path."

"And?"

Greg took another sip of the wine. "I discovered I was wrong."

"In becoming Johnny Saturn?"

"To try to become John Underhall." Greg drained his glass and sat the empty vessel on the table at his side.

"Everything I did was based around the 'What would John Underhall do?' question. Not once did I ask 'What would Greg Buchanan do?'"

Greg leaned forward and picked up the poker. He used it to shift a log in the fireplace, watched the shower of sparks as they rose and crackled, then leaned back, poker still in his hand.

"I believed that John Underhall would just wade in and bash his way through the throng of bad guys and come out on top. I should have known better. I knew your background as an Army Ranger, as a cop, as one of the best detectives on the force. I should have realized that you succeeded because of brains, not necessarily brawn. I also realized you were able to do all you did because of your desire to see it through no matter what, or how long it took." Greg weighed the poker in his hand, then sat forward and replaced it in the stand.

"Somehow, I feel like the last six weeks of being with you and following your training plan, has been a condensed version of what it has been like to be you," said Greg.

"And?"

"Johnny Saturn is one individual: you've been him, I've been him, and I'm sure someone in the future will be him.

"I don't want to be you. I want to be me. But I want to be a smarter me than I have been in the past. I no longer want to play by my old rules and screw who gets hurt because of it. That really made me no better than Wissenschaft."

John sat silently waiting.

"You are right. I have made a huge blunder with the whole Tactical-Wissenschaft thing. I let my arrogance lead me down the easier path, and that path was into Tactical's grasp. I didn't see it at the time, but I do, now."

"And what are you going to do about it?"

Greg thought about that. "How much time do we have left before I should go back home?"

"Two weeks."

Greg leaned forward and placed his elbows on his knees. He looked square into John Underhall's eyes.

"I need your assistance to bring peace to Spire City again. I want to help you undo my damage and to get things back on the right path. I'm ready to take guidance from you rather than try to be you. Hell, no one can be another you!"

John drained his own wine glass and sat it down next to him. He, too, leaned forward, and said, "Then I need to tell you what I've been remote orchestrating these past six weeks in Spire City."

Greg listened in amazement as John outlined his activities remodeling Greg's apartment building interior and levels beneath the ground into a strategic headquarters. He told Greg how he had a tunnel built with its own subway system to connect Greg with the Tailor, the underground city of Elysium, and other exit points around the city. He explained the network of mole people who worked for him in obtaining information, supplies, and technology. He described the micro intranet he had constructed and how the mole people were working beneath the city creating a working intelligence network that far outshone anything the international governments could do.

"Why do you think this is all working as well as it is, Greg?"

Greg thought for a moment. "Because it is on their home turf?"

"Exactly! If Tactical loses this fight and survives, he just moves on. If he destroys the city and survives, he just moves on. No skin off his teeth. No ties, no connection, just apathy and an every-man-for-himself mentality. And that's what will make him risk it all in the end and lose!" John's eyes were shining with the fervor he felt.

"What about Wissenschaft?"

"We'll get him when the time is right. He's a minor player in the overall scheme of things. Besides, he's old. Give him time and he'll be dead anyway, and his organization will crumble with his body. We've already put a stop to his mole people abductions. He has to change tactics, and that's when we'll nail him."

Greg sighed. "I'm not so sure. I think you underestimate him."

John stopped to consider this. "Perhaps, I do. Then we'll have to make plans to stop him as well. Like I said, we'll pit the two of them against each other, if we can, and let them do our dirty work for us. I believe they have sufficient animosity toward one another that something can be arranged."

———

For the next two weeks, John and Greg worked together, monitoring the intelligence network created and maintained by the mole people in Spire City, supervising the renovations at Greg's apartment building and the tunnels beneath it, and working to head off some of Tactical's worst victimization of Spire City's general population. Lastly, they both agreed that it was important for Greg to continue to keep his job in the Spire City police department for the time being. That gave Greg access to the City's computer system and allowed them the chance to throw the corrupt members of the city's government and civic employees off the scent.

Finally, the day arrived for Greg to fly back to Spire City. Marco gave him one last massage in the luxurious bathroom-spa, and Greg dressed one last time in clothes tailor made to fit him. Over the last two months, his clothes had to be remade several times as his shoulders widened and his muscles grew. After breakfast, Greg descended into the garage one last time to say goodbye to the Harley-Davidson that he had used during his stay. Man, was he going to miss that machine!

The wait at the airport was short and soon his flight was ready to leave. Greg and Victoria were flying back together and it was the first time he had seen the sometime metahero since that first night after her arrival. Somehow she seemed different, more relaxed. Greg wondered if she were going home as changed as he was.

Once in the air, Greg and Victoria talked of their lives and Greg was surprised to learn about Victoria's many failed relationships and her research at the university. She seemed excited to be going home and resuming her life. Greg leaned back and smiled. It was funny. He was looking forward to going back as well. But as Greg Buchanan and not as a John Underhall wannabe. And he was looking forward to the work that he and John had planned out for him.

Yes, life was good.

JOHNNY SATURN AND THE OLD WOLF

D eep beneath Spire City, below the maze of abandoned subway tunnels, access passages, air vents, and forgotten basement chambers, persisted the shadow of a wolf. Now nearly spent after all his countless millennia of existence, the Old Wolf rested, his yellow and red eyes gleaming in the preternatural darkness. He was older than mankind, and it had been he who taught the humans how to hunt by example. In his time, he had been called Teppe'n of lost Ultima Thule, and, later on, the nightmarish loup garou of Western Europe. He'd been a man, a wolf-man, and, before that, he'd been the grandfather of all wolves. When he howled, the sky quaked, the trees recoiled, and the earth whimpered. Now, he was part of the shadows, and he dreamed of ancient days.

I had travelled a long way to see this elder elemental, this wolf-man.

I had several names, but these days I called myself Johnny Saturn, and I was a sort of wolf among men and metahumans myself. I had determined I would find this Old Wolf—as he was called—and learn his secrets, or I would die trying. I didn't care, really, because the manic joy of chaos churned in my brain, and the smothering depression that usually held me in its thrall had been drawn back, leaving me with a wicked grin and the desire to break things. I was not a nihilist by nature, but when I got like this, I wanted to see everything crumble to dust around me.

Let it all fall, my mind seemed to say, *leave not one stone upon another.*

I was not a sane man, but what healthy, well-adjusted person would don the cowl of a mystery man and fight crime one punch at a time?

For that matter, what sane man would descend into the earth in search of the Teppe'n of Ultima Thule, also known as the Shadow Wolf and the Old Wolf? I would face him, and I would emerge from the earth reborn, or I would embrace my demise. I was no stranger to death, after all, for I had walked the shores beyond life once before, learning things that cannot be expressed with words.

And I had returned.

I had paid a price for this wisdom, for, as a man once dead, all mysteries were now open to me. All I had paid for this dubious reward was my left leg from just above the knee down. I'd replaced my lost leg with a mechanical one, but it was a poor trade by any reckoning.

Spire City's underworld was rich with the lost souls of men and women who had fallen between the cracks in the society above. Called the mole people, they lived in the dark, either because they had turned their backs on the American dream, or because of mental illness, drugs, alcohol, or human trafficking. These people were humanity's rejects, yet they were not without a tribe of their own.

Elysium City, the city beneath the city, lay in a cavernous chamber deep in Spire City's forgotten infrastructure. Elysium City, somewhat of a shanty town, was built in a space large enough to produce rain. When first experienced, the underground rain seemed odd and out of place, but this was not so. All great structures, such as the interiors of zeppelin hangers or monstrous caves, were large enough to develop micro climates and precipitation.

No one could remember what this series of wide, tall, interconnected subterranean spaces had been originally—a forgotten reservoir here, an abandoned power station there—now it housed a settlement built from recycled materials, all scavenged from what the surface world had thrown away. The mole people had built rickety buildings atop older rickety buildings. Electricity was pirated in, and, where the town wasn't illuminated by light bulbs, it was lit by fires. This was a community that was simultaneously wondrous for its absurd improbability and terrible for its poverty.

I had been down to Elysium City many times, and I had allies here. In a central area that served the town as a sort of forum and administrative center, I was escorted to see Doc. Charles "Doc" Ledmun was the under city's custodian, though he didn't claim that title. In his former life, Doc had been a surgical nurse, but now he was an unofficial street doctor and a man of undeniable wisdom. If you suffered from a broken bone, or needed a tooth extracted, a sore dressed, or a gunshot wound treated, Doc was your man. If you needed arbitration, or access to the city's limited resources, he, also, was the man you needed to see.

"Johnny Saturn," said Doc, "it's a pleasure to see you, my boy. How are you doing?"

I returned Doc's greeting, and we stood for a moment in awkward silence. He could see that I was in a dark place mentally, and he waited for me to continue. Finally, I said, "I've come to see the Old Wolf. This is my last stop before I approach him face to snout."

"Greg," said Doc, calling me by my civilian name, "it's not a good thing to go looking for the Old Wolf. That's for madmen and those who are sick of life. Nobody within living memory has seen the Old Wolf and returned to tell the tale."

"I wonder why the Old Wolf's lair would be here, under Spire City?" I said. "I mean, it seems like everything happens here."

"From what I've been told," said Doc, "The Old Wolf's lair can be found in any dark, deep place that you search for it. I'm not one for spiritual clap-trap, but the message is clear—the Old Wolf's lair is everywhere and nowhere as needed."

Doc and I spoke further, although I stopped paying attention to the conversation. If I were going to continue wearing the cowl of the mystery man called Johnny Saturn, then I had to face down the Old Wolf. I had lost my way in this life, and the Old Wolf, with his great wisdom, could set me on the right path. Or, he would devour me. It didn't matter all that much to me at this point which way it went.

I left the warm glow of Elysium City behind and traveled a rugged road of steam tunnels, sewer access shafts, and the pilings of massive skyscrapers that pierced the earth like stony roots. For a while I passed graffiti-painted walls, mole people camps, and the remnants of human habitation. Then, I was alone, passing among the trash, dust, and shapeless, angry ghosts. I was truly by myself then, climbing and walking where no one had dared to tread in many years.

I entered a long vault, the use and origin of which I could not guess, and walked among its crude support columns. The cool, damp air reeked of decay and mold. At the far end of this space there was an open, iron door, and beyond that lay seemingly impenetrable darkness.

I stopped before the door, and I listened. Something breathed heavily in the darkness beyond, and I was sure I caught sight of... I'm not sure what. It was a shadow against darkness, a sort of hyper-opaque blackness in a sea of shadow.

"My name is Johnny Saturn," I said. My voice sounded hollow to my own ears. "And I have come to see the Old Wolf, he who was once Tebbe'n of Ultima Thule."

I heard a dreadfully deep growl, and a huge shape shambled into view. Even I was impressed.

Approximately twelve feet tall, walking on long, canine back legs with each paw as big as a desk, the werewolf entered my lantern's radius. Hugely muscled, with massively thick arms that almost scraped the floor and talons longer than the leg I'd lost, the werewolf walked upright, yet there was no semblance of man in his face, with his prodigious jaws, flattened ears, and otherworldly yellow eyes. As giant monsters go, this thing was awe-inspiring. I thought I'd seen it all in my career, but this werewolf was the size of a box truck and infinitely more menacing.

"You should leave this place, Johnny Saturn," came the werewolf's voice. It was almost melodic, yet impossibly deep. "But I suppose it's too late for that, really. You can't possibly outrun me. Now you shall be my supper—bones, armor, and all. I am Fiernor, son of Fenris, and your way stops here."

"You bore me," I said, because he did. "I come to see the Old Wolf, not trade words with his door man."

The giant werewolf's growl was almost deafening, and he shot at me with the mass and speed of a freight train. He was fast, but not faster than my shotgun.

My custom automatic AA-12 fired six grenade cartridges in quick succession, and each projectile pierced the werewolf's hide and exploded from within. It was a gruesome sight, and I laughed maniacally. Maybe I should have been afraid of dying again, but I wasn't.

I was having the time of my life!

"Silver bullets? Booyah!" I cried as the werewolf stumbled and fell back. Since my shells weren't silver, I could see the horrific wounds I'd inflicted begin to heal almost immediately.

"You'll regret that," said the werewolf, its eyes now glowing red with rage.

"Maybe," I said, firing the tasers with which I had armed each of my gauntlets. "Maybe not."

Fiernor lit up like a lightning storm, and then he fell down, his fur smoking. He appeared to be dead.

"I believe I'll continue now," I said, perhaps too smugly.

The werewolf wasn't dead, of course, and his massive clawed hand shot out and grabbed me by the torso, pinning my arms to my sides. Only my armor saved me, because Harvey "The Tailor" Torres had quilted it from layers of a Kevlar-Nomex blend impregnated with shear thickening fluid over ceramic micro scale mail on top of gel impact dispersion cells over a Kevlar-Dyneema weave. Honestly, I don't know what half of that means, but I did know my suit was incredibly bullet and puncture resistant.

Using the retina display in my visor, I activated the unique power coupling circuitry I had gotten from Captain Barometer, initiated my scalar force field, and expanded it until the werewolf's claws popped open and I was free. The lycanthrope was quick, though, far quicker than me, and he was on top of me again, ripping and shredding at me and bearing me down beneath his massive weight.

I threw a desperate throat punch, but there was too much fur, gristle, and fat between my fist and the werewolf's windpipe to make a decisive strike. I still connected, though, because my kinetic transformer knuckle duster empowered my blow with enough momentum to snap back the werewolf's head. He collapsed in a huge pile of fur and claws.

The wolf man tried to rise once and failed, and then he tried again. He was a werewolf, so he would rapidly heal, but for the moment he was down.

"I don't want to kill you," I said. "Let's say I passed the challenge, and you and I both live to tell the tale, eh?"

The werewolf stared at me for a moment, and then a canine smile spread across his muzzle. "Agreed, Johnny Saturn. Go forth."

"No hard feelings?"

"None," said Fiernor, son of Fenris. "Good luck when you meet the Old Wolf."

I winked a quick salute to the werewolf, and then I marched into the shadows beyond the door.

In the space beyond, neither my electric lantern nor my LED penlight could pierce the darkness around me, and the same was true of my helmet's night vision lens. It was disorientating at first, but I had spent my life in a darkness of sorts, within the murky depths of depression that deadened my senses. You probably would call it clinical depression, but I call it every day, every week, and every year. What surrounded me now was only a physical darkness, and, when compared with depression, it was almost comforting.

———

Something rustled in the blackness, something big. I heard claws on the stone floor. Whatever else could be said of the Old Wolf, he was huge. I could sense his bulk, for such things are often a function of hearing, not sight. (As a vigilante, I had spent a lot of time listening to the pitchy blackness, and I had learned to "hear" mass and movement, though I was hard put to explain how this was so. I believe these days they referred to this ability as "passive echo location.")

"I've come a long way to meet you, Tebbe'n of Ultima Thule," I said. "May I see you?"

"No," whispered the Old Wolf. "You may not. There is nothing left to see. I am only a shadow, after all."

Shadow or not, that deep, bottomless voice seemed powered by lungs as big as industrial blowers, and moist heat rolled over me with each word the Old Wolf spoke. I was a mystery man, so I was used to impressive things. Something told me that this being put all those other things to shame.

"When I was dead, I was told to seek you out, Old Wolf. I didn't expect to return to this world, but..."

"Now all mysteries are laid open before you, is that it? That may be true, human, but I am no mystery. Your kind has forgotten me, yet was it not I who taught mankind to hunt? Did they not learn to speak by imitating my howls? Was it not I who taught your first shamans how to journey to the spirit world, speak with the spirits and gods, and return with their wisdom?"

"We know the answers to those questions, Old Wolf," I said. I knew from experience that you had to let mythological figures work their way up to the point.

"The world has changed. No longer do I run with my lupine children. Men half remember me in faerie tales, telling stories of how I blew down houses and ate cloaked travelers and their grandmothers, and infiltrated mankind in my many guises. They have forgotten my claws of iron, my scimitar-sized fangs, and my fur tougher than any human armor. They have forgotten the Wild Hunt, or how I ate Wotan during Ragnarok. They have forgotten Tebbe'n of Ultima Thule."

"I feel your sadness, Elder, but I have to hear your message." I stood in the darkness, listening to the Old Wolf's massive lungs draw breath, and centuries passed disguised as seconds.

"When you died," began the Old Wolf, "you returned as the avenger, marching beneath the banner of Saturn. You have slain your monster, and your vengeance is done. Now you have descended deep into the earth. You have faced your mortality in the form of Fiernor at my abode's gate, and you have asked for wisdom from the Old Wolf beyond its threshold. Clearly, you see the metaphor of death and rebirth in this journey, Johnny Saturn."

"Yeah," I replied. At first I was puzzled that the Old Wolf knew my name, but then he seemed to know everything, and I had announced myself when I arrived here.

"Now, I shall ask you a question. Your response will determine if you return to the world of men and metahumans so far above us."

"Hit me," I said. My mania was withdrawing, and the confidence in my voice did not sound as true to me as it had before.

"If you wish," said the Old Wolf, "I will lift the heavy malaise that chains you down, and you may walk forth healed in mind and heart. Is this your desire?"

"Of course not," I replied thoughtfully. "If I lost my mental issues, then who would I be? I certainly wouldn't be Johnny Saturn, and I doubt I would even be Detective Greg Buchanan of the SCPD. I'm not trying to be flip, but my depression and mania define me. I hate my illness' crippling effects, and the suffering, but there really is no Greg Buchanan without it."

I thought I heard the Old Wolf chuckle, but I couldn't be sure, for his canine larynx was ill-suited for human vocalizations, so maybe the chuckle was a growl.

"Then it is settled," said the Old Wolf. "Once you were an avenger, but now you are a shaman. You led your tribe to war, and now you will see to the tribe's spiritual needs. You have traveled beyond this illusory world, and now you have returned with answers to the questions that vex others. Mystery men and metaheroes will turn to you, for you have seen past this flimsy life to the greater reality, and, as much as it will pain them, you will speak truth. Your new life begins today, and your tribe awaits your ministrations."

I smiled ruefully, because this was not really what I had expected.

"Old Wolf, what if I had asked you to take away my mental illness?"

"You would not have. The seeds of what you now have become have always been in you. Do you remember what you saw the first time that you, in your role as Johnny Saturn, approached Karl Wissenschaft?"

"Always," I replied. "Instead of the man, I had a vision of an avatar of death with a halo of radiating graves around his fleshless skull. I can't ever forget that."

"That was your first vision as the shaman you would become. Now, leave me, Johnny Saturn. Your tribe needs you, and I would return to my dreams of hunting with my brothers, running like the wind, our howls filling the endless horizons."

Armed with new goals, and perhaps new reasons to live, I turned my back on the Old Wolf's dark chamber. I leave you to decide what lessons I walked away with. Sure, I could prattle on about what I learned, but I knew by now that there was little point in it. No matter how profound the lesson, your answers are not mine, and my answers are not yours. One man's wisdom is another man's foolish platitude, and I have no desire to share my tired expressions with you.

Nothing more needed to be said, so I left that place, returning to the world of sun, men, and metahumans.

SKORN

SKORNED

Mr. J. William Medal, Esquire, did not have the look one typically associated with the word "hero." It was not that he was not handsome, because he was—thick, brunette hair, a strong jaw, and piercing blue-gray eyes confirmed that. He was twenty-eight, upwardly mobile, with powerful arms, and a promising future at the Spire City branch of the law firm of Gray, Gray, and Gris. His office wall was covered in framed certificates and awards, such as Young Lawyer of the Year, the ISBA Laureate Award, the Diversity Leadership Award, and Super Lawyer Awards from 2010, 2011, and 2012.

Will could have looked like a metahero, but for one thing—his wheelchair. Will was a paraplegic. He had lost the use of his legs to a childhood spinal cord injury. His accident had not been anything remarkable or heroic—he did not push a blind man out of the way of a careening truck, nor did he take a bullet intended for someone else. Nothing like that. He merely had fallen into an old well at his Grandfather's farm, breaking through the rotten wood that covered it and onto the pile of stones that had been used partially to close it up.

Will did not remember much about that day, and he did not dwell on it. His mother had done her best, and if he had a father... Well, he had a father, but one that was not around. John William, aka Will, was born out of wedlock, and Medal was his mother's surname.

Tragedy did not slow Will down. Illegitimate, and "differently-abled," he had tackled life and taken it on. He had excelled at everything he ever tried, and he had a real talent for law and business. He had been the class salutatorian at the Indiana University Maurer School of Law, and he had clerked for a judge in the United States Court of Appeals. In his short career, Will already had earned the reputation as the corporate lawyer to watch out for; a real up-and-comer.

Will did not feel like an up-and-comer today. He sat in his small, private office and held a letter in his hand. If anything, he felt terribly conflicted: sad, angry, jealous, lonely, or a potent mix of all these emotions. He had the group secretary, Mrs. Marsh, draw his blinds and close his door. Will took a deep breath and lifted the letter again, reading it for the third time.

> *Dear Will:*
> *You have no doubt heard reports of my death, and that I died in battle with Dr.*
> *Horatio Synn."*

True enough. Johnny Saturn's demise had been featured in the headlines for weeks: John Underhall, mystery man, had given his life to foil the plot of terrorist Dr. Horatio Synn. The news had rocked Will's world. He had not known his father well, yet the old cop and crime-fighter had been his hero. Johnny Saturn, the street-level avenger, belonged to the city, and now to history, but to Will, this was his biological father. The two of them had had times together and conversations that were just their own. These were memories that were special to Will, a connection that belonged to the two of them and no one else. The world had lost a hero, but Will had lost his personal hero and dad, and that was a huge distinction.

Logically, Will should have resented his father, even hated him for being absent. Logic did not play a large part in this, however.

> *"Since you are reading this letter, you know that I am not dead. It's complicated,*
> *and I will try to see you as soon as I can. I may not be dead, but I can't go on,*
> *either. I guess you could say that I'm retired. I have Persephone, and she will*
> *take good care of me—or kill me, maybe. You never know."*

Will wasn't angry when he got the letter. His father was bigger than life, and if John Underhall could have saved his natural son the hurt of the old mystery man's apparent death, then he would have. But, heroes are often tied up with struggles bigger than themselves, and the side-effects can be convoluted, and hard to explain, to say the least.

> *"You've undoubtedly heard of the new Johnny Saturn. That's not me. I have*
> *it on good authority that he's an honest but troubled police detective named*
> *Greg Buchanan. I'm okay with him carrying on the tradition—it's an honor, I*
> *suppose—but he's got a lot to learn. I wish I could tell you more, but all I can*
> *say is I've got a bad feeling. If the criminals don't kill him, his personal demons*
> *will."*

Will considered this as he sipped his coffee. The attorney may well have sat in a small but well-appointed office, dressed in an expensive gray pinstriped suit, and seated in a state-of-the-art wheelchair that cost more than most peoples' cars, but his mind could not have been further away.

It was true that Will had followed the exploits of the new Johnny Saturn, the so-called "Giant Killer." The new hero, who had no metahuman powers of his own, had already built a solid reputation for taking down dangerous, powered criminals, thus earning his "Giant Killer" title. Will had figured out early on that this new man was not his fallen father, because this new Johnny Saturn played well with the police, used a different martial art (Krav Maga, not boxing), and was less taciturn than the infamously frowning John Underhall.

Will was jealous, of course—there was no way around that. He could not discuss it with anyone, but, in his heart, Will believed that he should have been the new Johnny Saturn. The fact that his paraplegia made that impossible only soured it further for him. Will had learned to live with his disability years ago, but now he had to face it all over again. He had a recurring dream where he suited up as the new Johnny Saturn, tracked down the pretender, and then claimed his birthright as his father's one true heir. Upon waking, Will's mood would shift from the muzzy glow of validation to the deepest dregs of self-recrimination and guilt.

To make it worse, Will knew the new Johnny Saturn was a good person trying to make the best of a rotten situation. Greg Buchanan could have no idea that there was another man out there who felt cuckolded by fate. Indeed, a deep and driving conviction must have burned Greg into picking up the mantle of a fallen hero, putting his own life on hold, and facing danger night after night without recognition or recompense. All this made Will even guiltier for his dark, vindictive dreams. In short, Greg Buchanan did not deserve Will's ill will, and Will was too fair to go on feeling that way.

> *"Will, I would not have wished my life as a vigilante on you. It is a hard career, with a hard ending. You would have been a great hero, though. I know heroes, and you have the seeds of greatness in you. This path was denied you, and there is nothing I can do about that. Yet, you are a warrior—you face your challenges fearlessly, like the samurai of old. Like one already dead. I'm not great with words, so if you don't understand what I'm saying, look it up."*

Will felt like crying, but he did not. He had not cried since before he injured his spine. He would not cry again. He understood what his father meant, of course. The warrior who fought as one already dead, with fearless abandon, with no concern for self-preservation, was unbeatable. Such a man would fight until his last breath was spent; fight until all his blood had drained away. He had the will to win no matter what the cost. It was the highest compliment John Underhall had ever paid him, and it was a testament to his father's life as well.

> *"Son, I'm going to ask something strange of you. Help this new Johnny Saturn. He is going to need it. As an attorney, and a good one, you can advise and shield*

him. As a money manager, you can relieve him of the stress of daily need. Greg Buchanan is a brave man, but he's not me.

Okay, you may think this request is cruel or insensitive. It may be. But, here's the kicker. I am not asking you to play sidekick to a man who has claimed your birthright. It's time for you to be the hero.

As much as I might have wished it, you cannot get out of that chair and take my place. But, you can rise up as the mastermind behind Johnny Saturn. You can be the force that takes our title and keeps it alive. If Greg Buchanan falls, then it will be up to you to choose another to wear the Saturn crest.

That wheelchair be damned, Will, it's time for you to be the hero of your own story. I built my life around a commitment to my mission and the belief that the absolute will to succeed at any cost is superior to any ridiculous, metahuman power. By now, my message should be crystal clear.

I look forward to the day when I see you again. It may take months, but I believe we will meet again in this life.

Your Dad, John Underhall."

Will folded up the letter and put it in his inner suit coat pocket. He sat in silence with his eyes closed. He felt a great weight of impending fate, or imminent change, resting on his head. When change comes, you can dig your heels in and fight it, or you can abandon yourself to it and see where the winds take you. Will had been happy with his life and what he had made of it, but no more. Something bigger than him had come, and J. William Medal could feel that there was no turning back.

————

Will was no fool.

Just because his father wrote him a rousing letter, Will had no intention of supporting an unproven mystery man's mission without the attorney in him first doing his due diligence.

The research was easy. Detective Gregory "Pretty Boy" Buchanan was a media favorite, and the photographers loved him. He had a knack for landing the high-profile cases, and his closure rate made him a city darling. Once you got past Greg's Brad-Pitt-good-looks and colorful reputation, though, another picture began to emerge.

A trust-fund son of old money, the Buchanan's were as old as Spire City and as wealthy as they were well-connected. Greg's uncles included one Catholic archbishop, a city councilman, and several prominent leaders in the business community. Greg's immediate family history was tragic, though. When he was eight years old, his older brother, Pete, was kidnapped and killed by one of his father's enemies. Soon after that, police officer Thomas Buchanan, Greg and Pete's father, took his own life. The specific details were messy, and they marked young Greg's life from that point forward. As a police officer, Greg was the cop no one could touch—his connections were too great, and his successes were too public, so the police brass shielded him from his failings.

Will rolled over the threshold of his favorite pub, the Leather Mug on South Clinton Street. The staff knew him there, so they showed him to his preferred table and brought him a glass of his preferred wine without asking. Will did not have to look at the menu because he already knew what his favorite dishes were.

When Will spoke with some of Greg Buchanan's associates in the 23rd Precinct, another, darker layer to the detective was exposed. "Pretty Boy" Buchanan got his nickname out of spite, not comradery. Buchanan could not keep a partner because no one could put up with his perceived arrogance, crazy hours, grandstanding, and secrecy. Detective Buchanan worked when it suited him, and he kept his counsel to himself. His primary defender was Lieutenant Detective Harry Brezneski, and that was likely because the "Brez" had been close with Greg's father, Thomas Buchanan. Greg had no close friends in the police department, just allies, and enemies. This "Dirty Harry" ethos had tainted Buchanan's whole law enforcement career.

Then there was the depression. You did not have to be a trained mental health professional to see that Greg Buchanan suffered from long-term clinical depression. Some of his detractors had waited years for the detective to eat his gun, but he never had. Detachment and depression was Buchanan's lifestyle, but he had never succumbed to the pain and ended his life.

Will finished his second glass of wine and helped himself to some of the fresh-baked bread and herb-infused oil that the waitress had delivered to his table.

Greg Buchanan was a huge question mark, one that Will was not sure he should support in the role of Johnny Saturn II. His father's letter had made that much clear—it was Will's choice who took the name Johnny Saturn.

A shadow fell across his table, but it was not the waitress. Will looked up, but he already knew who would be standing there.

"This is not a big town," said Detective Buchanan in a flat, menacing tone. "You've been asking around about me. You knew I was bound to hear about it."

"Have a seat, Detective."

"I'll stand," replied Greg.

"Fine. But, I think we should talk, and it would be easier if I didn't have to keep looking up at you."

Greg sat down opposite of Will, but the detective seemed taut and expectant. "You are J. William Medal, Attorney at Law, no criminal record," Greg said flatly. "Why are you poking around my past?"

Will's meal came, and he began eating his Irish stew. He was used to tense negotiations—in the world of corporate deal-making that was the standard. Will had developed an unbreakable poker face and a calming air that could defuse most tensions.

"Detective, I'm going to cut to the chase. The new Johnny Saturn has been quite effective at making enemies. Many of the criminals you've taken down have teams of lawyers. As of the last count, you, in your role as Johnny Saturn II, have thirteen civil cases filed against you, two criminal cases, and the police commissioner is being pressured to place your vigilante license under review."

"I've heard enough," growled Greg, rising to his feet.

"Please sit down, detective—you haven't heard nearly enough. The image of the lone mystery man is romantic and all that, but it's not an accurate picture anymore. The bad guys all have attorneys, and the good guys now need them, too. You need someone to make all those charges against you go away, as well as someone to deliver your statements to the police and the press."

Greg had not sat back down, but he had not left, either. Will knew enough about human nature to know that Greg was hooked, and now he just had to be reeled in.

"I'm not saying that it's fair or right," continued Will. "That is just how it is anymore. Nothing gets done without lawyers."

"So, what do you want?" asked Greg.

"I'm not looking for you to hire me if that's what you are asking," replied Will. "I'm looking for a partner. You need someone like me."

Greg took his seat again, and the two men sat in silence for an extended moment.

"Assuming that you are the real deal," said Greg, "and not the hired pawn of someone out to get me, what's in it for you?"

"Great question. This alliance will do nothing for my career as a corporate attorney, I'll tell you that. I will have to start my own practice."

"And?" pushed Greg.

"Well, look at me," said Will. "I cannot fight the bad guys the way you do, but I know I can make a difference. You cops may not think much of lawyers, but some of us got into this business for the right reasons, and I sure as hell didn't ace law school just to negotiate the finer points of leases and mergers."

The two men sat without talking for a bit until Greg ordered a beer.

"Thanks, by the way," offered Will, "for not insulting my intelligence."

"About the secret identity thing?" said Greg. "Don't worry about it. With facial recognition software, voice recognition programs, and not to mention DNA, it won't be long until that's all a thing of the past anyway."

"Don't forget satellite surveillance," added Will. "Privacy is—"

Will never finished his sentence, because that is when a massive explosion rocked the Leather Mug's front door and shattered the plate glass window next to it.

———

Chaos.

Glass exploded into a thousand hungry knives, and people near the front of the restaurant fell before the glass's glittering razor onslaught. Pierced and lacerated bodies tumbled through tables, chairs, and carts. Will and Greg were far back enough in the pub to avoid getting cut.

Will immediately lost track of Greg—where had he gone? Had the detective fled toward the kitchen? Will could not be sure, and he had other things on his mind now. He and his chair could handle most obstacles with the ease of long practice, so he rolled to the front of the restaurant. The chair itself was rigid styled, manually powered, built of ultra-light aircraft aluminum, and fitted with cambered wheels that were tilted wide at the base for maximum stability. That was a real blessing with all the broken furniture, shattered glass, and chunks of busted decor that choked up the floor.

There was not much Will could do for the wounded, but he could make for the street to find the source of the carnage.

Was this a terrorist attack? A bomb seemed like the most likely explanation.

What he found surprised him.

A giant woman, an Amazonian figure a foot taller than most men, was pulling herself from a mound of rubble and the ruins of a flatbed truck out in the street. She was a frightening creature, all muscle, tattoos, and leather. Even her face was tattooed, and she wore leather thigh boots, leather forearm-length gauntlets, a corset and a thong. An impossibly long ponytail whipped around behind her head as she moved. Her tattoos did not look like run-of-the-mill skin adornment, but more like a mix of mystic symbols.

Her identity came to Will quickly, because this woman was one of the city's most wanted criminals. She was called Skorn, and she was one of the top lieutenants to the city's premiere crime lord, Tactical, master of the Iron Brigade. She was a ruthless enforcer.

Someone had tried to kill her by throwing a truck at her, but now she shrugged the massive vehicle aside. The concrete beneath her had been caved in partially by the force of the impact.

Will rolled onto the street, awed by what was taking place. Was this the world his father had inhabited? One where gods and monsters battled?

In the sky, several city blocks to the south, a metahero in powered armor (Deco, if Will remembered his heroes correctly) had just hefted another truck at the woman. The rocketing semi-tractor hit the Amazon with the force of a bomb, and its fuel tanks exploded. Black smoke billowed into the sky and obscured everything for a minute.

"Is the fight finished?" wondered Will.

He heard the screech of tortured metal, and something at the core of the fiery, smoking wreck moved.

Filthy, angry, and cornered, Skorn emerged and ripped the semi truck's engine block out. With a ripple of muscle and a titanic heave, she sent her steel missile careening at the hero in the sky. Deco was not fast enough to avoid this, and the burning engine winged him, sending him spinning out of sight. There were two loud reports in the distance, one as the engine block smashed into a building, another as Deco crashed onto a roof blocks away.

Will was not sure what he should do—it never occurred to him to flee, or that he had rolled himself into the middle of a metahuman war zone. He should have been terrified, but it was as if his mental wires had crossed. Instead, Will was... fascinated, mesmerized.

The giant woman turned to leave, but again she was knocked off balance.

"Hello, Skorn," said a newcomer.

Johnny Saturn II, dressed in his blue and green armor with bronze fittings, had jumped her from behind, and he swiftly wrapped his staff around her neck in a cruel choke hold. He was using his new carbon fiber bo staff (a useful weapon that he also could employ as a pole vault, crowbar, and shield) to strangle her.

Skorn tried to dislodge Johnny Saturn, but his staff was lodged securely under her chin, and it was painfully cutting off her air supply. Skorn threw herself backward, trying to pin Johnny Saturn to a wall, but he climbed her back and leaped forward. She hit the wall, but he landed nearby and faced her.

Sirens filled the near distance as the police approached, and most onlookers fled. This was Spire City, and civilians knew better than to get caught in a meta-throwdown. People died, or worse.

Skorn and Johnny Saturn traded blows, and Will watched, rolling closer and closer. Skorn was fast, very tough, superhumanly strong, and a trained wrestler. Johnny Saturn dodged her every strike, deflecting here, turning his body there, and avoided damage with an exceptional economy of movement. He landed several blows on Skorn, but as yet he had not gotten the right leverage and angle to deliver a decisive strike. He actually seemed to be faring reasonably well against a metahuman who far outclassed him.

Giant Killer, indeed!

Johnny Saturn delivered a jab home to Skorn's tattooed stomach, knocking her back, winding her. She returned a savage, backhanded blow that knocked Johnny Saturn away with such force that he bounced down the street like a rock skipping across a lake. He disappeared from view and landed somewhere behind the hastily erected police barricade.

The police were choking off South Clinton Street's north and south exits and boxing Skorn in. She had a momentary breather, but her situation had turned desperate. With a mighty stomp, she sent shockwaves out and away from her. Windows shattered, fire-hydrants erupted, and cars knocked this way and that. Her force wave drove back the police, at least for a few minutes, but it was only a matter of time before Johnny Saturn or Deco returned.

Skorn's force wave also had knocked Will and his wheelchair to the pavement. He lay on the street, still strapped into his upturned conveyance, his hands bloody, and helpless.

That is when it happened, something that would haunt Will all his days. He would look back, over the years, and he would marvel—it all seemed so implausible, so unlikely. Surely, no one would have believed it. In a world of flying humans, raging mutants, and arcane wonders, something incredibly odd happened.

Will looked up from where he lay, and his eyes locked with Skorn's eyes. It could only have been a moment, in retrospect, yet for the two of them, it was millennia. He looked down the Amazon's line of sight, and he saw her as he had never seen another living being. It was as if he had been blind, and he was granted vision this one time, this bare moment, and Skorn was who he saw.

Will did not see a muscle-bound metavillain, that walking engine of mass destruction that everyone else saw. He saw a scared girl, a prisoner of fate, a precious person in real pain and confusion. It made no sense, but these things are not required to be reasonable.

Skorn, looking back, must have seen something in him as well, because she looked startled, thrown off kilter. At that moment, these two unlikely people had built a bridge between them that would stand for a lifetime.

Then, the moment had passed, and both Will and Skorn shook their heads, dazed. Police were forming up a new line, and Johnny Saturn reappeared atop a cop car. Johnny Saturn looked uninjured and eager to rejoin the battle.

Will looked at Skorn, and he said "Run! Go through the restaurant! Out the back! Run!"

She ran.

———

Will remembered the first time she came to him. It was later on the same day they met, the day he had helped her escape.

Will's apartment was dark, and he sat on his terrace, feeling the night air, listening to the sounds of the city rise from below. He wore a robe, and his bottle of wine was close at hand. His hands were taped up where he had scraped them up on the street. He had a lot to consider.

The doorbell rang, but he was not surprised. If she wanted to find him, all she had to do was read the report about the battle in the evening edition of the *Spire*

City Gazette, and then look up J. William Medal in the phone book. Will had told the doorman to ring her in, just in case she used the street entrance. Will had known she would come.

Will opened the door, and there she stood, beyond his threshold: A tall woman in an overcoat, the brim up. She wore dark sunglasses, which obscured some of the tattooed hash marks that reached diagonally across her face, from her chin to her forehead.

"Hi," she said, sounding a little hesitant. "I'm Michelle Breemer."

"Hi, Michelle, I'm Will. Come in."

Will rolled toward the terrace, but she stopped him. "Don't go into the light," she said, and she removed her sunglasses. She sat on the couch near him, and their faces were close together. All the air seemed to have gone out of the room as their eyes met again.

"I don't know why I'm here," she began. "I couldn't help it. I... This is all wrong."

Will leaned in and kissed her, and they did not speak for a long time.

That night, they were like one person in a single skin, safe in the dark. It was as if they had been alone all their lives, and now they had each other. It was a humbling, frightening experience, and they held each other with all their might and will. There had been other women in Will's life, but those early experiences did not even rate with this one. Those had been fumbling encounters, dorm rooms liaisons, second dates, laughing awkwardness. This time was different.

"So, it does work," said Michelle as her hand cupped his manhood.

"Like a soldier," said Will, "and reporting for duty."

"I thought, with you being in a wheelchair and all, that—"

"The effects of a spinal injury can vary a lot," he said.

Will skipped work the next day. The two of them stayed in his bed, the drapes pulled tight, safe in the gloom and alone with each other.

"This is all wrong," Michelle said. "We are from two different worlds. I grew up in a doublewide, under power lines, next to a toxic waste dump. Until recently I shared a bed with two psychopaths, at the same time. I... I have tattoos on my face. I'm not like you..."

"Hush," said Will, trying to subdue her with kisses.

"My father used me. I hooked and used until the thing that gave me the power happened. I didn't finish tenth grade…"

Will listened to her. He did not care about any of that. He was caught in a magnetic field with her. He was mesmerized and obsessed with her, and nothing else mattered.

"You poor dear," he said, "have you ever been happy, even one day in your life?"

Michelle wept, her sadness overwhelming her.

"Never once," she said. "Until now."

Will begged her to give it all up, to go away with him. She could not. The police wanted her on innumerable counts, which included scores of first-degree murder, second-degree murder, and manslaughter charges, and a bucket load of others that included aggravated assault, larceny, resisting arrest, intimidation, vehicular theft, criminal damage to property, and so many more.

Death was the only way out of the Iron Brigade. No one was allowed to walk away from the organization or Tactical's rule. Besides, it was not as if a six-foot-six, heavily muscled woman with tattoos could change her name and assume a new identity. She was trapped, well and truly. Michelle Breemer had never had a chance for a normal life. She had never gotten one fair break or even one person willing to take a gamble on her future. Her road had been paved with sharp stones, and her feet were bruised and cut, but it was the only road open to her.

"This is it," she announced. "We can't do this again. We'll get caught. Tactical will kill me, or you, or worse."

"Stay," pleaded Will. "We can work it out. There's always a way."

Michelle, dressed and ready to leave, touched his face tenderly. "There's no way, Will. I'm sorry for complicating your life, but this is it. Thank you, and goodbye."

With that, she was gone, and Will was more alone than he had ever been in his life. Not since those bitter nights in the Children's Ward at Spire City General, when he lay alone in the dark, feeling disembodied from his legs, did he feel so at a loss.

But, it did not end.

Michelle came back again and again. They could no more avoid each other than a moth could resist a flame. Together, they were spiraling in, getting closer to the fire all the time, and it was only a matter of time until they got burned.

———

For a while, it all worked like clockwork, and Team Saturn (as they privately called it) became the model of efficiency.

Greg Buchanan left the police department and got his private investigator's license, but he often still worked with the police as a hired consultant. In many ways, he worked with his old department more now than when he had been a full-time detective. Will took Greg's finances, shaped them up, and turned them into a small fortune, just in case the day came when Greg decided he no longer could work both sides of the fence.

Will and Greg had it all covered.

The rest of the unofficial team was a colorful band of misfits. There was Staff of Life, aka Victoria Shelbourne, co-founding member of the Squadron Premiere and the dean of Theoretical Physics at Spire City University. She provided scientific backup, and she was Greg's girlfriend. There was Denny Chambliss, aka Triops, Greg's best friend, a former member of the Iron Brigade, now reformed and a member of

BOMBASTIC AKA NILS ZILCHER

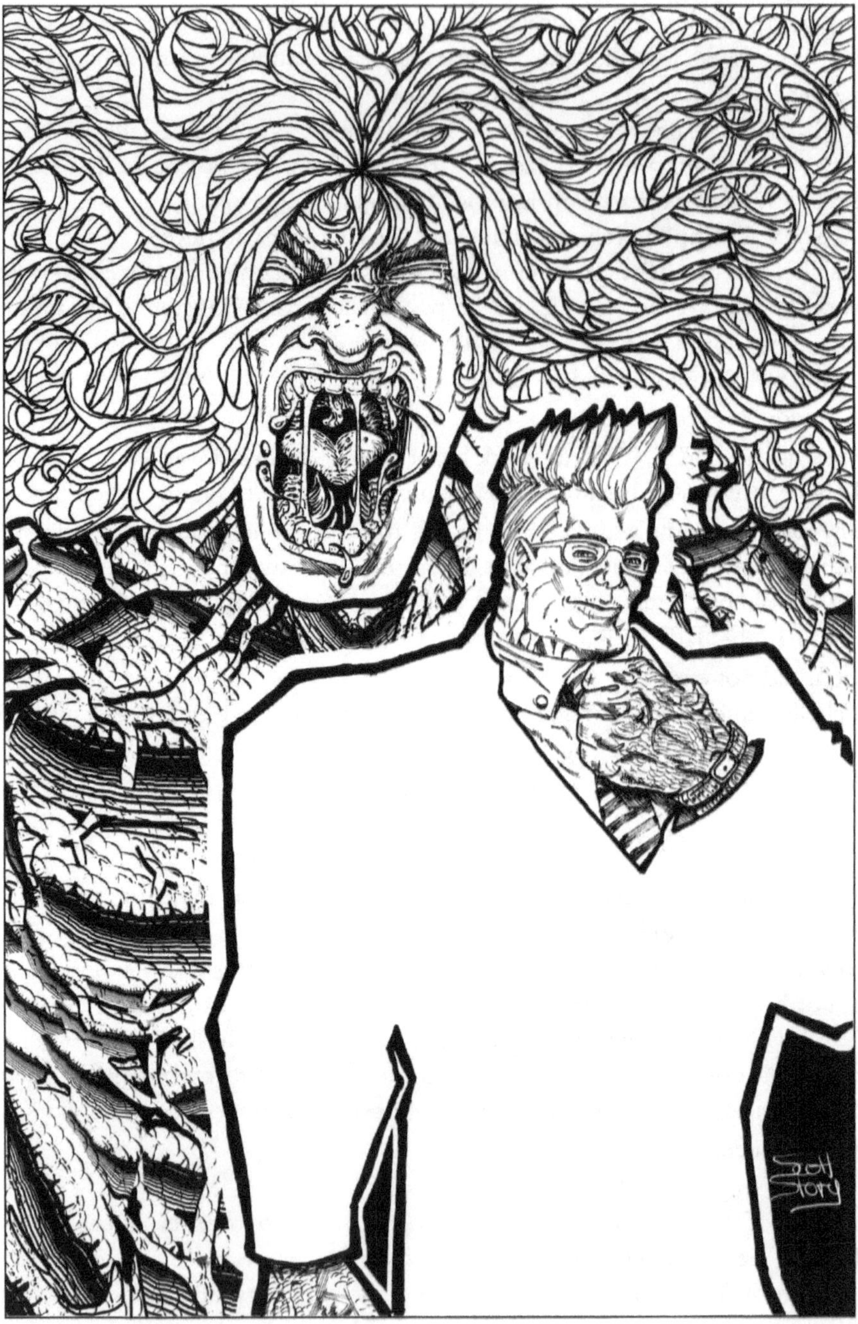

the Squadron Premiere, who helped out on the psychic front. (If Triops ever read Will's mind and found out about Skorn, the little metahero never betrayed him to the others. As far as Will knew, Triops respected his privacy and did not go rooting around his or anyone elses' brains. He had the power to ruin everyone he ever met, and apparently, he chose not to because of his solid ethical character.)

There was also Charles Ledmun, aka Doc, who provided emergency care. He had been a surgical nurse, but after he had become homeless, he turned into a well-respected street doctor and one of the leaders of the mole people. Mollie Andreeson was Greg's computer guru, researcher, and remote coordinator. She had been a teenage runaway captured by Dr. Wissenschaft and brutally transformed into a cyborg, so now she was part girl and mostly machine. Harvey Torres, called the Tailor, was a brilliant gadgeteer and materials engineer who built Greg's cutting-edge armor and equipment. Dr. Sandra Nagachi took care of Greg's long-term physical wellness and therapy. She was the former Spire City Coroner, but now she ran the Squadron Premiere's health program and clinic. Finally, John Underhall, the previous Johnny Saturn, who was rarely ever seen, although his seemingly endless resources, properties, and alliances played a crucial role in maintaining the team. To the public, Johnny Saturn was still a lone vigilante; no one knew that it took a support staff of dedicated experts to keep him in the field. It was as if Johnny Saturn were a race car driver, and the others were his pit crew.

When it came to enemies, the Greg Buchanan incarnation of Johnny Saturn was an overachiever. He had an intense, sometimes manic vendetta against Dr. Victor Wissenschaft, an untouchable old monster who ruled Spire City from his bank accounts, but all that finally ended with the mad scientist's death. Johnny Saturn also had an ongoing war with Spire City's crime boss, Tactical, formerly known as Nicholai Demetr. For a long time, Johnny Saturn, Dr. Wissenschaft, and Tactical had made up a three-way hate-fest that boiled like a cracked cauldron, always ready to break and spew burning bile across the city. Wissenschaft was gone, but Tactical was still out there pulling strings and choking Spire City.

Will's life had changed, too. He had quit his position at the firm of Gray, Gray, and Gris, despite an offer to become a partner, and he had established his own firm. He was successful enough in his first year to add a partner, Abraham Rosenblatt, Esq. Will was good at what he did, and soon all the charges and suits filed against Johnny Saturn had been dropped. The statements Will issued to the media brought in a steady stream of positive press for the mystery man, as well.

Will, by association with Johnny Saturn, now had his share of enemies too, and a bodyguard became a necessity.

Will hired a metahuman named Nils Zilcher, an ex-con who had found religion during his prison time. Nils, once called Bombastic, was a mountain of grotesque musculature, and he almost was indestructible. He had been augmented in the nineties by Dr. Wissenschaft, and Bombastic had once been a lieutenant for the terrorist, Dr. Horatio Synn. All that had changed since prison, and now Nils was an oversized nerd with a well-thumbed Bible and a taste for comics, B-Movies, and collecting science fiction memorabilia. Nils needed the work because it took a potent (and expensive) cocktail of pharmaceuticals to keep the pain from his implants and modifications at bay, and Will was glad to provide the big man employment.

Will liked the monstrously outsized man. He had given Nils bonuses on numerous occasions, helped him find an outfitter who could make decent suits for someone so large and bulky and provided him with the apartment next to Will's. Nils responded with iron-bound loyalty, and the giant bruiser now had saved Will's life on at least three separate occasions. As an ex-convict, Nils could not legally own a firearm, but he did not need one—his hands and gargantuan strength were plenty. Wherever Will rolled, he did so with his hulking shadow, Nils Zilcher.

Will and Greg got on well. Will could not manage Greg—that "Dirty Harry" loner instinct was too ingrained in the vigilante—but the attorney could advise and guide the hero at times. When Will needed a private investigator or a mystery man, Greg was there. When Greg needed a lawyer or a financial advisor, Will was there.

Team Saturn worked like a finely tuned timepiece for a time. Then, it did not. Cogs caught, springs uncoiled, and gears got stuck.

Autumn arrived, yet the year had been too dry, and the leaves turned brown until they broke free in the wind and floated to the earth. No riot of color this year for the trees of Spire City.

Team Saturn had made real inroads into the local crime terrain. Johnny Saturn managed to disrupt human trafficking rings, the illegal arms trade, and he even broke a large crack cocaine ring. He repeatedly had gone toe-to-toe with the local metahuman population, trading blows with Lacerater, the Rogue Statesman, the Scary Men, and more than a dozen other costumed, powered criminals. Johnny Saturn won more of these metaduels than not, and he never lost outright. The press loved him, and the metahuman community, which had always fostered nothing but dismissiveness, disdain, and contempt for non-powered mystery men, viewed Johnny Saturn with hard-won respect.

Will, accompanied by his ever-present shadow, Nils, rolled over the threshold into the Rafert Governmental Annex at the Spire City Municipal Complex. As an attorney, Will was able to flash a pass that allowed him immediate entry into the building, bypassing the long lines of resentful, glaring people who stood in the queues waiting for their turn with the metal detectors. Will and Nils approached the elevator terminals, and that is where Will noticed a familiar man.

The "Coat Man," as Will called him, was a homeless person who spent his days in the Municipal Complex's lobby to keep warm. He was a frightening figure, large and broad-shouldered, and made larger yet by the heavy winter coat he wore in the humid lobby. His hood was up and cinched tight, leaving only an oval of his face showing. That face was almost true black, his skin darker than that of most African-Americans, and it framed his eyes in a way that made them seem enormous and intense.

Will had noticed the Coat Man maybe a dozen times. Will often gave money to homeless people, and he donated money to the local missions annually, yet he had never given money to this man. He had heard from people that worked here that this fellow was mute: something terrible had happened to him overseas while serving in the military, and he had never spoken again. Now, the Coat Man filled his long days by sitting in the lobby and writing poetry in a small notebook. He would stare at people, then write, flip a page, and write more. All in all, it was quite unnerving, and it made people leery.

Will secretly was ashamed of the apprehension he felt for this man, and today he determined he would do something about it. He turned his wheelchair and rolled into the Coat Man's line of sight.

"Morning, sir. I heard you were in the military."

The Coat Man looked at Will, and then his gaze fell to his notebook where he quickly wrote something. The Coat Man ripped the page out and handed it to Will.

"I'm sorry, but this is not going to end well."

That was all the note said, nothing more.

Will regarded the message, and then he folded it and slipped it into his coat pocket.

"You're right, of course," Will said to the big man. "I knew that from the beginning. But, what else can you do?" He handed the big man a twenty dollar bill, then turned and rolled away.

"Boss," said Nils, "can I ask what that was? What did that guy give you, a stock tip or something?"

"Yeah," replied Will, "a stock tip. Come on. We've got court."

———

Will and Michelle lay in bed, the drapes pulled, with long spears of light lying across them from wherever there was a gap in the drapery. Michelle had introduced Will to the joys of smoking condensed hash, and they took turns drawing in deep lungful's of the pungent smoke, holding it for a time, and then exhaling. She always had a variety to choose from, because she claimed to "know some people."

"When I was a kid," mused Will, "I used to listen to Patti Smith's song 'Horses.' I would play it again and again, trying to figure out what she was talking about. It made me feel... I don't know..."

"Crazy, alive," Michelle answered for him. "I had that album too. It was just so out there. I'm not surprised you had it, too."

They kissed, but there was a sense of urgency in the room, an air of desperation.

"Our luck is going to run out anytime," said Michelle.

"I know. It can't go on like this. It's probably already too late."

They lay in silence for a moment, just touching. The rest of the world, all the people beyond the bedroom's walls, suddenly seemed dangerous, sinister, like coiled things ready to strike and devour their happiness and security. The Sword of Damocles was always out there, waiting to drop and end their fragile happiness. The two of them had stopped talking weeks ago about ending their affair. They knew better. This thing would be the end of them.

They had been doomed from the start. Michelle's boss was Tactical, the underworld czar of Spire City. Will's partner was Johnny Saturn, Tactical's sworn enemy. Will had shielded Johnny Saturn again and again, and he had used his legal prowess to confound Tactical's legal team too many times.

'I'm sorry, but this is not going to end well," the Coat Man's note had said. How right he was.

"Will, I want to try something."

"I'll try anything with you," replied Will, his handsome face bent in a knowing leer.

Michelle laughed, and then she sat up. "Not like that, silly. Something else, but you might not like it."

"What?" said Will, using the bar installed over his bed to pull himself into a sitting position. This bar, and other handles like it here, in his closet, and in his bathroom, gave Will the leverage to pull himself from bed to the wheelchair, the wheelchair to the toilet, wheelchair to shower, and so forth.

"I don't understand the thing that gave me powers," began Michelle. "It's like, I don't know, a green spotlight that crawled in through my mouth. It made me big, strong, and nearly invulnerable. I don't have any idea where it came from, but..." Michelle seemed at a loss for words, trying to explain something outside her vocabulary.

"You're its host, is that what you are trying to say?" Will said. "It lives in you, and in return, it gives you the ability to defend yourself and it."

"Yeah," said Michelle, nodding her head. "Well, what if I gave some of it to you—do you think you could walk, then?"

Will sat for a moment saying nothing, considering his response. If such a thing were even possible, he would refuse. He had no intentions of compromising the thing that made Michelle distinct. Before he could put this to words, Michelle gently lifted his chin with her hand and kissed him.

This kiss was not one of passion, but more an open-mouthed sealing of lips and a meeting of skulls. Green energy lighted their cheeks from within, and an intense pulse of power passed from Michelle into Will.

Will pulled away slowly, marveling at the stinging warmth that passed through him. He should have been angry because Michelle had taken liberty with him without his consent, but he was not. Will pulled off the sheets that half covered his naked body. Green tattoos, much like those that covered Michelle's body, momentarily flashed across his abdomen, pelvis, and thighs. His legs began to quiver, and painful needle stings stabbed at his legs and feet.

"Good Lord!" said Will—he had not felt real pain, or anything, for that matter, in his legs and feet for years. He understood phantom pain, and this was no phantom! His first impulse was to draw up his legs, pull his knees under his chin, and hug his legs to him. To his surprise, his limbs, uncoordinated and rubbery after so many years disuse, began to move and shift in response. His lower extremities were not as wasted as they could have been because Will regularly saw a physical therapist who worked the muscles and tendons to keep his legs from shriveling up and freezing.

Michelle, appearing a bit smaller after having siphoned off some of her power, reached out to help him. A flash of green pulsed when their skin came into contact, and it was all over. All unbidden, the portion of Michelle's loaned power snapped back into her, and Will's legs went limp again. Apparently, her metahuman energies had no desire to be divided up.

"Oh, I'm sorry," moaned Michelle. I, well I—"

"Don't apologize," said Will. "Look!"

They both stared at Will's feet, but nothing happened.

Then, his toes moved. Not much, but a little.

"I did that," exclaimed Will. "That's me. Get something sharp—I want you to help me test my reflexes and nerve endings."

Will smiled as Michelle ran to the bathroom to find a sharp implement. Maybe the Coat Man was wrong. Maybe things would turn out alright after all.

———

J. William Medal, Esq. rolled into Spire City Superior Court Three followed closely by his bodyguard Nils Zilcher. The huge man was invaluable because it often seemed like criminal enforcers were anxious to take pot shots at the crusading attorney. Will was in court today to deliver a signed and notarized affidavit by Johnny Saturn about a trafficker in black market human tissues the vigilante had busted.

Nils took his customary seat just behind Will's chair in the courtroom. The Honorable Judge William Strathmorne threw Will a hard look. Something was up, and the judge was not happy to see the wheelchair-bound attorney.

"Counselor, I'd like to speak with you in my chambers. Now."

Will followed the judge out the court's back door, down a short hall, and into his offices. Will had been here many times before, and he admired the beautifully polished oak woodwork, Italian marble-topped desk and end tables, and custom leather furnishings. He wasn't concerned about being separated from Nils, because what could happen here? This room was a superior court judge's chambers, after all. Even if trouble did present itself, Will had had a panic button installed on his chair's arm, one that would set off Nil's pager if he were needed.

Judge Strathmorne took his seat behind his desk, and Will rolled close.

"What's up, Bill? What have—"

"Can it, Will!" replied the judge angrily. "Why couldn't you have just played nice? Instead, you had to go all hotdog on us, prove a point, and make waves."

A cold chill crawled up Will's spine. "What's this about, Bill?"

The judge sat back, a look of guilt, shame, and conflicted emotion crossing his face for an instant, after which his look of stern disapproval returned.

"You've pissed off all the wrong people, Will. Why you felt the need to do this is beyond me, but now you've done it."

"And, your point is?" asked Will, himself growing angry.

"You don't get to be a superior court judge without powerful backers, Will. You've ticked off my biggest supporter one time too many."

"Damn it, Bill! I respected you! Who is it? Who pays your bills?"

The judge did not reply directly, instead saying "Don't bother to hit that panic button on your chair, Medal. I've had this room electronically blocked. What happens in these chambers stays in these chambers."

The judge pressed a button on his desk, and a section of wooden paneling on one wall popped open, revealing a secret door.

Out stepped an aggressive looking woman.

Will had never seen anyone remotely like this person. She looked as if she was the thematic love child of a porn actress, dominatrix, and an alpha predator. Her outre' appearance suggested that she could have fake porn sex with you while she multitasked and flayed you alive with her teeth.

"Will Medal," announced the Judge, "allow me to introduce you to Vox Malaise, leader of the Scavengers. Whatever happens now is out of my hands."

The woman raised a small object that might have been a can of mace but was not. She blasted Will in the face with the aerosol weapon in a perfunctory manner. "Call me Vox, dear. Everyone else does."

Will could not reply because then the lights of his world went out, and he went far, far away.

———

"That's the last of your appointments today, Nicholai," said Skorn.

"Good. I am tired of all the idiots," said Nicholai Demetr, aka Tactical.

Skorn drew close to her boss and put her hands on his shoulders. Her impersonal movements were those of a masseuse or caregiver, not a lover. He shrugged her away and instead chose to light up one of those foul, unfiltered Eastern European cigarettes he loved so much.

"Get out," said Tactical. "I can't stand to look at you! Get! Out!"

This treatment was nothing new to Skorn, and her face did not betray any emotion. It always had been their sex partner, Alaric, that Tactical had loved, not her, and he had kept Skorn in his menage a trois more for Alaric's entertainment. The giant brute had been a vigorous bull of a man, after all. Now Alaric was gone, and Skorn and Tactical had been forced to find a way forward without the great beast.

Tactical no longer acknowledged Skorn's presence as she excused herself. Once she was gone, he sat alone for a time, rolling delicious tendrils of acrid smoke around his mouth. He felt something with Skorn was not right since he had come back from near death. Something, but he was not sure what.

Tactical was Spire City's reigning crime lord and master of his own, private metahuman army. Like many metavillains, the crime boss had an incredibly convoluted history. In his Balkan homeland, he had been a patriot, a general, and then a war criminal; in America, he had been a terrorist for hire, a crime lord, and the leader of Spire City's Iron Brigade, and most recently an invalid and coma patient.

Tactical was six foot two, with a full head of blond hair, and a handsome but cruel face. He had not always been so. Until recently, he had been a short, one-eyed, bald cripple with half his body covered in scar tissue and all but disabled by a stroke. After a disastrous battle with Tactical's archenemy, the Utopian, the crime lord had been burned beyond recognition and kicked off a skyscraper to be splattered across the street below. It had taken an army of nanobots, extensive 3D bioprinting, and genetic vats liberated from a military black site to rebuild him from the cellular level up. In a rare show of vanity, he had a few genes activated here and there so that his rebuild gave him a full head of hair and his substantially increased height. No more was he the grotesque burn victim or broken-tongued stroke victim. Now, he was a Luciferian beauty and a rakish heartbreaker.

Tactical owed his rebirth to Skorn. She had rescued his charred, mutilated remains and collected most of the outlandish medical gear needed to rebuild him. She had kept the Iron Brigade together during his "convalescence" and returned the organization to his hands when he was reborn. She showed little ambition for herself, and commendable loyalty and resourcefulness in bringing him back to health and power.

Was Tactical brimming with gratitude for her fidelity? Hardly. If anything he resented her for it. He couldn't stand being in another's debt, yet he owed her everything. Tactical barely could tolerate his surviving enforcer, and he scorned her at every turn. Truth be told, he had always hated her, and giving her the codename "Skorn" was an excellent example of his unsophisticated yet blacker than black humor.

Tactical despised Skorn, but he also needed her. She was his strong arm, the iron-fisted enforcer that kept all his riotous followers and enemies in place. She protected Tactical and his reign over the Iron Brigade with ruthless efficiency. Theirs was a complicated relationship, a potent mix of need and hate. In Tactical's mind, Skorn was his property. She was the dog that you kicked and abused at will, yet it would still kill for you unhesitatingly.

What had changed with her? She still performed her role with merciless economy. She still attended to Tactical's needs. Was she distracted by something else? Tactical could not tell. Her old enthusiasm for violence and mayhem seemed intact, as did her copious appetite for smoking high-grade cannabis.

Somehow, something about Skorn was different, and Tactical realized that he really did not know her all that well. She was a mystery to him. He did not know her because he did not care. He never had.

––––––––

Will snapped back to reality with a jolt, instantly awake and hyper-alert. He was face up and restrained on a hospital gurney by heavy, blood-stained straps. The chamber that he now occupied was built of stained cinder blocks, and the buzzing fluorescent lamps hanging above gave the room and everything in it a dirty, greenish cast with zombie-pale highlights. In the near distance, maybe just down the hall, cries of torment rose and fell in a hellish cadence. Will hoped it was the television turned up too loud, but he knew better.

He was at the gates of some private hell.

Near Will, Vox Malaise adjusted the intravenous drip that was inserted into his arm. He did not know what was in the IV, but it had snapped him wide awake, made him feel flush, and produced a strong, chemical aftertaste in his mouth.

"Blargh," coughed Will. "It tastes like melting tires and model glue."

Vox Malaise shot Will a predatory smile. It was more the kind of grinning leer one would associate with a repeat sex offender than most women.

"This is the weirdest kidnapping ever," said Will.

This failed to elicit a response from the criminal overlord.

Vox Malaise ran her hands down Will's supine body. She wore finger jewelry that ended in long, vicious looking claws, and their contact seemed simultaneously sexual and imminently threatening. Her touch made him want to squirm out of his skin.

Vox Malaise loosened Will's shirt and exposed his chest. She stuck out her impossibly long tongue and ran it down his stomach, tasting him. The end of her tongue was forked like a lizard's, and Will could only guess that she had gotten the

surgery to cut the frenulum, the tissue that restrains the tongue from extending too far.

"J. William Medal, Esquire," she said. Her voice had the sibilant, lisping quality.

"I wonder if this still works?" said Vox Malaise, sliding her clawed fingers over Will's genitals. "Maybe we should find out."

"Let's not," said Will. "Why should you care about my, um, capacity anyway?"

"Care? I do not care at all, Mr. Medal. Your erectile functionality is beside the point, as far as I am concerned. What I do care about is the damage you and Johnny Saturn have caused my supply network." All the teasing and assumed coquetry had fled her voice. Now she sounded pissed.

"Do you think it is easy to obtain the constant supply of human test subjects, tissue samples, illegal drugs, and radioactive isotopes?"

Will said nothing, looking at Vox Malaise with contempt.

"It is not cheap, I promise you. You and Johnny Saturn have made a point of confounding me at both the street level and in the courts. I am not a happy businesswoman, Mr. Medal."

"So that's it then," said Will. "You plan to kill me, or use me to get your hands on Johnny Saturn."

"Good try," replied Vox Malaise. "But, we have not reached that stage yet. Instead, this is the part of the dance where I offer you a job."

Will could hardly believe his ears—*a job?*

"While I am sure that working as a crusading attorney is quite, ah, lucrative, I think you would find working with my legal team more to your benefit. I can make you a full partner, pay a salary that would make most American C.E.O.'s blush with envy, and offer you and your dependents an excellent health care package, including sight and dental. Oh, and I would use my magic to restore your mobility. Would you like to walk again, Mr. Medal?

"The alternative is death, I suppose?" said Will.

"You are so impatient! No, not yet," said the Vox Malaise. "I'm going to give you a week to think it over. I am supremely confident that you will accept my offer."

"You're insane," retorted Will. "You know I won't play along!"

"You will," snapped Vox Malaise, "because of this."

She produced an unmarked DVD and flourished it before Will's face. When Will said nothing, she continued.

"This DVD contains footage of your many romantic trysts with Michelle Breemer, aka Skorn. Can you imagine how much my wasp-sized drones were able to record? Everything, I can assure you."

"You vile bitch!" Will swore, struggling futilely against his bonds.

"Accept my bargain, or I deliver this DVD to Skorn's master, Nicholai Demetr.

What will he do to her? What form will his vengeance take? What will he do to you?"

Will had never been so enraged, and frightened, in his life. He had finally seen Damocles sword, and it had taken the form of a simple DVD. Will struggled to rise, to get his hands near the woman's throat, but he could not. The straps were too thick, and he was immobilized.

"I have you, well and truly, counselor. You are mine, now. You will work for me, and gain the world, or you will refuse and lose everything. You have one week before you report to work at my private law firm, Grim, Gravel, and Samuels. Or, should I say, Grim, Gravel, Samuels, and Medal?"

"You bitch, you bitch," swore Will, his voice now dry and cracking. His face was red with anger, and his eyes were shot with veins. He was more helpless at this moment than he had ever been in his life.

"So it's 'no,' then," said Vox Malaise. "You are so stubborn that you would rather die by Tactical's hand than play along with me. Impressive, but stupid."

She regarded him for a moment, giving him one last chance to change his answer, and then she shrugged.

"I still win," she said. "Tactical will kill you and his lieutenant. This act will weaken his hold on the Iron Brigade, and give the Scavengers the opportunity to wipe out Tactical's little meta army. You might have been a useful tool, but I still get what I want, and that's all that matters.

"Goodnight, Mr. Medal."

Vox Malaise smiled sweetly, and then she adjusted a valve on Will's IV, and he was instantly unconscious again. Almost as an afterthought, Vox Malaise tucked her copy of the incriminating DVD into Will's pocket.

"Don't worry, dear—I've got a copy for Tactical as well."

———

Tactical watched the DVD. It had arrived at one of the Iron Brigade-owned banks by special courier earlier that day, and then it was delivered to him by one of his men.

Tactical ejected the DVD from his computer. He had seen enough. Initially, he did not know who Skorn's wheelchair-bound lover was, but the DVD included helpful captions between scenes. The paraplegic man was J. William Medal, Johnny Saturn II's attorney.

"Interesting," thought Tactical. "Unexpected and interesting."

Tactical was known for his sudden, violent temper. To call him mercurial was a gross understatement. He was more volatile than a bottle of nitroglycerin tossed around by blindfolded drunks in a powderkeg. He had killed dozens of men in fits of red rage. He had shot them, strangled them, blown them up, tossed them off buildings, thrown them down elevator shafts, pushed them under trains, buried them alive, and smashed their skulls open with stones. If the resolve and grit to kill were

fossil fuels, Tactical could have drained the world's dinosaur deposits in a matter of days.

This time was different. Now Tactical seemed thoughtful, at ease with the situation. There was a glacier forming in the ice-glazed cavity of Tactical's soul, and it had been freezing into Skorn's likeness for a long time.

Could Skorn have betrayed him to the enemy? Was she an informer on the Iron Brigade?

Tactical had chosen not to jump to conclusions. This was just the type of trick a bitch like Vox Malaise would pull to destabilize the Iron Brigade and make him destroy his most formidable henchwoman. Upon further reflection, Tactical remembered that Vox once had owned a successful pornography studio and that she had easy access to all the performers and technicians needed to fake such a DVD with ease.

Something this serious called for independent verification. Tactical reached for his phone. He hit speed dial and whispered a command into it.

"Bring En Camera to me, now."

Soon the hapless metavillain arrived.

En Camera looked like a cross between a robotic human and a digital camera. Not an expensive DSLR camera, either, but one of those silly looking compact cameras that kids and tourists used to take lots of appalling, fuzzy pictures. He had a big, telescoping lens for a face and a meek, downtrodden posture that betrayed his painfully low self-esteem. In an age when everyone carried digital cameras in their phones with them, how did being a hybrid android/camera make him anything but worthless? En Camera looked ridiculous, and his fellows in the Iron Brigade never let him forget it. To them, the sad-sack robot was a half-assed idea made stupid. The bullying and teasing never stopped.

En Camera's tormentors were wrong. He may have had the unfortunate distinction of being an anthropomorphized camera, but his outer form was an expression of something else. Something valuable. En Camera was the manifestation of accurate, repeatable remote viewing. He could look across time and space and see anything. If he had a mind to do so, he could have perused the Hall of Records hidden beneath the Sphinx at Giza, the mind-blowing vistas of Mars, and futures beyond all comprehension. He could record what he saw in mind-boggling high definition audio and video, and he could project his findings for others to view.

Tactical looked at the pathetic android camera. The crime lord understood all the implications of En Camera's abilities. He knew that Iron Brigade's most useless member was, in reality, its most useful.

"I've got a task for you," said Tactical. "So, don't screw this up!"

"I... I..."stuttered the brow-beaten robot.

"Shut up," said Tactical. "I have heard enough of your pathetic mewling for two lifetimes!"

Tactical steepled his fingers and gathered his thoughts.

"Skorn has been 'off' since I came back. I can't put my finger on it, but something has not been right about her. I want you to use your worthless powers and check what she has been up to in her free time. I want details, and I want you to project the results for me. Do you think you can do that without screwing it up, or are you truly as worthless as I've always suspected?"

"I c-can do-dd…"

"Shut up and do it now," said Tactical. "If I hear one more excuse, I'm going to blow you to bits and put you out with the recyclables. You disgust me, and I have no idea why I've put up with you this long."

En Camera collected himself as best he could and cast his gaze across space and time. When done correctly, this ability took advantage of the non-locality of the universe at a quantum level as well as the causal power of observation. What the robot saw surprised him, and it scared him as well—would Tactical destroy the bearer of bad news? En Camera did not have a choice.

"H-here's what I've got," said the robot, and he projected the damning results into the room in a high-resolution hologram.

Tactical leaned forward and watched. His eyes flashed red, and an ugly frown twisted his beautiful face into something baleful.

————

Will moaned softly, twitched, and he tried to open his eyes. It was hard at first because his eyelids had gummed together.

He was in a hospital bed in a pleasant, private room at Spire City General. He would find out later that he had been dumped unconscious on the hospital sidewalk around midnight. His chair was nowhere to be found, and his wallet and keys were missing. Luckily for Will, the police easily were able to identify him, and he received excellent care.

It seemed like everyone Will had ever known was in the room. There was his mother, Loraine Medal Kendall, and his stepfather Raymond Kendall. Nils was there, of course, full of apologies and self-recrimination for a kidnapping that he could not have stopped anyway. There was Will's law partner, Abraham Rosenblatt, and his lovely wife Sheila, and their daughter Samantha. There was also Sandra Nagachi, chief physician with the Squadron Premiere. Everyone important was there but Greg Buchanan and, for obvious reasons, Michelle Breemer.

The doctors declared that Will was in good shape after his ordeal, and he could go home in the morning after they kept him in the hospital overnight for observation.

Visitors came and went, as did members of the press, looking for a juicy story, and detectives from the Spire City Police Department. Will knew it was pointless to implicate Vox Malaise, the Scavengers, or Judge William Strathmorne. They would all have airtight alibis, and Vox was virtually untouchable anyway

Greg appeared in the door to Will's room.

"Everyone out," announced Greg, not unkindly, but with a note of authority. "The counselor and I need to talk."

Everyone, even Will's mom, removed themselves to the corridor, and Greg closed the door and pulled up a seat next to the bed. Will said nothing at first. This was no well-wishing visit, and he knew this was going to be unpleasant.

"Ready to cut the shit and tell me everything?" asked Greg. He held up the unmarked DVD that had arrived at the hospital with Will. "I have friends here, so I was able to intercept this before the police got it." Greg did not seem overly cross. If anything, he seemed disappointed.

"What do you want to know, Greg? There's a lot to tell. There's a lot I should have explained a long time ago."

"Let's start with Skorn or Michelle Breemer," said Greg.

"Does everyone know about this, now?" asked Will, following up with a sad smile.

"Probably. Remember we once talked about privacy and secret identities? It was extreme arrogance on your part to think that you could keep something this explosive a secret. Surveillance cameras, X-Ray or laser eavesdropping devices, satellite tracking, human intelligence resources—this whole damn city is wired."

"Don't forget drones," added Will.

"Yeah, them, too."

Before Will could explain, Greg rose and started pacing.

His face flushed with emotion, and his eyebrows tightly knitted in anger. "My own partner consorting with the enemy! Do you know what that did to me? Yeah, I figured out you weren't in bed with Nicholai Demetr—you were in bed with one of his chief lieutenants and lovers! You were not only betraying me and everything we've worked for—you were stupid about it!"

Will took in all in silently. He was hurt and ashamed, but he knew he deserved it.

"You are not a bad guy, Will. In fact, you are one of the best men I've ever known. But you are dishonest, and you took that whole 'man of mystery' thing, and you abused it. I can't tell you how many times I had decided to cut you loose because I couldn't trust you. But, I didn't. I had to believe you were a good guy in a bad situation. Besides, we were doing so much good in the city. Maybe Skorn was a secret project, and she was feeding you inside information about the Iron Brigade that helped you pursue them in court! Maybe."

Will smiled half-heartedly. "Nope, none of that. She wasn't my spy. I didn't want to jeopardize her position. It was just too risky for her."

Greg sat down again. "Then, it was all about a woman. It wasn't about recruiting an inside person, or an intentional betrayal, or anything else. It was the girl."

"Yes," said Will.

Sixty seconds of awkward, heated thought passed. Both men knew the next words were important.

"You lied from the very beginning, Will," said Greg. "Why didn't you tell me about John Underhall?"

"Wh-What?"

"The first Johnny Saturn. He's your father. I assume you know that."

"How did you find out?" asked Will.

"I'm a detective, you idiot. That's what I do. I would never have teamed up with you in the first place without first doing my research. I waited for you to tell me, to explain your real motivations, but you never did. I assume that's why you set yourself up as my minder, because you believed the Johnny Saturn persona was your birthright, and you had to manage your intellectual property."

Will and Greg talked for an hour, and Will told him everything. Will gave up all the power he had held over everyone by selectively parceling out information. He realized that he had wronged Greg by omission and should have trusted the detective from the beginning. Will should have done a lot of things differently. He was amazed that altruistic intentions had led him into a wilderness of lies, half-truths, and deception. Will had wanted to be like his father, yet this was not how John Underhall would have handled anything. This realization was the most self-damning thought of Will's life.

The suite's door opened, and Nils let himself in.

"Sorry, boss, but this couldn't wait. A bicycle courier just delivered this, and I signed for you."

Nils handed Will an envelope. He opened it.

> *"If you want Michelle Breemer, you can have her. She's waiting for you in the warehouse at 33rd and Hardy. I can't wait to see you.*
>
> *N. D."*

Will's blood froze in his veins, and his stomach tried to crawl up his throat. He was paralyzed, this time with dawning horror, not injury. Everything he had feared for so long was now coming to pass.

"Well," said Greg, reading over Will's shoulder, "Either Vox Malaise played her hand early out of spite, or Skorn screwed up and got caught."

"No..." whispered Will, his face screwing up in anguish.

"I'm going to suit up and end this thing once and for all," said Greg Buchanan, rising as he did. He was already starting to slip into his Johnny Saturn persona, growing more intimidating and menacing by the moment.

"Wait," said Will. "Here's what we are going to do…"

———

When Team Saturn arrived at the warehouse on 33rd and Hardy, they were not surprised to find that it was an old, vacant Wissenschaft Inc. facility. Maybe Tactical chose this location to send a message to all his enemies—what is yours is mine! Once, Wissenschaft had been Tactical's primary competition for the job of being Spire City's crime boss, after all. Maybe Tactical merely found it amusing.

Johnny Saturn led the way, ferociously kicking the building's aluminum door off its hinges. With him were Will and Nils, who had smuggled his wheelchair-bound boss out of the hospital.

A vast gloom waited within the warehouse, a cavernous space punctuated only by an orderly forest of steel support columns and tons of scattered trash. Dusty light filtered in through holes in the sheet metal roof, and the place smelled of mold, old grease, dust, and stale air. It looked empty, except for its lone occupant. Skorn hung from the rafters, heavily chained and motionless. A pool of blood had collected beneath her. She was naked and covered with burns, cuts, welts, and all-over bruising.

"No!" hissed Will, who set his chair into motion, covering the hundred yards between him and Skorn on wheels faster than his companions could run.

"Careful, Will—we're not alone here," said Johnny Saturn. "My night vision lenses are picking up shapes in the distance."

Will got to Michelle Breemer. From below, it was impossible to tell if she were still alive.

"Nils, get her down—Give her to me!"

Nils found where her chains were anchored, released them, and lowered Skorn into the waiting arms of her lover. It was an odd sight because she was out of proportion with him, and she was heavy enough that his wheelchair sagged beneath their combined weight.

"Michelle! Michelle! Can you hear me! Please be alive! Please!" Will held his breath, waiting, hoping against hope.

Skorn's eyelids fluttered, revealing unfocused eyes.

Johnny Saturn stood, his carbon staff at the ready, looking into the distance. "Be ready, Nils. They're coming. There are a lot of them."

Nils leaned forward, flexing his massive arms as would a gorilla. "Let 'em come, Johnny. Let 'em come."

Will knew none of this. He held his broken, dying lover in his arms, and nothing else registered.

"Hold on, Michelle! I'll get us out of this!"

"Shh," said the giant woman through bloody, swollen lips. "I'm not getting out of anything this time."

"Yes, you are!" said Will, pushing some of the now slackened chains off her. "I'm here! I'm going to save you."

Skorn tried to smile, but her face was not functioning as it should have, and one of her eyes started to turn red as it hemorrhaged from within.

"Will?" she said.

"Yes, my love?"

"Have you ever been happy," she asked, "even a day in your life?"

Will smiled sadly.

"Never once," he answered. "Until I met you."

"It's the whole Iron Brigade," said Johnny Saturn. "There must be forty metahumans here." Indeed, the Brigade had surrounded Team Saturn, and even now they were tightening the noose. "I'll hold them for as long as I can, Nils. You get Will out of here."

Nils looked at Johnny Saturn, realization dawning on his face. He said nothing, though. He did not have to.

"It's okay, Nils," said Johnny Saturn. "I blew my 401K on this armor, so I knew retirement was out of the question for me anyway."

The cordon of menacing metahumans had closed around the little group. They were all there, Lacerater, Subwoofer, Boltz, Mr. Meridian, Ambiguous, Dr. Somnambulism, Terra Rosa, Celerity, the Hypodermic Man, and all the others. It was a metahuman army, and most of them had grudges to grind with Johnny Saturn. Their master, Nicholai Demetr, stepped forward.

"Greetings, Johnny Saturn," said the Balkan fighter. "When last we met, you used my army as leverage against Dr. Wissenschaft's mercenaries. I wonder, what will you do this time?

Johnny Saturn stepped forward, facing off with the yellow and brown armored crime boss. Saturn's bearing was menacing, his frown magnificent, and many of the Iron Brigade fighters shuffled back several paces under his baleful glare. This Johnny Saturn was the 'Giant Killer,' after all, and he had survived long enough for his reputation to far outstrip his reach.

"Last time we met," said Johnny Saturn, "you were much shorter and uglier. I'm impressed."

"I guess you could say that I'm a new man," said Tactical. "You, conversely, are about to become a dead one."

"If you knew me at all," growled Johnny Saturn, "you would know that I'm okay with dying."

Tactical grinned.

"Then, you will die. Alone and without allies, you all three will die here."

Johnny Saturn smiled, and it was a chilling sight.

"Did I say I was alone?"

There was a thunderous rattling, and the warehouse roof peeled back as if it were an oversized sardine tin. Above, framed in the sunlight, was the Squadron Premiere: Utopian, Staff of Life, Iron Claw, and Triops. Torch Song, Ms. Meme, Silverwing, and Hotfoot were there, as well as others that included Charge, Velvet Cipher, Deco, Pummel Horse, Anvil, Hyperspace II, Lady Fishnet II, Skyshark, and the Ghost of Benedetti. They circled in from the sky like brash, primary colored birds and formed up in a cordon with Johnny Saturn and Nils Zilcher, surrounding Will and Skorn.

"I brought some friends too," said Johnny Saturn.

"Damn you, Saturn," swore Tactical, then he raised his gun and took a wild shot at the vigilante. The battle joined with a deafening impact, and soon weird energies permeated the air, balls of plasma shot here and there, and a multitude of assorted projectiles in motion turned the atmosphere dark. The cement flooring cracked, shifted, and became perilous under the combined force of the two teams, and the warehouse began to collapse in sporadic, drunken waves. Fires started here and there, smoke and haze cut visibility to a few yards, and the sounds of metal rending, stone crumbling, shrieks, challenges, death rattles, and horrific moaning filled the space.

Before Nils joined in the battle, he scooped up Will, his chair, and Michelle all at once, and then carried them to the conflict's outer perimeter. He shielded them with his own body as he ran, and he moved with a speed and nimbleness no one would have expected from the over-muscled giant. Once he had deposited the lovers in a relatively safe location, he turned and began fighting. No one was going to harm Will without first killing Nils!

Will was oblivious to all this. He felt Michelle shudder, and he instinctively knew she was about to slip away. "Hang on, Michelle! Hang on!" He pulled Skorn closer, intent on kissing her one last time. Their lips locked, and with her last reserves, Michelle responded to his touch.

Will's kiss was savage—it could not end this way! It must not!

The battle in front of Will and Skorn had reached a rolling boil, but none of the fighters noticed that something very odd had just happened. A strobing pulse of green energy, much like a spotlight, yet unveiled only for a moment, flashed around the two lovers. Space seemed to warp, and now it appeared that Will was far bigger than the woman he held in in his arms, not vice versa.

Will unsnapped the seat belt that held him in his chair. He stepped forward, and he gently laid Michelle into the chair he had just vacated. He did not see any life left in her, and he could not tell if she were still breathing.

Will rose to his feet, and he stood under his own power. His clothing grew so tight that it popped apart at the seams with his every movement, and his once unmarked skin now was covered with the same mystical tattoos that previously had adorned Skorn. (Will once had wondered how a tattoo artist's needles could have pierced an invulnerable woman's skin, but now he knew—they had not. It was the tattoos that made her skin nearly unbreakable. It was a chicken-and-the-egg story where the chicken came first.)

Will raised his head and locked his gaze on Tactical

"You!" bellowed Will. "You killed her!" His voice had become a roar, cutting through the noise of battle like a fog horn.

All the fighters froze for a moment. These men and women lived in a world full of magic, miracles, flying humans, and mad science run amok, but even these people were given pause when the disabled lawyer stepped from his chair and rose up as a tattooed giant.

Will charged Tactical with bullish ferocity, knocking aside the metahumans that blocked him. They flew this way and that, bonelessly flopping like rag dolls fired from a cannon.

Will grabbed Tactical, lifted him overhead, and then smashed him into the floor with such force that it pulverized the surface to sand and rubble. The violent kinetic energy radiated out, liquefying concrete, toppling some of the combatants, and even breaking some metahumans' legs in its passing.

"Never touch me again, you cretin!" screamed Tactical. His armor had taken the brunt of the attack, though he was still rattled by the attack's ferocity.

Will ripped away chunks of Tactical's armor, but he was not quick enough. Tactical opened fire with both gauntlet guns. Like all the weapons Tactical preferred, these firearms were compact but delivered disproportionately powerful payloads. But for his new metapowers, Will would have been blown to bloody red gobbets!

As it was, he was momentarily stunned, and the bullets blew small divots in his skin.

"You can't kill me," bragged Tactical. "I've seen more war, blood, and pain than you could witness in a million years! I am—"

"Shut the fuck up," cried Michelle Breemer. She caught Tactical in a chokehold from behind and yanked the crimelord off his feet.

By all appearances, Skorn should have been dead, but the random mystical tattoos on her skin showed that she hadn't passed all her magic power into Will, and she had kept some for her own use. She smiled through her swollen, bloody face as she tightened her grip on Tactical's throat.

"Uk, uk uk!" cried Tactical, and his face turned red and then purple. His beauty had been twisted into ugliness by rage and agony.

"Were you going to chop me up and leave me in a refrigerator, you disgusting little man? Were you going to kill me to inspire Will into becoming a tragic hero? Was I just an incidental plot point for you and your twisted little narrative?"

Skorn twisted, and Tactical's neck loudly snapped. Tactical's tongue protruded out, and his eyes almost bulged out their sockets, then they went dark as his inner light began to flicker out.

Will had regained his feet, and he approached.

"Michelle—" he began. No one would ever know what he might have said. Would he have urged his lover to kill Tactical? Or, to release him to stand trial? In an instant, it did not matter.

"I had you brought back to life, restored your power," whispered Michelle in a dry croak to Tactical. "That was my mistake."

With a mighty tug, she ripped Tactical's head from his body. She cast his corpse aside, and then she stomped Tactical's severed cranium and brains into a frothy red paste.

No one in the Squadron Premiere or the Iron Brigade moved to stop her. The battle had halted, and everyone watched Skorn's terrible vengeance play out. Some of the witnesses were sickened, some were envious, and some just impressed.

Michelle looked down at the mess she'd made.

"You won't be coming back to life from that, you sadistic pervert."

Then she slumped into Will's waiting arms.

The battle had been more or less even, but after Will and Skorn had defeated Tactical, the Iron Brigade began to panic. It was soon a rout, and those villains that had not fallen in battle fled by foot, wing, stealth, teleportation, or whatever means they had at their command. A third of the bad guys were captured before the day was out and the Iron Brigade's power in Spire City was broken forever.

———

When the surviving Iron Brigade metavillians still at large straggled back to their home base beneath the Gold Building at University and 12th street, Vox Malaise and the Scavengers were waiting for them. Vox had known about Tactical's stronghold for some time, and she had captured it while the Iron Brigade were off getting their collective asses kicked.

All the Scavengers were there, from hellish Ventilator Angel to Tapeworm, Tripartite, the Drunken Prophet, Rancid, Dr. Dissection, down to the Bacterium Twins, the Skold's Brank, the Hideous Handmade, and scores of others.

For the surviving Iron Brigade members, the choice was a stark one—swear allegiance to Vox Malaise and her reborn criminal order, or be fed to the Ventilator Angel. When faced with that genuinely horrendous thing with all its rusty, pitted, iron blades and pinchers, only a few chose death. Those that did had cause to instantly regret their stubbornness, both in the dying and in the long, screaming afterlife.

Vox Malaise settled onto the ugly, industrial-themed steel girder throne that Tactical had recently occupied. Old wrongs had been overturned, and her day was upon her now. She once again was the undisputed criminal overlord of Spire City. The chill smile that spread across her face had all the warmth of a cadaver in the morgue's freezer.

————

The next five years passed quickly for J. William Medal, Esq.—five years of intense work. Earlier that day he had been sworn in as mayor of Spire City, and he and his transitional team were settling into his new offices in the Rafert Governmental Plaza. Will had made good use of his four-year term as the Spire City prosecutor, and his war on crime had vaulted him into the public consciousness in a big way. Mayor Jeremy Newstead's administration had been disintegrating for a while, collapsing under an avalanche of scandals and corruption, and pushing him out of office had been easy.

Will walked to the windows of his corner office on the twenty-fifth floor and surveyed the city. He could hear his security chief, Nils Zilcher, organizing the police officers assigned to the mayor's security detail in the next room. The huge man may have been an ex-convict, but there was no one the new mayor trusted more, and the officers worked with him without a fuss. The opposing party had tried to use Will's association with Nil's as the subject of attack ads, but the public never latched onto it and had elected Will anyway.

The mystic tattoos and metahuman strength that had come from Michelle Breemer were all gone now. Those symbols and the magic they represented had never been intended for Will anyway, so over time, they had drained away. Michelle eventually regained most of her power, and once again she was covered in those mystic markings. For Will, the power was gone, but its legacy remained: Will was no longer a paraplegic. His spine was healed, and he was fully ambulatory.

It had not been easy, but Medal had gotten Michelle Breemer, aka Skorn, a pardon for her crimes, and now she was Michelle Breemer-Medal, Spire City's first lady. She was never going to fit the template of a mayor's wife, not even close, but Will didn't mind. She was one-of-a-kind, and the city came to love her as she was. The people of Spire City loved a good redemption story.

Will thought of the others who had helped him in his quest. He considered Greg Buchanan, and Will smiled. Greg was going to make an excellent Spire City Police Commissioner, and one of Will's first acts as mayor had been to appoint his old partner to that post.

Will's mind wandered to his father, John Underhall, the former Johnny Saturn. His dad lived with his wife and daughter in their villa in Monaco these days, but he also kept a secret apartment on the Squadron Premiere's campus. He knew that his dad had a hand in almost everything that happened in Spire City and that the one-time mystery man continued to work behind the scenes. John Underhall had had a few health scares, but overall his well-being had improved after he beat his addiction to painkillers. He was enjoying a fruitful semi-retirement collecting vintage Harley-Davidson and Indian motorcycles, deep sea fishing, and being wrapped around his five-year-old daughter's little finger. Will and his dad still corresponded regularly, and he valued the older man's advice.

Will's Mom, Loraine Medal Kendall, had also become something of a local celebrity. She had become a regular on a social issues talk show, wrote prominent editorials on the *Spire City Gazette's* website, and hosted fundraisers for her many causes. Will didn't know what to think about all this, but he was proud of his mom and loved her, so that was what counted.

"It's time for your luncheon with the Barr Association, Mr. Mayor," said Abraham Rosenblatt, Will's longtime law partner and now the deputy mayor.

Will, Nils, and Will's personal assistant, Carley, rode the mayor's private elevator to the ground level where the mayor's limousine waited. As they crossed the short, marble expanse from the elevator to the front doors, Will saw someone he had not seen or thought about in years.

The Coat Man.

He looked much the same, a big man in a thick, threadbare coat, the hood pulled up and cinched close. As before, the Coat Man was writing in his notebook.

Will stepped away from his entourage and approached the homeless man. Will did not know what to say, yet he felt it was important to acknowledge the Coat Man. Will sat on the marble bench next to the imposing figure.

"Well, old friend, it's been a long time. Do you remember the note you gave me five years ago?"

The Coat Man looked up from his notebook, his huge eyes framed by his dark brown skin. It was an unnerving stare, one that spoke volumes, but said little. The Coat Man slowly nodded. He remembered the note.

"It said, 'I'm sorry, but this is not going to end well,'" quoted Will. "Truer words were never written. Things did not end well at all. We survived, though, and that says something."

The Coat Man nodded in understanding. He was mute, by choice or some other cause, but he could make himself understood well enough.

"What's next, then?" asked Will. "I've got a lot of work to do. Will I succeed?" Will did not feel the slightest bit silly or odd asking the Coat Man this. Over the years Will had come to believe that their first meeting was almost oracular—fate had brought them together.

The Coat Man looked at his notebook, and then a frown creased his brow. He tore a blank sheet of paper free from the book and handed it to Will. There was something sad about the big man's eyes, a look of hopeless resolve, perhaps.

Will took the sheet of blank paper, then he stood up to leave.

"Thanks," said Will to the Coat Man. "I hope we meet again, but if we don't, you have my gratitude." Will gave the man some money, asked him if there was anything else he could do for him, to which the Coat Man shook his head "no."

Will rejoined his patiently waiting party.

"What was that about, boss?" asked Nils, understandably perplexed by what he had just witnessed.

"The future," replied Will, holding up the blank page for the others to see. "It's up to us to write the future. It's wide open."

JOHNNY SATURN II

I ALWAYS WANTED A GIANT ROBOT

It was June 24, 2012, in the dark watches of early morning after business hours at Corky's Pub, yet long before the Spire City dawn. Corky's was a cop bar I used to frequent back when I was Spire City Police Detective Greg Buchanan, and Corky himself was one of the few friends I had left from my pre-metahero days. Now, I was Johnny Saturn, and it was really hard to have normal friends.

After my apparent death saving the city from the Graf Zeppelin III and the machinations of Dr. Karl Wissenschaft, I was sort of the city's darling. There had already been two really bad movies made about me, and several equally fallacious books. In all fairness to the producers and writers of these movies and books, they could not have asked me for my version of the events because I was "dead" at the time they were written. The truth was not all that important to them anyway because sensationalism sold much better than truth. Bread and circuses, and all that.

Anyway, this morning I sat at the bar with my old friend Corky, a congenial middle-aged ex-cop who always reminded me of a black Dick Van Dyke. Corky had been a beat cop back in the day when my mystery man predecessor, John Underhall, had been on the police force. I had removed my mask and pulled down my cowl, and I was simply Greg Buchanan not Johnny Saturn II.

Corky refilled my glass with Scotch whisky. "So, this invisible robot?"

"Well, it's sort of convoluted," I said, "and it hasn't gotten any easier to explain in the retelling."

"Start at the beginning, Greg. I have got to hear this one," said Corky.

"Okay," I said. "It began up north in Chicago. Something big and unidentified tore down at least one firehouse and a post office a few months ago."

"And it was invisible? How did anyone know it was a robot?"

"Well," I said, "it left giant, mechanized, three-toed footprints wherever it moved, and it chugged as if powered by diesel engines. In the fires that followed the destruction it made, the robot's outline was exposed in the waves of heat. It was about one hundred and fifty feet tall, basically humanoid in shape, or maybe gorilla-like, and heavily armored."

"Armored, huh?" said Corky.

"Sure," I said. "They didn't find that out from its outline though. They discovered that when the Illinois National Guard tried to stop it with cannon and tank fire, and when their aircraft tried to blow it away with air-to-surface missiles. Nothing stopped it, or even slowed it down. The local metaheroes, and some of ours too, tried to contain it, but they were all unsuccessful.

"Then, after each battle, the giant robot disappeared," I said.

"I don't get that part," said Corky. He followed up his statement with a smile and then another round of whisky. "Mmm, smooth," he said, obviously pleased with his drink.

"I know, I know," I said. "It's really weird. It made no sense until much later when the robot attacked Spire City."

———

When the giant mechanical gorilla plowed into a wealthy bedroom community named Asphodel Heights on the north side of Spire City, it tore its way through town with the ferocity of an F5 tornado. The local metaheroes were quick to respond, and Titanium Tom's Squadron Premiere led the charge. The Squad's combined might managed to bring the robot to a stop, creating a temporary stalemate.

I was there, too, but I didn't take part in the direct assault on the giant mecha.

I'm not that kind of metahero, and at best I would have squeezed one of the really mighty metas out of place in the battle lineup. My value really comes into play when I serve as a scout, strategist, and detective. I am a traditional mystery man more than a metahero, and I had no intention of arm-wrestling the damn robot. I had thrown in with the Squadron Premiere on numerous occasions, but I was not one of them.

From what we could tell, the robot's "head" was a rotating turret mounted with some sort of advanced particle beam weapon. As the mechanical beast tore through one building after another, trying to get at the metaheroes, its "death ray"—as they dubbed it on Action 4 News—blew away random buildings within a two mile radius. It seemed like the heroes were causing more harm than good by baiting the robot. Of course, what else could they do?

The robotic titan tore into I-60, the interstate that separated Asphodel Heights from Spire City to the South.

I got a pretty good view of what was going on as I helped with the evacuation and cleared the way for first responders to reach the injured and dead. I had no reason to prove myself fighting a big metal monster, and I think I saved more lives working on the sidelines. As it was, that day proved to be the last for heroes like Stellar II, Tidal Force, the Ravenous Raptor, Sureshot III, and the Silver Age great, Lightspeed.

Keep in mind, I am not criticizing the metaheroes. They are not always all that imaginative—especially Titanium Tom—but they deal in force, and stopping the titanic, invisible robot seemed like a very good idea. I do not think it was their fault as individuals that the problem escalated, but a fault within the metahero institution itself.

Once the robot broke into downtown Spire City, it did its disappearing trick again. Had it teleported out? There was no visible gate, and no sucking "whoosh" as air rushed in to fill the robot's voided space. Had it all been an illusion, and only then had someone thought to disbelieve it? This seemed too unlikely to consider. The truth was nobody knew, and it was not 'til much later we discovered the answer was much, much stranger.

That night, as we all assisted the folks trapped inside the destruction zone, I ran into one of my best friends in the metahero community. His name is Triops. I had once done him a favor, and we had become friends as a result. This time we found each other in the coffee line at the Red Cross's emergency shelter. Triops was a member of the Squadron Premiere, and he had been there for the frontal assault.

At less than five feet tall, Triops claimed to be a hybrid of a gray alien and a short prehistoric long-tailed brine shrimp called a triops. He looked like an olive-green-skinned gray alien with three eyes and a long conical head; he was one of the most powerful psychics in the city and most likely the world. He countered his odd appearance by dressing in a dapper business suit and answering to the name "Denny."

"That was the damndest thing, Greg," Denny said.

"Yeah?" I replied.

"That robot was physical, but not physical like we know it. It's hard to explain, really. I almost felt like it was a tulpa."

"Say it in English, Denny. I have no idea what a 'tulpa' is."

"A mental construct," said Triops. "An artificial being built from someone's thoughts or imagination."

"That is pretty weird," I said.

"But, it's not a tulpa. It 'felt' different."

"I'll take your word for it, psychic guy."

Triops sipped his coffee, and added, "I mean really different. Like ancient technology, or alien technology. I'm not really an expert on either, unfortunately. I grew up in Nebraska, and they didn't really cover those topics in public school."

Ancient technology? I was not an expert either, but I knew someone who was.

This was not going to be fun.

———

Up until a year ago, Wissenschaft Inc. had owned Spire City's healthcare network, the *Spire City Gazette*, several television stations, and the NBA team, the Spire City Ferrets.

After Dr. Wissenschaft's apparent death, the company was mostly subsumed by Synn Tech, a multinational conglomerate based out of Brazil. Wissenschaft Inc.'s odds and ends that escaped the takeover were still substantial, and it still owned several hospitals, television stations, a national trucking firm, and a controlling interest in the Spire City Ferrets. To illustrate its continued presence in Spire City and the considerable economic power it still held, the company's stockholders had seen fit to build Wissenschaft Plaza at 21st and Banks.

At 163 floors, Wissenschaft Plaza was currently the tallest building in the world, though that record changed almost daily as other hulking monstrosities were erected around the Middle East and Asia. To my eye, this building did nothing for Spire City's skyline, and it seemed a gross misuse of funds and materials. For all I knew, they had to raid the earth's core and the Sahara Desert for all the steel and glass it took to erect this sad testament to alpha dominance.

High above the city streets perched the office of Wissenschaft Inc.'s CEO and CFO, Tara Wissenschaft. I did not look forward to seeing her again. Our last parting, over the bleeding, headless body of Dr. Karl Wissenschaft, had not been all that amicable. I could only hope I would be admitted to see her, and I did not know what to expect.

I wore my civilian clothes and came as Gregory Buchanan. To my surprise, my name alone allowed me no-questions-asked passage through the security checkpoint, onto a high-speed elevator and past a secretary to see Tara. I could only assume I was on some sort of short list. Maybe she just wanted to gloat some more. Or, maybe, she wanted to toss me a hundred and sixty floors to the street below. Twice. It was hard to tell.

In a lavish office big enough to contain a grocery store and the strip mall next to it, Tara Wissenschaft waited for me. She wore a severely-cut ash gray business suit, and her blonde hair was slicked back and short. She looked as approachable as a venomous snake and as warm as an ice sculpture, yet she was attractive in the way only danger could seduce you.

I offered Tara a smile. I had been there when she was "born." She was an incredibly lifelike android, a one-of-a-kind prototype so expensive another like her would never be built. Her programming was based on a real human girl, Mollie Andreeson, and I had been Tara's first victim—and her first love.

Unrequited love, I should add.

"What do you want, Greg?" There was an angry edge to her tone and... something else. I cannot claim to understand all the nuances of a typical human girl, and in a lifelike synthetic girl said nuances were beyond mysterious.

"Hi, Tara. I've got a couple questions."

"So?"

"Questions only someone with a crystal skull and access to the wisdom of the ancients can answer. May I sit down?"

"Do whatever you want," she said, but then took a seat, too.

"I assume you've followed the story of this giant, invisible robot?" I said. "Triops tells me it is some sort of really, really old technology. Something antediluvian."

Tara said nothing.

"Is it yours?" I said. "You have access to that kind of know-how."

"I do," said Tara. "But it's not mine. I'm not the only source of the old wisdom on Earth."

"I believe you," I said. "You are too busy trying to establish your power base to risk it for... well, I don't know what. Wissenschaft Inc.'s involvement makes no sense. Unfortunately, we don't know the motive, so that makes these bizarre spree attacks hard to pin down."

"Thank you," said Tara. Her synthesized voice rang with irony.

"Can you tell me anything about this?" I said. "You must have a clue, considering everything you know."

She snorted in derision, and said, "Yes, of course. But, why should I tell you?"

"Let's not do this," I countered. "We have history between us, and we both have the same blood on our hands. I get that. But I'm not your enemy, and innocent people are dying because of this robot thing."

"You look like hell, Greg." She was trying to divert me, but I wasn't playing.

"Well, I'm wearing a replacement leg, my hair is turning prematurely white, and I have the scars of second and third-degree burns on my back from the last time we said goodbye. So, yeah, I hardly look twenty-eight anymore."

Tara did not respond. The office lights dimmed and a projection screen descended from the ceiling. As a walking computer, she was silently tied in with all the office's automated features. For all I knew, she was also negotiating business deals, accessing the Internet, and hacking a mainframe somewhere while she talked with me. For a moment her eyes glowed a clear blue, and then they projected a two-dimensional image onto the screen.

"Handy," I said.

"Shut up and watch," said Tara.

An alien world flickered to life on the screen, its simple, two-dimensional projection seeming almost three-dimensional because of its excellent depth of field. Like all the emanations from the incredibly ancient crystal skull encased in Tara's head, it was monochromatically blue. Schematics flew by, slowly resolving into the plans for a giant robot. I could not read the plan's accompanying measurements, but the man standing as a reference point next to the monster automaton hinted at a scale of about twenty-five-to-one, or one hundred and fifty feet tall.

The robot's proportions were not exactly human, though it did have two arms, and it stood upright on two legs. Its head appeared to be more a like a gun turret, with a cannon-like apparatus protruding from it, but no obvious "eyes." With its long, thick arms and relatively short legs, it reinforced my previous perception of an upright gorilla.

The robot was covered with thick, armored plates, and there were all manner of pistons, winches, and gears at its joints. Its overall styling hinted at ancient Greek, Egyptian, and Aztec aesthetics, but that made sense in light of the fact these three cultures were the Atlanteans' most direct descendants.

"In the antediluvian period," began Tara, "when Atlantis was at its cultural apex, scientific knowledge far exceeded what we know today. People travelled through the skies and even to distant planets and stars on vimanas. The planet itself was a giant computer, with all its veins of ores the rough equivalent of circuit boards. Crystal skulls were a type of home computer, and working star gates were laid out on the planet's surface as collections of astrologically arranged minhirs and dolmens. Modern science considers these people to have been Stone Age primitives, yet their mastery of the cosmos still dwarfs our own even now.

"These days, traditional scientists and historians flounder in confusion when asked to explain the cyclopean weights the ancients were able to move and manipulate. Who or what could have moved the stones of Baalbek into place, for example? Aliens? Sonic antigravity technology? The answer is stranger than you might think.

"Giant thought robots did all the heavy lifting," said Tara. Either she had the ultimate poker face, or she was being serious.

"Thought robots?" I wondered, although I could not wholly banish the incredulity from my voice.

"Indeed. Thought robots. These were not the tulpas later created by the Tibetan monks, nor the phantasmata created by wizards during the European Renaissance. Those skills may have been offshoots of the old thothbot technology. With tulpas, for example, monks manifested semi-independent, sentient creatures and people from intensified thought to carry out their wishes. Thothbots, unlike the tulpas, never became sentient, and they were created through mechanical means, not mystical ones."

Tara continued. "These robots were formed of coherent thought, with conceptual pistons and imaginary gears, all powered with potential energy. These robots could be as large or small as the thought engineer intended them to be, with seemingly unlimited power. When you wanted to store a thothbot, you simply forgot it, and it ceased to be until remembered again."

"Tara, this makes no sense. I guess I can handle giant, invisible robots, but this is more like something an LSD-soaked British writer would come up with!"

"Not so," said Tara. "We have found so little evidence of antediluvian machinery because it was all forgotten, leaving only their works, but not the machinery itself. Tectonic forces broke apart the world's rock circuitry, and the sea-based data banks scattered without the coherent electrical force to keep them in place. How humanity survived the inky blackness of the dark ages that followed is a testament to your mindless stubbornness."

"So, you are telling me the invisible robot that is terrorizing the Midwest is a 'thought robot'? Are you having fun at my expense?"

"Yes and yes," said Tara. "It pleases me to see you confused, but the thothbots are most certainly real. Thothbots later lent their name to the Egyptian deity of wisdom and thought, Thoth. He often appeared in legend as a baboon, hinting at the ape-like robots from which his name was derived."

"If all this were true—and I'm not convinced yet, not by a long shot—how would you destroy a thothbot?"

"You can't," said Tara, turning off her blue projection and letting her eyes return to their normal appearance. "You cannot destroy a thought. You can't even forget it away because you are not the one who remembered it back into action."

"Remembered it... back into action?"

"Enough," she said. "I'm in great demand, and I have given you more than enough time."

"But—"

"But nothing," she said angrily. "Check your tablet computer when you leave here. I've emailed you a document that should answer the rest of your questions. If you cannot figure it out from that, then I don't know how you ever managed to work as a Spire City detective."

I rose, and the door I had entered her office by opened again.

"Go," said Tara. "And do not bother me again."

Our interview was over, so I walked away.

"I've got a new battery for your prosthetic leg at the will-call desk," she called after me. "You should check in with my people at Wissenschaft Prosthetics on the 43rd floor. Your leg needs some upkeep and fine tuning."

As unlikely as it seemed, Tara still cared about me, at least a little. I saw her turn away, and I left her office. The least I could do was leave her dignity intact. Tara was right—the document she posted on my tablet computer was enough for me to figure out what had happened and who was responsible. Before I could follow through on this information, however, the thothbot struck again.

This time the invisible robot chose a major exchange along I60, the interstate that ran along Spire City's northern flank, and began to tear through the city's infrastructure. This would be the second time the thothbot had attacked the interstate. The giant mecha focused its attention on the road itself, not the drivers, but that was not enough to prevent fatalities among the afternoon drive-time traffic. Overpasses exploded under giant fists, a stretch of highway was ripped out, and buildings on either side were pushed over by the invisible attacker. Rush hour was always a bit crazy in Spire City, but this was something else!

A semi-trailer loaded with giant steel beams plowed into what must have been the robot's left leg, and the force was sufficient to drive the robot to one knee. It was easy to see the thothbot's outline by now, because the destruction it caused had thrown up a huge cloud of particulate matter. As the dust settled on the thothbot, the mechanical behemoth's outline became partly visible.

I had arrived on the scene in my guise as Johnny Saturn just in time for the speeding semi-trailer to make the robot stumble. I had hitched a ride with my girlfriend, Staff of Life, carried by one of her scalar force fields. Staff of Life was Victoria Shelbourne in her civilian post as a doctor of electro-gravitational physics at Spire City University, a blonde Welsh woman in her mid-thirties. Victoria never claimed to be as wildly brilliant as the great Nikolai Tesla, but she had been clever enough to figure out variations on some of his most arcane technologies and use them to transform herself into a metahero. More recently, Persephone Synn Underhall had made some rather amazing upgrades to Victoria's gear, and now Staff of Life was arguably the most powerful metahero in the city.

The Utopian came with us. He was Victoria's best friend and an old-school metahuman with enough power to make Greek gods burn with envy. The Utopian could break the sound barrier when flying, lift a Boeing 747 and give it a toss, and see through most materials at seemingly impossible distances. He was a handsome, late-twentysomething with blond hair and a serious sense of entitlement.

Not bothering to wait for my opinion on the matter, the Utopian plowed ahead, his fists held in front of him as he hurtled out of the sky at the giant thothbot. Under ideal circumstances the Utopian should have waited to coordinate his plans with Staff and me, but he did not, and I was smugly fine with that. I really was curious what the big blue and gold hothead could do against this elder tech.

Have at it, golden boy! I thought.

The Utopian slammed into the robot, creating a concussive shock wave that shattered windows in a one-mile radius; the robot was tossed back about six blocks, tumbling through tall buildings like a wrecking ball into houses of cards. The thothbot finally smashed into the gargantuan Pantheon Inc. building at Union and 24th, carving a vertical, robot-sized crater out of the skyscraper's north face, and then fell to 24th Street below in an avalanche of stone, glass, steel, and dust.

The Utopian also was affected by the impact, and he rebounded out of the city and into the farmlands to the north. Maybe he would bounce like a skipping stone until he hit Chicago, I don't know. He was tough and determined, so he would be back in no time.

Going mano-a-mano against the robot was not my style. I could have, sure—my harness was based on Captain Barometer's old rig, powered by zero point energy and it granted me the power to fly, generate powerful force fields and fire powerful impact beams. Dr. Horatio Synn had upgraded my systems, giving me all sorts of little perks; then it was upgraded again by Staff of Life, giving my impact beam a devil of a punch; and then Harvey "The Tailor" Torres had tuned it all up and repackaged the whole thing into a couple of stylish and comfortable bracers.

I did not often use all these powers as would a metahero— instead, I rarely resorted to flying; I used my force fields to replace my old body armor; and I used my impact beam to back up my fists with one hell of a punch, like brass knuckles that hit with the force of dynamite. So maybe I could have tangled with the robot, maybe not. As far as I was concerned, a head-to-head fight like that was a waste of my real abilities.

"Victoria, can you keep the robot busy 'til the Utopian gets back? I think I know how to end this without too much more property damage. If the Utopian does it his way, there won't be a city to protect, you know?"

I jumped, and I was airborne under my own power. I hated to break character and take to the air, but this was the exception that proved the rule.

————

I did not have to fly the friendly skies very far; just four blocks to the Major Sam Jefferson Federal Health Care Center at 26th and Yew Street. This was a local Veterans Affairs hospital, primarily devoted to the long-term care of veterans. I guess you could say this facility was something of a military old folks' home, and you would be pretty much correct.

I landed on the hospital's roof and let myself in through an access door.

Four blocks away, ominous plumes of black dust bloomed into dark columns in the sky, and the massive bass *whump* sounds of the thothbot and the Utopian playing punch-the-sandbag with each other shook the entire city. Here and there, the yellow blasts of Staff of Life's energy beams gave the whole tableau a glaring sense of menace. I was armed to deal with crazy threats, but even I felt uneasy with what was going on. Too much had happened in Spire City in the last few years not to be afraid.

Inside the Jefferson Center hospital, doctors, nurses, orderlies, and even patients ran this way and that with mad resolve, doing their best to evacuate the building before it got knocked over by the giant robot. I was one of the city's most famous metaheroes, but such was the chaos I was able to walk through the building unnoticed. I found my way into the hospital ward, and, in room 5035, I spotted my prey.

An elderly, weathered man sat on the edge of his bed, bent over a dog-eared magazine, his hand running over some of the black and white illustrations printed within. If I did not already know this man was in his mid-sixties, I would have guessed he was in his eighties. Life on the street can do that to you.

"*Astounding Epics* magazine, the 1974 June edition, right?" I asked.

The old man stopped what he was doing and looked up from his well-worn periodical in amazement. When he stopped fingering the charts and art in the old pulp periodical, the cacophony of the nearby battle ceased for a moment.

"Wrong," said the man. "It's the January 1976 edition, my second story, 'Marvels of an Elder Earth.' How did you find me?"

"I got a tip," I admitted. "I've got copies of both your stories stored in my mobile computer. With those, it wasn't all that hard to track you down."

The old man said nothing, but his weathered hand slid across the paper, and the nearby battle began again with massive booms.

"You are Richard Rush," I said. "You were wounded in 1969 at the Battle of Hamburger Hill in Vietnam, suffering a concussion and traumatic brain injury from a bomb that went off too close to you. After an honorable medical discharge, you came home to Spire City and wrote at least two stories for *Astounding Epics* magazine, 'I Remember Atlantis' in 1974, and 'Marvels of an Elder Earth' in 1976. After that, you lived homeless on the streets until 2011 when you were admitted to the Major Sam Jefferson Federal Health Care Center. I found all this out after a few searches on the Internet."

The battle outside had gotten a city block closer, and out the window I saw another building collapse and the Utopian knocked back. The Utopian looked very dirty, well-pummeled, and put-upon, but he flew back into the fray almost immediately.

"You don't know anything, Saturn!" cried Richard Rush. "You've only got part of the story!"

"I'm all ears," I said.

"In 1970, I got sucked into the infamous MKUltra as a patient! They repeatedly dosed me with a really nasty batch of LSD and locked me into sensory deprivation devices for weeks at a time! You have no idea what that will do to a man! It was then, cut off for weeks from anyone and everyone and even my own body, tripping on lysergic acid diethylamide, that I first saw it. There I was, a disembodied intelligence in a sea of nothingness, watching reality unravel and weave itself back together again and again, a screaming white vertigo of horror! That is when I first saw the script."

The script. I knew what he was referring to, at least on one level. There was an alien alphabet of some sort, or an alien font or pictograms, printed alongside Richard's stories. It was very odd looking, full of intricate letterforms that looked like a mix of mysterious math symbols, musical notation, and M. C. Escher-esque motifs. It was incredibly intricate and it reminded me a little of blueprints or schematics to some unidentifiable machine.

"At first I didn't understand what I had discovered, or where I had found it. Maybe it is encoded in our DNA, or maybe it is some quantum graphology that may only be seen from the correct psychological angle. Perhaps it was so huge that we could not make it out with our own eyes, or maybe I had remotely viewed it from some impossibly distant past."

As he ranted, Richard Rush stopped stroking the symbols in the old magazine, and the booming sounds of mayhem now just a few blocks away died down again.

"It's inconceivable, but this alphabet is not a language—it is the individual parts of a working machine! If you can write it down, then you can manipulate it and make things happen. Watch!"

I was stunned enough to doubt my own eyes for a moment. This was madness!

Richard pulled his finger across one of the symbols, and it rotated on the page. What was just ink and paper was also some sort of machine controller at the same time, a dial Rush could twist and adjust. It made no sense whatsoever, even to someone mired in the crazy world of metaheroes, but the inked symbols on that mundane newsprint rotated, interlocked like a watch's gears, and moved at his touch.

This text was a device, and this device was text.

I thought maybe my eyes had fallen prey to some sort of autosuggestion, that this was an optic illusion, or I had psyched myself into seeing the crazy man's visions. But I knew it was not the case. Richard Rush was controlling the invisible robot from here, and the mechanical text in an old magazine was his control pad.

"First I flattened the neighborhood up in Chicago where I grew up. Then, Asphodel Heights here in Spire City, the one-time neighborhood of the woman who left me at the altar and broke my heart forever. Now, I am destroying that part of I-60 where they tore down my family's ancestral home—all for a stupid stretch of interstate! And, I did it all from right here in my bed!"

I knew what I had to do. Rush's hand began moving across the page again, and another building tumbled beneath the thothbot's titanic blows.

"Why now, Richard? Did you keep this magazine all these years, waiting for the right time?"

"Of course not, idiot!" He was screaming so hard now his face turned red and purple. Maybe I would get lucky and he would keel over from a heart attack.

"A magic woman gave it to me, a woman made up of blue chaos swirls! She called herself Eris, and she told me to have fun with my old story and machine-o-grams."

I felt like I should have known who he was referring to, but it did not matter—undoubtedly an LSD flashback of some sort. I put Eris onto my mental "to do" list, because I had more immediate issues to attend to.

The thothbot was just across the street now, and it was looming over the Jefferson Center, blocking out the hazy light in the room. The Utopian and Staff of Life had tried to hold the line, but so far they had failed. The robot rang like a huge steel drum beneath the Utopian's blows, and Staff of Life's particle beams scored the robot's outer shell, but it was not enough. Gears churned, hydraulics hissed, and I knew it would all be over in a moment. Richard Rush intended to die, and he was taking me and the hospital with him.

I snatched the magazine out of Rush's hands.

"Give that back!" he cried. "Give. It. Back!"

The thothbot's attack never came.

"Sorry, Richard, no can do." I rolled up the pulp fiction serial and stuck it in my inside coat pocket.

"No... no..."

"It's over," I said. "You have had your vengeance, but now it's time to forget the thothbot. Can you do that?"

"I... I've already forgotten..." Tears freely rolled down Richard Rush's face, and he crumpled back into his bead, pulling into a fetal position. He sobbed uncontrollably.

"Nobody understands vengeance better than me, Richard," I said. "You will find a way to move beyond this. I know."

Utopian and Staff of Life entered the hospital room and took up positions behind me. It was easy for them to find me, because Staff of Life could follow my equipment's energy signature. The two heroes said nothing, and certainly the scene had to be very strange to them, but they were real pros, and they somehow could sense we had won.

"I'm not turning you in to the police," I said. "There is no way they could prove your crimes in a court of law. It's all too weird. Instead, I believe the fair thing is to leave you here, to spend the rest of your days in this room, attended by people who have no idea what you have done, and what you have been through."

We three metaheroes turned to leave, but Richard Rush's wracking sobs cut through even our leathery metahearts. His agony was very real, and it recalled to me my own dark places of despair.

"Don't you dare judge me!" screamed Richard at our backs. I turned around. He pulled an army service revolver from under his mattress and lifted it to his mouth.

"Richard, no!" I yelled.

Too late. The thinking parts of Richard Rush were splattered over those drab gray walls in a huge, shiny red arc. It was over like that.

———

"So, that's the story of the thothbot," I concluded.

"Well," said Corky, "I've spent my whole life in Spire City, so I've heard some really odd stories. That one has them all beat. I always thought some weird weather phenomenon was behind all that destruction, or bombs or something. Not a giant invisible robot. Too weird."

Corky took a drink. We were polishing off the bottle of Scotch.

"What happened to this 'thothbot'?"

"When Richard died, the robot was forgotten, and it ceased to be real," I said.

"And the magazine?" Corky followed up.

"I stuck it in a drawer. I don't know how many copies are still out there on the collectors' market, but no one alive knows what those mechanical symbols do, or how to work them."

"No one?" asked Corky, his eyebrows cocked in doubt.

"Well, not exactly," I said. I rolled up my left sleeve, and there, etched into the metal bracer I wore, was a duplicate of those elder pictograms.

"What?" said Corky, taken aback. "You don't mean—"

"Well," I said, "I've always wanted a giant robot, so..."

CITY OF THE BROKEN GATE

Our beginnings are always with us. Life happens, and years speed by, but it is always our beginnings that remain our most vivid memories. It might have been one of your parents' offhand comments; perhaps the doll you lost in the pasture beyond the gate you were told not to open; or the feel of your grandmother's nightgown. Life may have awarded you multiple doctoral degrees, and just as many husbands— four if you are counting—but your character and your journey began long before that. It is not just that way with people, but with countries, cultures, maybe even the whole human race. I almost am sure of it: the problems that plague us now began a long, long time ago when humanity was in its tumultuous infancy. The nature of our struggles has never changed, only their circumstances.

My name is Victoria Shelbourne. I am the dean of the Spire City University Physics Department. I call myself an explorer and science adventurer, but the world calls me a metahero. That is inaccurate, of course: I have no metapowers, just my mind and my inventions. I do not fight crime, but I always have been in the forefront of the battle when it comes to saving lives or averting crisis. As a metahero, I have worked under the title Victoriana and Power Staff, but these days I call myself Staff of Life. I am not completely satisfied with "Staff of Life," because I am not a healer bearing a caduceus, nor am I bread. Once you have branded yourself successfully, though, it is not easy to change.

For purposes of full disclosure—and to satisfy my editor—I will briefly describe myself. I resisted this in earlier drafts because I believe my words and knowledge better define me than does my superficial appearance. I am Welsh born, and still have a Welsh accent, but I have been a citizen of the United States of America for years now. I have an athletic build, chin-length blonde hair styled in a bob, and I suppose my face is well-proportioned and symmetrical enough to qualify as pretty. I have been known to wear light makeup, but my appearance would not qualify as "high maintenance." I wear glasses because I cannot abide contact lens, and my look tends to be more functional than fashion-based. As I mentioned, this makes me uncomfortable, because I prefer to get by with my brains, not my looks.

The story that follows is not about me specifically, although I was a key player. Every narrator is partial, and I claim to be neither balanced nor unbiased, but what matters here is that this story is true. It is about our beginnings, and it may not sit well with you.

————

July 23, 2012, I flew low across Spire City en route to my boyfriend's apartment building. I flew close to the rooflines because I did not want to interfere with all the helicopters, drones, and flying metaheroes that frequented the sky above Spire City. I still had to keep a watchful eye out for cables, wires, and pigeons, so I kept my speed below sixty miles per hour. When you fly this low, you could really feel the city beneath you as if it were a living thing.

If there is an archetypical Midwestern American town, it is Spire City. It squats on the north shore of Lake Avernus, which is the southernmost and smallest of the Great Lakes, on the Illinois side of the Illinois/Indiana border. Located more or less in the middle of North America, the city is connected to the Atlantic Ocean by Lake Michigan and the Great Lakes Watershed to the north, and to the Gulf of Mexico by the Mississippi River System to the south. It also is linked to the East and West Coasts by Interstate 60, which splits off Interstate 65 that connects Indianapolis and Chicago. At one time, Spire City was the primary hub of a vast railroad network, although Chicago has taken that distinction in recent decades. The Hesperides International Airport is one of the largest of its kind in the world, covering more ground and runways than London's Heathrow and Chicago's O'Hare combined, as well as being the central hub of National Express, the world's largest courier service.

You could call Spire City the crossroads of America, or you might as well call it a rustbelt city, or part of the Corn Belt or the Bible Belt. It all works well enough. About four-and-a-half million people call the city and its nearer suburbs home. Like other Midwesterners, these folks are friendly, conservative, and maybe too polite. They also are tough and proud of their battle-scarred metropolis.

Spire City, along with Manhattan and Los Angeles, is one of the three main concentrations of the metahero culture in the United States, and thus the world. Manhattan may have the Collective of Champions, and Los Angeles the San Andreas Sentinels, but Spire City boasts the Squadron Premiere, as well as a few smaller metahero groups and several metavillain gangs such as the Iron Brigade and the Scavengers.

Along with the Utopian and Tilt, I was one of the founders of the Squadron Premiere, and so I would have remained if the group had not been co-opted by the Department of Homeland Security. When that happened, all the foreign-born metaheroes were expelled, and I was no exception.

Let me clarify a couple of items: as I have mentioned, I have no metapowers of my own, but the power staff that gives me my codename can encase me in an electro-magnetic levitation field that allows me to make short-range flights. I did not invent electro-magnetic levitation, but I did design this staff and its micro-toroidal power plants. I based it on years of my own research; the missing notebooks of Nikolai Tesla; a few pieces of technology from my friend and colleague Gary Redman; and recent upgrades from one of my mentors, Persephone Helios Synn Underhall. Expressed technically, the staff is a combination of hyper-quantum couplers with a psycho-active operating system all projected from a geosynchronous satellite and a virtual array holographic core. If that sounds like presumptuous technobabble to you, then I do not blame you.

My second point of clarification is this: I am 37 years old and calling Greg Buchanan my "boyfriend" seems silly. Life partner, significant other, special friend, they all sound insufficient or patronizing. Greg is everything to me but my husband, and that will never be an issue because I will never get married again. Four times is enough, thank you. I am not going to jinx a fifth relationship by making it legal.

I flew low across Spire City on my way to the Baumgarten Building where Greg lived. I descended toward Union and 3rd Street and maneuvered in to land. Before I could touch down on the Baumgarten Building's roof, there was a huge popping sound followed by an explosion of glass. I just was in time to see Greg blown out one of the Baumgarten's fourth floor windows; he plummeted toward Union Street below amid a shower of glass. He was falling backward and his arms were flailing about, and he looked as surprised as I was.

I aimed my staff and caught Greg in one of my patent-pending mag-lev spheres, and a millisecond later I laid a scalar force field over the streets below to catch the falling glass. It was not a great volume of shards, but I could not risk any bystanders getting seriously injured. I neatly deposited Greg, me, and the pile of glass onto the Baumgarten's roof.

"Thanks," said Greg. I do not think he was scared for himself, but if anyone below had gotten hurt then he would have felt responsible. "I bet a lot of people are dialing 911 right now, and I'll have to explain this to the police somehow. Ugh."

Greg had been a police officer himself until recently, so he knew the boys in blue were not going to be amused. He was right. They were not amused, not even a little bit. Greg had not been popular during his time as a police detective in the 23rd Precinct, so his reputation did not put him behind the thin blue line. After a bit of bureaucratic red tape, and repeatedly assuring the police he had not blown up a methamphetamine lab or something, we were finally alone.

"What were you doing, Greg?" I asked.

"Huh?" he said. His ears must have still been ringing from the explosion, and he had not gotten all his hearing back yet.

"What. Were. You. Doing?"

"I was working with the thothtech again," he admitted. "Just when I thought I had made a breakthrough, Boom! I wrote something that blew up."

Greg was a handsome, late twenty-something. He used to be quite muscular, but now he was too thin, and his temples had gone from dirty blond to silver after his recent ordeals. Those same ordeals had robbed him of his left leg, and he now walked with a high-tech mechanized prosthesis. His shirt and jacket might have hidden it, but I also knew his upper back was scarred with multiple burns. The last year had not gone easily on him, but he was still very much the man I loved.

The "thothtech" he mentioned calls for some explanation, so prepare, dear reader, for an information dump. I already have ignored my editor's request to open this narrative with the explosion. "Hook them early!" he said, and so it seems only right that I further break the rules of good writing and lay some exposition on you. I do not claim to be a skilled writer, so forgive me. I am far better at writing thesis and grant applications than details of my life.

About a month ago, Greg and I, along with many of Spire City's other metahumans, foiled the attack of a giant, invisible robot bent on reducing the city to rubble. The robot was the temporary embodiment of an ancient Atlantean technology, a sort of machinery alphabet that functioned in real world space. I guess you could say it was a two-dimensional technology that manifested in the three-dimensional world. You could rearrange or compose the machine alphabet as you saw fit, and the configuration you wrote became a real world machine until you deactivated it. If a machine written as B, D, and X did one thing, then a machine composed of X, B, and D did something else, and so forth.

The thothtech script itself looked like a cross between ancient Sumerian hieroglyphs, a circuit board, and shapes reminiscent of precision clockworks. Writing this script out in ink and then watching it animate and function on the paper was surreal at best, and unsettling at worst. You could feel on a deep, instinctual level you were watching something inexplicable and alien. Not something *wrong*, per se, but very much a thing of some ineffably foreign *other*.

This technology sounds easy to employ, but it is not. Greg and I now possessed all the thothtech script or letters that composed the giant, invisible robot Greg had kept, but that did not mean we had the whole thothtech alphabet. Plus, we were experimenting blind, and we had no good idea how some of the symbols interacted with each other, what effect they would produce, or what form they would take when combined. Greg and I had been working on the script all month, but there was so much we did not know. For example, what was the thothtech's power source? Where did the machines go when deactivated? What were these devices made of when active? We certainly were not creating or destroying matter, because that would have broken one of the fundamental laws of physics. We were not even completely sure what activated or deactivated the machines.

I have some theories on all this, of course. A part of superstring theory or M-theory called brane cosmology postulates that all of reality is projected onto two-dimensional sheets or branes, and we only perceive our reality as three-dimensional because we are part of the projection. It thus follows the thothtech script is somehow a part of the two-dimensional projection, and activating it extrapolates it into three-dimensional space.

Activation comes from the observer effect—the potential for these machines already exists, and the act of observing them triggers whether they occur or do not. It is fundamental wave vs. particle stuff, Schrodinger's silly cat and all that. As far as an energy source goes, I am leaning toward a pure expression of zero-point energy. I know that thothtech would have to exist in an impossibly cold state of absolute zero, but I am still working out my ideas, so let us not get lost focusing on this aspect.

If what I just wrote makes no sense to you, then I am sorry. Quantum physics is very real, and it is every bit as complex as it sounds. So, if your physics IQ is up to snuff, great, and if not, then keep reading because I will endeavor to make everything clear in conversational English as this narrative goes on.

———

"So, let me get this straight," I said. "You were experimenting with thothtech on your own—"

"—Even though you advised me not to," Greg said.

We were now on the fourth floor. Greg was one of the Baumgarten Building's only two inhabitants, so he lived on the third floor and used the fourth as a private gym, workshop, and office.

Greg chose to ignore my disapproving stare. He continued, "It wasn't like I was unprepared. I had these on."

He raised his arms to show off his twin bracers. Gary Redman, the former Captain Barometer, built these, and when Gary retired from the metahero business he gave them to Greg. They allowed the wearer limited flight and effective force fields. Since Greg had taken to wearing them, I had made many significant upgrades to them, and they were now similar in function to my power staff technology. In other words, if Greg had not been stunned by the explosion, he could have used his Barometer tech to save himself and shield the bystanders below. In theory, anyway.

(Author's note: As the story progresses, I will refer to bracer's power as Barometer power. That is only because of who invented them. These tools have nothing to do with barometric pressure. I am not certain why Gary took the title of Captain Barometer. Metaheroes from the '60s and '70s were odd people.)

Well, there was no point in arguing free will versus predestation with Greg Buchanan because he was going to do whatever he felt he needed to. What he needed to do now, as it turned out, was spend the rest of the day with me. We stayed the afternoon in his distressing third floor apartment engaged in private time. Or, is the term "quality time"? Oh, Americans and their silly euphemisms. I suppose it is better than the British "bumping uglies."

———

If used responsibly, thothtech had the potential to change the world overnight and usher in an age of great prosperity. It would not get that chance, of course, because it was far too dangerous.

When you take metaheroes into account, then please consider the scores of outré technologies these people have collected from aliens, time travelers, ancient peoples, magic, pseudoscience, a wide range of impossible inspirations, and the side-effects of scientific faux pas. All these weird tools and weapons have baffling implications and the potential for massive world-wide change, but these technologies never reach the public. Instead, they get passed from hero to hero and are closely guarded. Imagine all the force fields, particle ray guns, super artificial intelligences, teleportation devices, perpetual motion machines, zero-point energy turbines, personal flight apparatuses, and so much more—why do these technologies never become available to the common consumer?

It is not that complex. Human cultures easily can be unbalanced and destroyed when presented with overly advanced technology. No one wants to initiate the next dark ages by exploding a cultural science bomb. Plus, consider each technology's hapless inventor; he usually is going to end up dead or in prison, not rich like Thomas Edison. The titans of energy cannot afford to lose their profits and power, so it is far easier to kill or imprison the inventors and then suppress their troublesome technologies. Remember Wilhelm Reich and his orgone energy? He died in prison, and the orgone technology was suppressed and discredited, eventually becoming little more than a cautionary tale. Consider the lost notes of Nikolai Tesla and the awful wonders written within. He died alone and debt-ridden while his notes held the keys to a fantastic future that never came to pass. These sad stories have a way of adding up like bodies in a mass grave.

When an exotic vessel of some sort crashed in Roswell, New Mexico in July, 1947, the U.S. military amassed a technological windfall. They distributed the ship's salvage to the great corporations of the time, and the reverse engineering that followed gave us lasers, microprocessors, transistors, cloaking technology, fiber optics, infrared vision, electromagnetic propulsion, and a great deal more, both mechanical and biological. The so-called military-industrial complex has continued to build upon these advances for decades, and the result has been an increase in convenience—and narcissism—as well as the slow crumbling of our culture, loss of privacy, the greater disparity between the wealthy and poor, and the ever increasing dissolution of human interrelationships and community. I suppose it was lucky the so-called black physics of Nazi Germany were destroyed when the Third Reich fell, because it would have probably been even more destructive. We can only hope this nefarious knowledge remains buried forever and never surfaces again.

All this was on my mind the next morning when I arrived at my office. I had been the dean of the Spire City University Physics Department for several years now, and while I attended to my academic duties I kept thinking about the potential consequences of thothtech. When I first encountered the thothtech symbols, I knew I had seen something before very much like them, but I could not place where. That afternoon, while I had a late lunch of salad with tea, I finally remembered.

Eustace Freemantle was the most important man in my life.

I loved my dad and my grandpa for all the right reasons. I had flirted with love during my four failed marriages. I loved my protégé, Brian Faraday, whom you may know as the Utopian, as I would have a younger brother. I loved my former protégé, Madame Fishnet, may she rest in peace. I loved Greg Buchanan, my latest—and most intense—romantic relationship. But, Eustace Freemantle was in a class all his own.

I did my undergraduate work at a community college near where I was born in Snowden, Wales. Then, I was off to Oxford to pound out my doctoral theses on exotic physics. Dr. Freemantle was my advisor, and he helped shape me into the academic and person I am today. He and his wife, Genise, were a second family to me.

Eustace Freemantle was a world-renowned astrophysicist, but that was only one side of him. He had an obsession with Stone Age megalithic sites, and he had some rather arcane theories that, had he been found out, would have gotten him drummed out of most institutions of higher learning in the world. It was not so strange there was a correlation between hard astrophysics and ancient megaliths, because the calendar functions and star alignments of the old henge sites were well known, but a deeper look took Dr. Freemantle down a veritable rabbit hole of weirdness. His theory was mad, but mad in a way only great minds like those of Archimedes, Nikolai Tesla, or Galileo could have conceived.

It went something like this: the Stone Age peoples of the world remembered an earlier age when the Earth was connected to many corners of the universe by stargates. Stargates are not well understood, but they appeared to have been two-way bridges between Earth and other alien worlds that dotted the universe. The gates were used for travel, shipping, and relaying messages between planets. They negated the vast distances in the universe and made intergalactic cultures a reality.

The fall of the stargate infrastructure necessitated the return of spacecraft and dangerous trips across the gulfs of space. I am somewhat reminded of more modern times, when the highly efficient interurban railway lines in America were pulled up to make way for interstates and inefficient, fuel-guzzling trucks and automobiles. These illogical patterns have haunted humankind from the beginning, and we rarely learn from them.

What were the worlds like at the other end of those cosmic tunnels? No one knows anymore. It is difficult to make an educated guess at this point. I will leave that kind of wild speculation to the so-called remote viewers, sloppy scholars, contactees, and conspiracy theorists of the world. Maybe they discuss it on that *Prehistoric Aliens* television show that goes on and on. I cannot say because I have never watched an episode nor do I intend to.

Each stargate was attached to a single, stellar destination, usually a small star system or cluster of stars. The wooden or stone menhirs on the Earth side of the gate would be laid out like their target star cluster, but in reverse, a mirror image of its heavenly configuration. When the Earth rotated down through time on its twenty-three-thousand-year precession of the equinoxes, each of the stargates came online as they passed directly beneath their corresponding star system. Such stargates dotted the Earth, located in well-known locations like Avebury, Stonehenge, Brittany, the Giza Plateau, and thousands of others. Most of these sites remain undiscovered and have been lost to time and/or rotted into non-existence.

Dr. Freemantle knew he was treading on dangerous ground, so he never published his findings. Mainstream consensus science is a mule that can deliver a hell of a kick, and those who prodded the beast never fared well. Instead, Dr. Freemantle kept his findings in a series of handwritten notebooks. If he had lived, I'm not sure what his final intentions for this research would have been.

I never lost track of Dr. Freemantle, and we remained close as I established my career. I managed to go through husbands with alarming rapidity, and gained two more degrees at the Massachusetts Institute of Technology or M.I.T. My own dangerous ideas were coming to me during that time, as my obsession with the lost notebooks of Nikolai Tesla led me to develop a miniature toroidal power plant that could have changed the world. Well, it could have, but the consequences of publishing were too great, so I began secretly to develop the technology that later would become my power staff.

I became convinced the only man I could trust to be my advisor for my fourth doctoral dissertation—this one on quantum toroidal mechanics—was Dr. Eustace Freemantle. By this time, Eustace had left Oxford behind and was now the head of the physics department at Spire City University. His relocation made little sense—it was comparable to an astronaut quitting NASA to become a crop duster pilot, or a bishop becoming a choir boy. There was no "hush-hush" scandal, no quiet but mandatory retirement. Dr. Freemantle simply had moved to east Illinois.

So, I followed. What else could have brought me to the Midwestern United States of America? It certainly was not the cuisine. No, I came to Spire City following my old mentor. He and Genise welcomed me into their home like the daughter I almost was to them.

"So," I had asked, "Spire City?"

"I know what you are going to say," said Dr. Freemantle as he fumbled with his pipe. He was a pot-bellied man in his seventies. He was congenial and given to smiling often. He wore glasses and had a wild halo of white hair that ringed his head but left him bald on top. He often wore brightly knit sweaters and caps because Genise was a prolific knitter.

"Well, it is a far cry from Oxford," I said. "I can't believe you left all that behind."

Eustace stuffed his pipe and lighted its bowl. "What a stodgy bunch of fusspots the other Oxford professors turned out to be." He became more serious then. "It sounds crazy, dear Victoria, unless you know why I am here. No one else would understand, but I can share the truth with you. I've discovered things here that will astound you."

"Well?" I said, pausing between sips of my Yorkshire Gold tea.

"You know my body of work. You know there are scores of forgotten or misunderstood stargates spread about the globe, and there are examples of them on every habitable continent. I've discovered something far more earth-shaking than that. There were stargates, but there were also mega-stargates. These were massive portals made up like the smaller, better-known type, but with parts composed of individual stargates spread over great geographical areas."

"No, really?" I said.

"Yes, really. There were colossal, planetary stargates, reverse pictograms of star systems that were made up of numerous individual stargates rather than simple menhirs or mounds or wooden poles. These mega-stargates could facilitate intergalactic passage on an almost planetary scale, allowing for wholesale cultural exchanges, xenoforming and terraforming, and mass sharing of genetic materials. It is very likely there was once a mega-world made up of scores of planets, all connected and thriving and trading. I think of it as a sort of cosmic Pangea. There were probably two or three of these mega gates on the planet, so old they were all but forgotten by the time of the great Biblical deluge. It seems the last of the ancients made a daring attempt at Carnac in Brittany to rejoin their lost compound world, but by then they had forgotten how to finish building it.

"One of the mega gates was here, in North America. Three of its component sites are of keen interest to me. About 350 miles south by southwest of here are the Monk Mounds in East St. Louis, which were built according to mainstream archeology in BC 1000 to BC 3000. They are much, much older, of course. Also, there is a much lesser known site of importance about 170 miles southeast of here built by the Adena-Hopewell peoples in what is now called Mounds State Park in Anderson, Indiana.

"Let me show you my collection of artifacts, and some symbols I've photographed throughout the region. I think you'll find them illuminating."

We rummaged through Dr. Freemantle's notebooks, and the symbols, crude in their weathered states, reminded me of clockworks, or parts of a circuit board. I would not see their like again until eight years later when Greg showed me the mysterious thothtech symbols for the first time.

———

Fast forward to the present day.

"Let me get this straight," said Greg Buchanan. He seemed a trifle incredulous, and I could not blame him. "In your personal library, you found a book that belonged to an old college instructor of yours, and that book just happens to explain where we can find a whole copy of the thothtech alphabet?"

"When you put it that way..." I said, dramatically rolling my eyes for his benefit.

"And, as it turns out, the place we can find the lost alphabet is here, in Spire City?"

Greg was stripped to the waist, getting ready to put on his Johnny Saturn uniform. Sometimes it broke my heart to see him like this. In addition to his left leg, he had lost around forty pounds of muscle since he had been resuscitated. For, in truth, he had been dead. That changes a man, and Greg was living proof of that. His eyes... I could not even begin to imagine the things those eyes had seen.

But, the whole picture was not bad. Greg's bipolar illness had gone into remission, and he no longer was impaired by manic, careless energy or crippling, black depression. I will admit, I am still holding my breath, afraid of a possible relapse because his mental illness could always come back. Maybe it is just a matter of time. Whatever the case, it was easier to live in denial about that than take a hard look at the future.

Before his death, his Johnny Saturn uniform had been heavily armored and laden with weaponry, all courtesy of the brilliant Harvey Torres, also known as the Tailor. Now Greg no longer resembled a modernized medieval knight, and he was at best lightly armored. He was not that sort of heavy combat warrior hero anymore, he said. He was a new Johnny Saturn, one who could reason and see things others could not. He claimed to be some sort of metahuman shaman now, but I chose not to dwell on it. I am a scientist, not a mystic. Magical thinking has little place in my world.

The new Johnny Saturn uniform was largely dark purple, and it still featured the deep hood and the Saturn symbol of the previous uniforms. It was designed for freedom of movement, but it need not have been because Greg was no longer going to be practicing acrobatics or Parkour. Those were just not feasible with a prosthetic leg, even one as advanced as his. Now he relied on the hybrid "Barometer" technology he wore, and sometimes on his thothtech robot.

"Two-hundred years ago," I said, "when this site on the north shore of Lake Avernus, or more specifically what would come to be called Sorrow Bay, was chosen to be the county seat, there was a major collection of Indian mounds already here.

In those days, you did not have to call on archeologists to dig a site before you proceeded to develop it. Archeology as we know it had not been invented yet, and the antiquarians that preceded them were usually gentlemen scientific dabblers, not government officials. The city founders tore down the Indian mounds and used the soil from that place to level out the site for the future town and to extend the land out into the bay. It is sad because we do not even know the name of the tribes that lived here, and archeologists now refer to them as the Quern people. Querns are grinding stones for making flour, and that is all that is left of those otherwise forgotten peoples.

"Dr. Eustace Freemantle, my mentor, made a quiet study of these things over the years, and he was convinced this was a key site in an even greater mega-stargate. When European settlers tore down the mounds, they broke the pattern and disrupted the region, and all its ley lines and geologic energies began to erupt into ugly discord. This is why Spire City has attracted one huge disaster after another. It sits on a broken stargate that has been shorting out and malfunctioning badly."

"So, we just happen to live in the 'City of the Broken Gate,' huh? That's why all the misery and weirdness keeps descending on our battered lil' city?"

"Exactly," I said. "I inherited Dr. Freemantle's papers when he died of melanoma in oh-eight, as well as his apartment. His wife, Genise, went back to London, and I was the closest thing they had to a daughter, so... Well, I finally remembered where I had seen symbols much like the thothtech letters, and they were in some of Dr. Freemantle's unpublished papers. When I dug deeper, I found he had funded and led some unofficial explorations under the city looking for evidence of the stargate. Those missions were before I came to Spire City. According to this," I said, holding up a ratty, beat up notebook, "he found his proof and a lot more. He discovered numerous unexplained artifacts, and he recorded symbols I now recognize as part of the thothtech alphabet."

"That's intense," said Greg. "It seems like such an unlikely coincidence, but—"

"It is no coincidence!" I blurted out. "Nothing that has happened here ever was a coincidence. Every weird, horrible, and near apocalyptic event that has gone on here happened because of the Broken Gate. Greg, we may be able to retrace Dr. Freemantle's steps, get the thothtech alphabet, and perhaps even fix Spire City!"

"'Fix' Spire City?" he said. He was clearly intrigued and caught up in my enthusiasm.

Greg looked up at me. "It's a shame we cannot ask Tara Wissenschaft for the rest of the alphabet," he said. "She probably has the complete history and all the technology of the antediluvian world locked away in her head. Unfortunately, she also has begun to claim all this ancient lore is the wholly-owned property of her company Wissenschaft Inc."

"Are you and Tara even still speaking?" I asked, feeling a little disappointed in myself for inquiring.

"No... yes... I don't know," said Greg. "She gives out a lot of double messages. I'm not sure if she hates me or loves me right now."

He paused. "We need to pack for a camping trip." His eyes lit up. "A camping trip underground."

———

Our journey began on the private rail car Greg kept under his apartment. Well, to be more accurate, Greg's sometime "boss," John Underhall, kept the rail car for Greg because it made an effective way for Johnny Saturn II to quickly get around the city. From there, we followed Dr. Freemantle's notebook maps through a series of cellars, closed subway lines, empty cisterns, forgotten basements, streets that mysteriously had been covered intact and sealed off, air shafts, crumbling access ways, abandoned underground parking garages, and many other subterranean spaces that were much harder to identify.

Thousands of homeless people, called "mole people," lived down here, and they had established several communities under the city. Someone with a sense of drama had named these little mole people towns after regions of the mythical Greek underworld, and the largest of these ramshackle villages was called Elysium City. Johnny Saturn II was on great terms with these communities, and John Underhall, aka Johnny Saturn I, was considered by many to be the king of the mole people. Johnny Saturn II was no king, but he made it a point to see to these peoples' needs, and they loved him for it.

Elysium City was located in a chamber large enough to have its own climate and occasionally to produce light rain. It was lighted with pirated electricity, fed with pirated water, and many of its homes had pirated cable television. The buildings all were built of materials cast off by the sun-lit world above, and these structures were cunningly constructed from all the scavenged brick, sheet metal, lumber, cardboard and canvas that could be scrounged up. The world above was well known for its material waste, and the mole people were more than happy to take advantage of these otherwise unwanted resources.

After a short visit with some of Greg's friends, we learned Dr. Freemantle had indeed passed this way a few years back, and many mole people remembered him. Greg and I were able to employ some of the same guides as we set out on our journey. It was good to have expert guides in the underworld, because many oddities lived beneath Spire City. There were rumors of wandering cyborgs left to their own devices after Dr. Wissenschaft died; a crocodile king; and a giant wolf proto-god Greg would confirm having met but about which he rarely spoke.

When we arrived at a well shaft that led into the black depths below, our mole people guides left us. They had no intentions of following us into that strange, other realm, and I could not blame them. Spire City's underworld ended here, and an impossibly ancient domain of darkness began.

I should mention we lighted our journey with my staff, its backup toroidal power plants providing illumination and protection. Usually, I got the bulk of the staff's power beamed wirelessly from a low orbit satellite that flew in a fixed position over Spire City. That was impossible here because we were too far below the city, and too deep in the bedrock, to pick up that signal. Consequently, it was all up to my standby toroidal generators.

I used my power staff to levitate us down the blackened shaft, and as the environment changed it felt as if we had entered another plane of existence. My first thought was this must be Alice's Wonderland, but this was the Midwest, so it could only be Oz. It was neither, but something far stranger. We were far into the bedrock below the city, and also far below Sorrow Bay that lapped up against the city's south flanks. It was cold, about 56 degrees Fahrenheit—as you Americans measure things— and very humid. Now we were in some kind of mine. The tunnels varied in width, but they looked to have been carved out of the stone by mechanical means, though the nature of those machines was far from obvious.

"We're getting close," I said. "These tunnels were part of a system built under the Quern people's city and the stargate. Dr. Freemantle's notes say no one knows how extensive these passageways are, and modern archeologists and historians won't even recognize their existence."

I was no archeologist, but I found it curious the walls and chambers were all undecorated. This led me to believe these subterranean places were service tunnels and warehouses, not living areas.

Eustace's maps were good and very helpful as we moved through a bewildering maze of cross halls, large chambers, and very steep stairways that required us to hop down step by step as if they had been carved for giants. From the scale of things, the "giants" hypothesis began to make more and more sense.

"Stop where you are," came a cold voice out of the dark.

A woman stood on a gallery above us. She had a menacing, high tech gun in each hand, and both Greg and I had red dots painted on us by their targeting lasers. My force fields were more than a match for a normal bullet, even a high-powered or explosive one, but this woman had technology at hand that gave me pause. I had never met her, but I knew her by reputation quite well.

"Hi, Tara," said Greg. "Bit of a coincidence, running into you down here."

———

Tara Wissenschaft, aka Tara 5.0.

This was no coincidental meeting, of that I was sure.

Although I had never met Tara, I knew a great deal about her. In the few short months since she'd been built and activated, she had racked up a very strange and convoluted history. I am not going to attempt to relate it all, only the parts of her story that have to do with this narrative.

Tara Wissenschaft was a very life-like android built by the Nazi war criminal Dr. Karl Victor Wissenschaft. When I say very lifelike, I mean she made for a very convincing teenage human girl, with no hint of the "uncanny valley" effect that makes most life-like robots seem "off" or fake. When she initially was activated the first person she ever saw was Greg Buchanan in his Johnny Saturn II uniform. From that moment forward she had been romantically obsessed with Greg. Honestly, it would have been sort of cute or sweet in a real human girl. In a high-functioning assassin android with superhuman abilities galore, it was anything but cute. Tara's creator, Dr. Wissenschaft, had possessed a crystal skull of great antiquity. After Tara had killed her "grandfather," she had claimed the skull and incorporated it into her own head. The skull, once possessed by Heinrich Himmler, was an incredibly ancient Atlantean computer, and it had changed her, granting her vast knowledge of the ancients and their lost technology.

Did I tell you her story was convoluted? This is the abbreviated version, I promise.

So, there Tara stood, dressed like a jungle adventure teenage fashion doll, and she had us covered with twin guns. Her "great white hunter" outfit was cut to show off her impressive—read: fake—legs.

"So, Greg," said Tara, "is this your Welsh girlfriend? I thought she'd be a lot prettier."

"Tara—" said Greg.

"And younger. You never told me she was so old."

"Oh, boy," said Greg, seeming to be temporarily at a loss.

"Ms. Wissenschaft, why are you here?" I asked.

"Why are *you* here, and with him?" cried Tara. She hopped the fifteen feet down to the floor and landed without even a bounce.

Greg and I both began to speak, but Tara shouted, "Shut up! This property and all technology or data you might collect here is the proprietary information of Wissenschaft Inc. You are trespassing, and I could shoot you both for breaking and entering!"

Greg shot Tara a reproachful look. "Tara, you can't lay claim to an epoch and its entire archeology."

"Your attorneys can discuss that with my army of high level lawyers," said Tara. "We can tie the issue up in court for decades!"

I smiled. I was an academic, so talk of attorneys and suppressing information was boring to me. I should add not only was it boring, but all too familiar. I had no patience for it. Long ago I had learned there were two types of knowledge in the academic world—the approved, mainstream, consensus knowledge taught at universities, and then all other knowledge. This forbidden "outsider" knowledge could end academic careers, and rob away tenure, publishing deals, and even one's life if the information was dangerous enough. After a rough-and-tumble career in academia's so-called ivory towers, I understood Tara's attorneys posed a serious threat, but I was not going to let my life be dictated by fear.

"Tara, you've placed a tracer of some sort into Greg's prosthetic leg, haven't you? You've been stalking him and his movements, and you followed us down here."

"Shut! Up!" screamed Tara, and she discharged both guns at me. The gun's futuristic design did not hint at what they were, but it became quite clear when she fired. They were laser-guided plasma discharge weapons, but you just as well might have called them straightline lightning blasters. My scalar shields turned the blasts. The two deflected beams, each about 500 megajoules strong, gouged two big holes out of a nearby wall. Both guns whined as they began to recharge for their next barrage.

I returned fire, but with an electro-magnetic pulse meant to burn out the little android's circuits. Lightning danced all over Tara, but it would seem she already was hardened to this type of attack. Her clothes began to singe and burn, but she wasted no recovery time at all, and she threw a vicious kick that managed to buckle, temporarily overwhelm, and short out my force fields with a loud *pop*. More by luck than anything, I managed to block Tara's next blow with my staff, and we both tumbled back against the wall. I really could have used the extra power I normally would have gotten from my dedicated satellite, but that just was not in the cards.

This would be a good time to mention I am not a hand-to-hand fighter. I have no combat training of any sort. I am a scientist, and I always have relied on technology for my defense. To put it bluntly, if this little fight went on any longer, Tara would've killed me.

Luckily for me, that did not happen. Greg leaped in and separated us using his hybrid Barometer technology to augment his strength.

"That is enough! Tara! Back down now!" he shouted.

Tara did back off, but not before she shot me a look of pure contempt. For an over-glorified robot, she had the whole bitch thing down pat.

"We're all here now," said Greg. "You both are very important to me, so I don't need you killing each other."

"Ludicrous" I said. Greg could not be suggesting we work with this little sex pot android, right?

"What?" blurted Tara.

"I don't care if you think it's ludicrous," said Greg. "I suggest we move forward on this expedition together. We'll have plenty of time to fight about who owns what later."

Tara and I looked at each other, and she appeared to acquiesce. I did not trust her for a moment.

"Besides, if you both care so much about what happens to me, then you should know that your little fracas almost brought down the whole chamber on us!"

There were cracks in the floor, wall, and ceiling, and colorless dust sifted out of deep fissures in the rock. He was probably right because these surfaces looked quite unstable now. Greg continued. "Tara, I don't know if you came here to find the same thing we came for—I kind of doubt it—but we'll all go forward and find it together, or not at all." Greg was not known for diffusing tense situations, but he seemed to be juggling this one pretty well. Or, was he? As powerful as Tara was, she did not have to accede to his wishes, yet she was.

Tara's face lit up with a cherubic smile and twinkling eyes, and she took Greg by the arm and said, "If you say so, Greg. Together."

Great, I thought. *Together it is.*

"Aw, man..." said Greg. "You two and your fight fried my watch. I paid a lot of money for this thing, and now it is ruined."

———

Two hours and fifteen minutes passed as we made our way through the cold, wet subbasement of the world. I had set my staff to record our route, which was a help because the galleries and the halls we passed through all looked pretty much the same. It seemed the ancients had the good sense to have cleared the complex out before they left because there was no old technology lying around. At least that is what I thought because I am not sure I would have recognized any ancient machinery for what it was. If an alphabet could be the working components of various devices, then perhaps the rocks were laced with micro transistors, or composed of smart stone, or it could only be viewed from certain angles, or inside a tesseract, or whatever. For that matter, maybe the crude Neolithic monuments dotted around the planet were complex machinery, and not just badly weathered stone and stains in the earth. Considering Dr. Freemantle's work on stargates, that seemed somehow much more possible.

Guided by Eustace's notes, we made our way down to a deeper complex of tunnels and chambers. This level was cut from the bedrock with laser accuracy that almost appeared modern. These passageways were not poured concrete over rebar, however, just stone that had given way to ancient miners. Dripping water dotted the ceiling with long stalactites and the floors with some corresponding stalagmites, and even with my limited knowledge of geology I could tell these tunnels had been largely undisturbed for what must have been tens of thousands of years.

There was evidence of earlier machines in this part of the site, mostly in the form of bolts or rivets that no longer supported anything in the stone, and grooved tracks in the floor that left us guessing about their original purpose. They reminded me of a childhood vacation with my family on the Isle of Malta, where miles of ancient

TARA 5.0 AKA TARA WISSENSCHAFT

railway track crisscrossed the landscape. No one on the island knew for what the railways had been used or who could have laid those mysterious tracks, but the most common folklore on the subject attributed them to Faeries and then simply dismissed the tracks existence from all the approved travel guidebooks.

We came upon a large chamber with a dock of sorts. Dark, almost still waters gently lapped up against it, and I was reminded of the mouth of the river Styx. My best guess was the water below the pier was a submerged access to Sorrow Bay. Since I knew we were well below the lakebed, I surmised this could only be a water trap—much like under most sinks in modern plumbing—or this place would have been flooded. Water lapped up to the stone pier, but the dense accretion around the walls hinted that this place had been abandoned for ages. By "ages," I mean geologic ages, but perhaps my imagination was running away with me.

I paused, looking thoughtfully at the water lapping against the stone dock.

"Something is not sitting right with me," I said.

"Forget to take your fiber this morning?" said Tara. "Old people can get out of sorts if they don't keep their digestive tracts regular."

"Shut up, you automated sex toy," I snapped. Greg shot both of us a glare and Tara and I both let it go.

"Here's the thing," I began. "The general nature of the great, enduring mysteries is you never find conclusive answers. Instead, you just learn enough to keep pulling you on further into the mystery. You know what I mean—"

"I have no idea," said Greg.

"Okay, no one ever catches a live yeti, and spaceships never land on the White House lawn, and a living camarasaurus is never discovered in the Congo. The mysteries are self-sustaining—there is no irrefutable evidence to prove them decisively, just enough hints to entice another generation of curious adventurers, free thinkers, and delusional people to keep going."

Greg looked at me, but he made no comment.

"No one ever captures a plesiosaur in Loch Ness, Scotland. Faeries do not show up on the evening news to announce their presence. No one ever conclusively finds the Ark of the Covenant, Noah's Ark, or the Moth Man. No one can establish if the Shroud of Turin is authentic, or if the Spear of Destiny is legitimate or a hoax."

"It's real," Tara said matter-of-factly.

"What?" I said.

"The Spear. It's real."

"How do you know?" I said.

"I just know," said Tara.

"Okay, whatever," I said. "My point is real mysteries remain mysteries, and they cloak themselves in what we call 'high strangeness.' This time they have not, and the three of us have walked virtually unopposed into a mystery that could turn mainstream history and science on their heads. All this usually is impossible to prove in any conclusive manner, yet here we are with proof galore."

"Are you saying mysteries are some sort of sentient tricksters?" asked Tara.

"Not at all. They are more like self-sustaining memes. Many of them even may hint at real truths, but their real function is to continue propagating themselves. That's why mysteries often become addicting, inspiring all sorts of obsessions, so they can persist for generation after generation."

"Okay," said Greg. "I get it. There's a perfectly good answer to your question."

"Oh?" I said.

"You are right. On your own, you would have never found the way into this place, or if you had you would never have made it out with proof. You'd have had a wild story that proves nothing, and you would have been snubbed by the scientific community and the public at large. At the same time, hundreds of dreamers would have come up with crazy scenarios and irrational thought games to prove you right. They would assess and defend your character, but in the end all the wishful thinkers never would be able to prove you were right. Your story would be told again and again until it became legend or myth, and with each retelling it would take on a further ring of truth. All the while, you would never get the satisfaction of proving anything to anyone but those who wanted to believe."

"You are simply making my point," I said.

"Yes and no," said Greg. "That's how it would go by yourself. You are not by yourself. You are here with me."

"And that makes a difference because?"

"Because I've been dead, and I returned. All the mysteries are open to me. High strangeness no longer cloaks reality from me."

"Is this more of that metashaman stuff you talk about?" I asked.

"Sure is," said Greg. "Consider this. I went to the Land of the Dead, and I learned things, but I was able to come back. A shaman is someone who sends his spirit to the other side, asks questions of the spirits and gods there, and then comes back with those answers for his tribe. That is me. My tribe is the metahuman community."

"I don't know," I said. I had little use for New Age thought and magical thinking. "What do you think, artificial girl?"

"I have the knowledge of the ages locked in my head," said Tara with an attitude that came off as both perky and condescending. "I already know all the answers to these questions."

"Fine," I said. If these two were not going to take me seriously, then it was time to terminate the conversation.

Greg, Tara and I proceeded from the submerged lock, and we followed a wide hall to its terminus.

Massive stone double doors loomed over us and were almost lost in the darkness overhead. They were pocket doors, each intended to recede into the wall when opened, and the hidden machinery that once opened and closed this immense gate must have been impossibly huge. I felt reasonably sure this door was built with more conventional technology, not thothtech, because the latter would not require all the moving parts in the door.

The walls on each side of the doors was made of monumental stonework that reminded me of the perfectly fit, dry stone walls of Cusco, Peru, with stones so carefully laid you could not slide a razor between them. The individual stones, many of them weighing twelve tons or more, were of irregular shapes and sizes, and they brought to my imagination a colossal vertical puzzle intended for giants.

Cut into the walls on either side of the gate were massive relief carvings of ancient astronauts. Mainstream scholars did not recognize these kinds of depictions, such as here or the Mayan relief carvings in Palenque, as ancient astronauts. In the context of our surroundings, however, the figures depicted certainly looked like astronauts strapped into space capsules, but as channeled through a primordial artist's eye.

Understand I am not suggesting the ancient Maya visited the North American Midwest and carved these walls. Far from it. Rather, I do maintain the advanced peoples of prehistory who inspired the pyramid-building cultures of the past certainly had been here. We often call this primordial race Atlantean, but they would not have called themselves this. In fact, calling them Atlanteans suggests they were all from a unified culture while I am reasonably sure there were many advanced societies in the forgotten past.

"This is incredible," said Tara. "Before Spire City, and before Quern people, this place was a spaceport. These carvings prove it. While I would have liked to say this explains a lot, it does not. It raises more questions than it answers."

"I thought you already knew all the answers?" I quipped.

Tara ignored me.

The light of my staff illuminated the space around us, but as I mentioned it was insufficient to light the ceiling so far above us. Broken stone and animal droppings littered the floor, and this place was so ancient that time and nature were taking it back, slowly covering it all with stalactites and stalagmites. The stone doors were etched with symbols, and each carving was about a foot square and six feet up.

"I recognize this one," said Greg, his enthusiasm on the rise. "I don't know all of them, but these are thothtech, and this letter symbolizes some variety of latch or access."

"Wait!" cried Tara, "don't—"

Greg had already reached out and activated the ancient symbol. On one level the thothtech symbol merely was a low relief carving with traces of badly faded red paint on the door; on another level, it was a machine, and touching it caused it to turn like a newly wound clock.

Massive vibrations rose from deep below in the earth, and we felt it more than heard it as they shook through the floor and up our legs. The tremors of a huge, hidden machine clicked into motion and then ground to a halt. The giant pocket doors shivered a little, tried to open, but they were in such poor repair they only cracked apart about a yard. Beyond the doors lay stygian blackness, and the dank, musty odor of old, stale air rushed out to greet us.

"Crikey," I said under my breath. I felt a sense of wonder I had not felt since I was a schoolgirl, and a sense of awe that usually is beaten out of us by the repetitive, mundane life that follows.

"You should not have done that," said Tara. "That thothtech pictogram triggered several more in close proximity to it, including one that I think was an alarm of some sort."

"Alarm?" said Greg and I at the same time.

"Yes," said Tara, "an alarm. I am not sure who it was intended for, so it is probably harmless now, but I don't know."

The three decided to set up camp just outside the gap in the old pocket doors.

"Be careful not to get nicked or cut down here," said Tara to Greg. "Ancient air often holds old, forgotten diseases. Your body won't have any defense against them."

I smiled to myself. It was nice Tara was so concerned about Greg's safety. My safety was a total non-issue to her, of course.

"Don't you think it's time for you to share the rest of the thothtech alphabet with us?" I said.

"Ha!" Tara seemed equally amused and irritated by the suggestion. She said nothing else on the matter, but clearly her answer was "no."

––––––––

Unbeknownst to us at the time, something heard the alarm Greg had triggered and began to awaken. In the deepest recesses of Lake Avernus, the southernmost of the Great Lakes and just below Lake Michigan, an elder thing started to stir with purpose. It was so old that it already had been forgotten by the time King Scorpion founded the Old Kingdom of the Nile, or Khemet. This being had lain in dreamless, deathlike sleep so long the sediment around it had compressed into rock, and so it would have stayed to the end of time if the ancient alarm had not summoned it. The lake bed cracked apart, and opaque, obsidian eyes opened.

––––––––

Greg and I took turns sleeping because the way beyond the gate looked like very challenging terrain, and we had already been awake for well over twenty-four hours. While Tara did not need sleep as we know it, she did slip into her "sleep" or "battery preservation" mode to recharge. I am sure she could have reactivated at an instant's notice, and I doubt she ever stopped monitoring Greg while he slept. I know I did not rest all that well because I did not trust her.

This is a good place in the narrative to set a few things straight. First, I scanned and recorded the thothtech symbols when we encountered them, and I uploaded them to the Cloud via a special ground-penetrating radar hookup I had devised. Because of this we had never been truly cut off from the surface world so far above. Sadly, I couldn't use the same radar to hook up with my satellite and my primary power source. The two technologies did not play well together.

Second, I should mention again Greg Buchanan was present in his Johnny Saturn uniform, and it was as Johnny Saturn II the world above knew him, but I thought of him only as Greg Buchanan. I know I touched on this earlier, but I think it is important we do not confuse the issue. His "Johnny Saturn II" persona was very popular with the public in general. To my knowledge, there had been a couple of movies made about him and half-a-dozen books written about his exploits. Most of these books and movies were based on speculation, and most centered on the time Greg had died fighting with Dr. Karl Wissenschaft aboard the Graf Zeppelin III. That was very dramatic stuff, so it was no wonder the crowds ate it up.

It is safe to say that he was Johnny Saturn II to the world, but to me he was Greg Buchanan, the one-time Spire City Police Detective who had overcome terrible loss and traumatic mental illness. I will continue to refer to him as Greg in this narrative.

"It's time," said Tara.

We three rose and ventured forth into the unknown.

———

In the sea gate and pier deep underground, the one we had recently vacated, the ancient monster rose from the waters and lumbered onto the dock. This being was almost sixteen feet tall and about seven tons of dense, granite hard muscle. Its powerful legs propelled him along as easily on land as they had in the water, and its huge, outsized webbed hands reached for the pocket doors that were frozen almost closed and ripped them out of the wall. Water drained off the creature's gray skin, and its dead, black, shark-like eyes probed ahead, looking for the intruders that had disturbed it.

———

The vast ceiling and gigantic walls beyond the pocket doors were true wonders of the ancient world, but we'd already seen some eye-opening sites, so this place did not make the impression on us it could have.

The chamber must have been truly colossal at some point in the past, but it had collapsed at an earlier time in history and completely blocked off most of the area. Only the space that was very near the perimeter walls was passable, making it somewhat like a tunnel that was very tough to negotiate. The walls themselves were much like those we had seen earlier, with the same unevenly shaped stones so finely fitted together that they looked almost like they had been poured into place, making a gigantic, interlocking rock puzzle. There were serpent-headed protrusions mounted on the wall at various intervals, but we did not have enough context to guess what they originally had been intended for. I got the impression they must have had a utilitarian purpose because they did not have the feel of pure decoration.

Greg had moved on ahead a bit, and Tara fell into step with me.

"You know Greg is really mine, don't you?" said Tara.

"Oh?" I said, maybe egging her on a bit.

"You are a temporary thing," said Tara. "He'll lose interest in you and come back to me. Sorry, dear, but it is kind of inevitable."

"A robot shouldn't suffer from such fantastic delusions," I said. "I think your databases need to be repaired."

"Cute," said Tara, shooting me a smug smile. "You cannot think of anything witty to say, so you belittle me."

"Truth hurts, sweetie," I said. "We can say your logic protocols are corrupted, or we can say you are psychotic. It's really all the same thing."

"Bitch!" hissed Tara, and she moved on ahead to be nearer to Greg.

Our bickering stopped when we came upon a wonder of the ancient world.

———

In my time as a metahero, I've seen some pretty amazing—even outrageous—things. I've seen men fly under their own power, heroes as mighty as the gods of old, and monstrosities to rival almost anything in mythology. I've seen horrors out of space, and zeppelins armed with super rail guns. I've seen men die and then return from the dead. I've seen things far, far beyond what most people ever see in their day-to-day lives.

This was of another magnitude. This was a bag of amazing wrapped in an awe-inspiring box.

Perhaps it would be best if I went back to where I left off. Before us, blocking our passage, was a primordial aircraft of some sort. About two-hundred feet of the craft was exposed, and the rest was crushed beneath the caved-in ceiling.

"Wow," said Greg. "Just... wow."

From what I could tell, the craft looked much like a cross of a space shuttle and a ladybug. It somehow appeared clumsy and aerodynamic at the same time. What we could see of its hull still gleamed after ages of lying in ruin. It was more than twice the size of one of our space shuttles and almost half-again the size of most jumbo jets.

"Fascinating," said Tara. "An Atlantean asvin. I didn't think any had survived into modern times." Clearly, she was accessing her crystal skull's memory banks.

"Asvin?" said Greg.

"Asvin is a more modern term for it. Its owners wouldn't have called it that any more than they would have called themselves 'Atlantean.' The asvins were much more advanced than the better-remembered vimanas of ancient India, and this ship was capable of flying through the air, underwater, and the interstellar gulfs between stars. It would have lifted off vertically, and could move in any direction, backward or forward as needed. It was easily as maneuverable as a modern helicopter or blimp."

"I've seen one of these in Dr. Freemantle's notes," I said. "There was a pre-Colombian model of one of these found, and when they tested it with a motorized mockup it proved to be aerodynamically sound."

As we got closer, the ship's hull, which was apparently without seams or visible rivets, was lightly decorated with flourishes and figures that hinted at some stylized antediluvian artist's vision.

I used my staff to scan the hull, but the results were incomprehensible.

"This metal is on no periodic table I've ever seen," I said.

"Orichalc," said Tara. "An Atlantean metal. You might have found a few odd samples in the Iraq National Museum in Baghdad before it was sacked during the second Iraqi War in 2003, but now even those pieces are lost, scattered among private collectors."

It also was apparent to us that since the vessel was jammed in our path, and we could not get around it, we would have to pass through it to continue our journey. There were several large holes ripped in the ship's outer skin that made it look as if we could at least enter it, but we had no idea if we could easily exit it one the far side.

Tara spoke. "Be careful, Greg! These things were partially powered with mercury, and almost anything in there could be quite toxic to modern humans."

I took some readings with my staff.

"Radiation levels are within safe parameters, and I am only reading trace levels of mercury," I said. "It's safe enough to go in."

"Whatever, grandma!" snapped Tara.

"There's been a persistent internet rumor," I said, "the American military discovered a vimana hidden in a cave in Afghanistan a few years ago, and the soldiers who tried to retrieve it met an unfortunate end. I think it is better to be safe than sorry, don't you think?"

"That story was exposed as hoax from 2010," Tara shot back.

"Probably," I said. "But how can we know anymore? The truth has become wildly subjective, and our media only gives us a heavily edited spin on the facts."

With the tail of the ship crushed under tons of rock, it was hard to estimate how large the vessel was, but our best guess was about 300 feet from nose to tail, and probably about the same length wingtip to wingtip. We entered the ship at a point where downward forces had split open the hull. The break in the ship's skin was clean, and there was no sign of individual plates or rivets. We climbed as much as we walked, for the craft seemed to have been designed for beings much larger than us, perhaps twelve to eighteen feet tall. We made our way through a series of bays and corridors, but it was very hard to determine what these spaces had once been used for.

In what we could only assume was the ship's engine room, there was a series of crystal spheres, copper coils and fittings, and strange arrays of graphite rods. How these things functioned was far from obvious, but none of us could deny how beautiful these alien contraptions looked. Mirrored walls made it hard to judge how big the engine room and the engine were, and some of the machinery could only be viewed from certain angles even when you had a clear view.

"Damn!" said Greg. "Look at this thing here, and you see it. Move an inch this way or that, and it is gone or invisible!"

"Some of these components are fifth-dimensional," said Tara. "We can only perceive the parts that intersect with our three dimensions, and the others just *seem* invisible. They are not invisible, though, they just do not exist in our three-dimensional reality from that angle. Our perspective just doesn't include the higher dimensions."

It took us the better part of half an hour, but we finally reached the asvin's bridge. It was mind-blowing, no doubt about it. The ship's pilot still reclined in his chair as he had when the ship was crushed. His cause of death was not immediately apparent, but whatever killed his ship had killed him, too.

OK, let me collect my thoughts. This was an amazing scene, one burned into my memory for all the days of my life. It also was very odd and alien, but I will try to do it justice with my words. Bear with me. The pilot was mummified, his flesh having collapsed into a leather sheath over his bones. He would have been about twelve feet tall in life, with bright red hair, a wide forehead, widely set eyes, and six fingers on each hand. His skull still rested in its helmet.

"He is a type of Nordic," said Tara. "They are a race of aliens that have been continually visiting this planet for a few thousand years. They are not really Nordic or from Scandinavia, but they bear a small resemblance to Scandinavian people. He's a giant primarily because he lived in an age of maximum genetic expression. In his time, the air pressure was greater, the oxygen content in the atmosphere was higher, and the heavier atmosphere shielded Earth's inhabitants from more radiation than it does now."

"Huh..." said Greg.

"You can find the remains of Nordic-human hybrids, giant red-haired peoples, all over the planet. They've been found in China, the American West, everywhere. Science has turned a blind eye to them for the most part. Their remains usually go missing after a short while. Conspiracy theorists believe there is some sort of multi-century cover up going on, and I suppose I cannot rule it out."

The pilot's chair was something like a recliner in full horizontal orientation, meaning the pilot was more lying down than sitting. The control surface above him was nearly as big as the chair below, and he was tightly sandwiched in between chair and control panel, giving the impression he was trapped in a modern magnetic resonance imagining device, or MRI. The pilot's chair was mounted on a column of unknown machinery from below, and the control surface was likewise suspended from a similar column that descended from the ceiling. Rubbery, organic-looking tubes like veins crisscrossed the floor and fed into the column that supported the chair. This detail would have seemed very odd in a traditional human cockpit, but here all the machinery had a creepy, techno-organic feel.

The cabin's upper walls were covered with half a dozen large screens. They were shaped in weird, wall-hugging geometries, and three of the six appeared to be no longer functional. One screen, which was damaged in one corner, showed a submerged pyramid with a crystal capstone and water that boiled above it as if the crystal were emitting a very high resonant frequency.

"That is in the Bermuda Triangle," said Tara. "Pay no attention to that."

The other functioning screen showed a giant, cigar-shaped mother ship crashed on the lunar landscape. The ship was twisted, broken, and in a poor state. Occasionally the screen would flicker and change, replacing the crashed ship with its pilot, a dead alien woman. Her skin looked too waxy to be real, and she wore a bizarre apparatus on her face that seemed more like a tribal decoration than the high-tech machine it must surely have been. The screen flickered, and the crashed cigar ship reappeared.

"That is a valixi or Atlantean mother ship," said Tara. "I am not sure who or what the woman is, but I assume she was the pilot. I won't know for certain until Wissenschaft Inc. is able to put down an unmanned spacecraft on that part of the moon. Give it a year and then ask me again."

The third screen displayed an image even more disturbing than the first two. A humanoid, larger than our moon by the look of it, floating in space, and it was carefully forming a binary star system between its raised hands. The figure was bulky, with bizarre protrusions jutting from his body, a red cast to his dull, metallic skin or space suit, and alien motifs adorning its body. Its size alone twisted my stomach with a sickening sense of wrongness.

"That is one of four known beings collectively known as the Incarnate," said Tara. "Almost nothing is known about them, but one ancient legend claims they each are aspects of the universal godhead, and gnostic legends identify them as the 'demiurge,' an evil co-god that rules this reality. I suspect they are cosmic hubs for pipelines for pure information. These things are so huge no one has ever been able to communicate with them. We might as well be amoeba to them."

"Why are they humanoid?" I said. "That makes no sense. The humanoid form is hardly designed for walking around outer space."

"Your thinking is too limited," said Tara. "These are eleventh-dimensional beings, and the part we perceive here in our three-dimensional world is practically impossible for us to make sense of. So, our minds try to extrapolate the impossible, and you get two arms, two legs, a trunk, and a head. Besides, humanoid is the most common shape of biologically-based sentient beings in the universe. It's not an elegant layout, but it works."

"That crystal skull computer of yours sure knows a lot of weird stuff," said Greg.

"Yeah," agreed Tara.

We looked away from the screens and their bizarre feeds, and back at the cabin around us. The command chair was surrounded by a semi-circular walkway, and that was surrounded by various workstations. The stations were each about six feet from floor to control surface, and that made sense for a crew that was probably each around twelve feet tall. Those control panels were labeled with thothtech script, and from what I could tell the entire mecha-alphabet was represented here.

"Bingo," I said, and I used my staff to levitate high enough to see all the thothtech letters. "I think they are all here, the whole thothtech alphabet."

Tara chimed in. "All twenty-three uppercase letters, fifty-two lowercase letters, eleven conjugations, nine possessives, and the sixteen numbers that represent the base twelve and sixty mathematical systems and their multiples. Remember, these are all the property of Wissenschaft Inc., and you are forbidden to copy or record these in any way or on any medium."

"Screw that!" I said, and then grinned as my staff emitted a 360-degree laser pulse that recorded everything in the cockpit in high resolution.

"Stop that this instant," cried Tara. "Erase that information, or I will tie you up in court to the end of your days!"

"Bring it on, robot chick!" I said. "As of now this information has been uploaded via my ground-penetrating uplink and is being distributed to hundreds of servers across the web. You do not own this history or technology. Everyone does."

Tara pulled her guns, I threw up a shield, and Greg tried to interpose himself between us. Honestly, I am not sure which of us set off asvin's security system. The ship's guard appeared before us as a green bar of light that rose from the floor, slowly revealing or materializing the figure beneath it as the bar made its vertical ascent. The effect was almost comical, as if it were six seconds of cheap special effects from a 1960's space opera drawn by hand with a marker on each frame of film.

"Cease your hostilities now!" boomed the ship's guard. "Aggression will not be tolerated aboard this vessel."

Greg, Tara, and I were all shocked and confused into a simultaneous moment of silence, and then we all erupted in speech together.

"He speaks English?" said Greg, perhaps more amused than worried.

"This ship's security officer is human?" said Tara at the same time. "That makes no sense at all."

"Eustace?" I said. "Eustace Freemantle? Is that you?"

———————

"Eustace," I cried, "you cannot be here! You're dead! I was there when you were cremated!"

"Victoria?" said the Eustace lookalike. "Is that you? Delightful!"

"What are you?" I demanded. "A clone?"

"No, no—" he said.

"A shapeshifter? An android? A replicant?"

"No, my dear—"

"An ultrasound phantom? An X-ray transmission straight to our cerebral cortexes? An evil twin? An undetectable mind-altering gas in the air inspiring hallucinations?"

The faux Eustace tried to object again, but I cut him off.

"A time traveler? Master of disguise? Doppelganger? Tulpa? Ghost?"

"Victoria, please," said Eustace Freemantle. "I'm not any of those. I am not even Eustace Freemantle."

"Then. What. Are. You?"

I was really confused now, because this was Dr. Freemantle down to the finest nuance, with all his mannerisms, speech, wild white fringe of hair, his glasses, everything. If this was some sort of cosmic joke, it would soon discover that Victoria Shelbourne was not a good sport with pranks.

"Please, Victoria, I can explain," he said.

"I'm waiting."

"Your mentor, Dr. Eustace Freemantle, visited this ship, and the ship carefully scanned him, including his genetic makeup, memories, personality, all that he was. Taking this form made it easier for me to converse with him. Once I recognized you from Dr. Freemantle's memories, I thought this form would make it easier to communicate with you, too."

"So," I said, as I got my breathing under control, and my racing heart began to slow, "you are an artificial intelligence?"

"Well, yes," he said. "I am the surviving fragment of the ship's AI, as expressed through a solid hologram."

"Solid hologram?"

"Absolutely. My creators understood how to project, stabilize and build various structures with photons. Solid light, like light sabers from the movies."

I was confused. This artificial intelligence had explained to me it was not my beloved mentor, yet my heart and all my senses told me it was him. I threw caution to the wind, and I hugged the old man. Hard.

"I've missed you so much, Eustace!" I said, and I might have shed a tear or two in happiness.

The faux Eustace hugged me back. It was a tentative hug at first because I think he'd gotten more than he bargained for when he took this shape and identity. He gave in after a bit and shared the happy moment with me.

"Did you say I was dead?" he asked.

"Yes," I said. "You passed away in 2008. Genise took your ashes back to London. I still live in your apartment here in Spire City, and I still have your papers. I even have your old job as Spire City University's Dean of the Physics Department."

"I am sorry for you loss," said not-Eustace. "The doctor was an admirable man, a great thinker, and he loved you very much. You were his only real successor."

"I know," I said. I hated to admit it, but I was still crying.

"I really liked the old fellow," said faux Eustace. "I guess I shall never see him again."

"Are you daft?" said Tara, intruding on our moment.

"Of course you won't talk to Dr. Freemantle again," said Tara, "because you are a perfect replication of him. You are him in all the ways that matter. You have his memories, his body, his emotions—you are Dr. Eustace Freemantle."

Tara seemed visibly upset, and it only made sense. She considered herself to be "real," but we all knew she was the copy of another human girl. Eustace had to be real as far as Tara and her sense of self were concerned. I really enjoyed seeing her squirm, though I am not all that proud to admit it.

"Crikey," said Eustace. "Your android is a lot more opinionated than I would have expected it to be."

"I am not anyone's android, you stupid projection!" Tara's anger was escalating quickly, so Greg stepped in.

"Apologies, Doctor," said Greg. "Tara is usually much more pleasant to be around."

"Don't help me, Buchanan!" cried an exasperated Tara.

"Eustace," I said, "is she correct? Are you tied to this place by a projector of some sort?"

"No, Victoria. I am a solid photonic hologram. I am scores of exowats tied into a Dr. Eustace-sized package. I only stay down here because it is my duty to look after this old ship."

"Well, that settles it for me," I said. "In fact, if the whole of reality is a three-dimensional hologram written on a two-dimensional brane as postulated in M-theory, then you are not very different than us. You are my lost mentor and friend, Dr. Eustace Freemantle, and I am not letting you go again."

Eustace gave me one more squeeze, and then he stepped out of my embrace.

"I appreciate your sentiment, dear Victoria, but I have to tell you why I am here. You've set off an alarm somewhere in the spaceport, and something really terrible has been activated and is on its way to eradicate you. You'd better run, or you will become as dead my namesake."

––––––

"We're not running anywhere, Dr. Freemantle," said Greg. "We're metaheroes, and we are trained and equipped to handle just about anything." As we talked, we exited the far side of the asvin that had been blocking our path.

"We will get whatever is coming when it emerges from the asvin. We have the drop on it, not the other way around," I said. "The high ground is ours."

We felt the earth ominously shiver, and then it shook again and again. Giant footsteps. Whatever was coming was heavy. We heard a loud roar that sounded more like two huge bricks being ground together, or maybe what a tyrannosaurus rex caught in a giant bear trap would have sounded like. Maybe you could say it sounded like a huge rockslide with a really bad attitude.

In war, all the well-planned tactics in the world only last until the first bullet flies, and then everything is up for grabs. So it was that our plans to get the advantage on the approaching enemy were overturned in an instant. Giant clawed hands each the size of a large automobile tore the asvin apart as the creature barreled through the wreckage. Eustace looked deeply pained at the ship's destruction because it had been stuck here, pretty much in one piece, for over thirteen millennia, and this was a sad ending to its long survival.

The creature stepped through the ruined ship and into my staff light.

This is the point where I explain how frightening this creature was, and try to impress you with a lot of adjectives pulled from H.P. Lovecraft stories. Forget it. You've heard all that before. What I will tell you is this—I've faced down the very real prospect of death, and the end of the world, and those were nothing compared to this. My legs turned to water, and suddenly I knew what it was like to be a tiny mammal that had fallen into the clutches of a huge predator. This was gutwrenching horror, and if I hadn't forced myself to hold my ground then I would have fled in a mindless surge of terror or, more likely, have been frozen in fear.

I am not sure what Greg felt. He had been dead once, and he had suffered a world of hurt many times, but all I could read from his face was determination and maybe a bit of resignation, too. I have no idea what Tara "felt," or what she at least was programmed to feel, but I could not care less. I cared more about what an old car loaded into a compactor might think than I cared about that little peacock of a robot's feelings.

The monster was about sixteen feet tall and probably around six or seven tons in weight, and it seemed like a cross between a killer whale and wide, gorilla-like humanoid. Its black hide was webbed with a lattice of veins, and it looked wet and shiny. Its head was cone-shaped as would be a killer whale's, and it had multiple rows of sword-sized teeth. Its small, black eyes were beady and opaque; impersonal, implacable. Those giant clawed hands were three-fingered, webbed, and sported claws long enough to puncture a bank vault. Its arms were also webbed to its flanks, giving the elder organism a manta ray quality, as well as being a further indication of the leviathan's semi-aquatic nature.

"Pathetic vermin!" it bellowed, "why have you disturbed my slumber?"

Great. It could talk. This was not a good sign.

I was shocked and scared, but not so much that I couldn't throw up a preemptive force field between us and the monster. The beast slammed my scalar field so hard my staff almost shook out of my hands, and I am sure I jammed some of my fingers. The second blow was so hard the force field broke, and feedback turned the staff into a lightning rod and blew me back down the passageway. I landed like a rag doll, momentarily disorientated, but mostly conscious. I am lucky I didn't break my neck. I have never been tasered, but this must have been similar. I was stunned, and barely in control of my limbs after that jolt, but I shook it off as quickly as I could. The staff itself dematerialized as soon as I let go of it, and I could only pray I would be able to reboot and rematerialize it.

Tara had turned her plasma guns to full, and she cut loose with slashing bolts of lightning that would have chopped a hole in a modern aircraft carrier. The monster was pushed back by the bolts, but the burning gashes they left in its hide almost instantly sealed back up. There was a weird, water-like ripple on the creature's flesh when its hide closed back in, like a pond swallowing a rock after a failed skip.

Eustace helped me to my feet while Tara took another turn at the monster.

"Stone the crows!" said Eustace. "It's a leviathan prime. There were only thirteen like it ever made." He sounded frightened, and it did not inspire much hope. We were as outgunned as a leaky canoe against a tsunami.

While Tara again blasted the monster to no effect, Greg exposed his left bracer by pulling back his coat sleeve. The bracers housed his Barometer technology, but that was not why he did it. Instead, the thothtech symbols for Greg's giant robot were etched there on the bracer's exterior, and Greg activated the giant mecha, controlling the giant automaton's movements with deft finger swipes over the machine alphabet's letters. In actual use, it was not so different from controlling a tablet computer's touch screen.

The results were not promising.

The Atlantean mechanical giant plowed into the leviathan prime, and the monster's huge fists grabbed the robot and began to crush it. The robot's head was much like a turret with a giant cannon mounted where a face should have been, and it swung its cannon around and blasted the aquatic monster again and again. The leviathan lurched back in pain, but each time the impact's damage healed instantly, and the whale monster grabbed the artillery and ripped it off the mecha's head. The leviathan pounded the giant thothtech machine to pieces, driving it into the ground. The individual blows were so powerful everyone felt the resulting vibrations radiate through the earth like incredibly huge bass drums.

"Thothtech?" roared the monster. "You hoped to stop me with thothtech? You must be as mad as you are stupid!"

Neither Tara nor Greg were stupid, but they were definitely mad enough to throw another barrage of plasma bolts and giant robots at the leviathan prime.

"That monster is not speaking English," I said to Eustace, "but, I understand every word it's saying. How's that possible?"

"He is speaking the human root language," said Eustace. "It is written in your junk DNA, and everyone on Earth spoke it until the Babylonian Crisis. After that point, it malfunctioned and subdivided again and again like a cell would, until thousands of languages were spoken across the world, all sharing an origin, but each new tongue was mostly incomprehensible to non-native speakers. Still, that original proto-language is at the root of all language, and still comprehensible to all humans even though none of you can speak it any longer."

There was a huge crash ahead, and a dense cloud billowed forward. Tara and Greg emerged, running hard in my direction.

"We stalled him for moment!" cried Tara.

"We caved in the passage on him," said Greg, "but that won't hold him for long. We've got to fall back."

"'Fall back?'" I demanded as my staff finished rebooting and rematerialized in my hand. "What do you mean 'fall back'?"

"Run!" cried Greg.

"Run for your life!" yelled Tara as she dashed past us, the Doppler effect making her voice tinny as she shot ahead down the passage and away from us.

We ran. It was no orderly retreat, nor was it a timely fall back to marshal our forces. We flat out ran for our lives. We were terrified to our very marrow.

Metaheroes are not supposed to run. That is what all the television shows, movies, comics, and web serials tell us. We are supposed to bravely stand against impossible odds, holding out for a miracle, somehow saving the day at the last possible moment.

Bollocks.

Ninety-nine percent of the time, that is an accurate description of what we would do. Then, there's the exception. That is when you run. And we ran exceptionally fast. In all fairness, I never knew a man with a fake leg could run that quickly—Greg could really move when properly motivated.

Behind us, there was a rumble as the leviathan prime began to free itself from the avalanche that had pinned him down. We felt a sickening tremor ripple beneath us as the monster shifted untold tons of earth and stone.

You might judge us harshly. Go ahead, because I am not here to earn your praise—I am here to save your life. Those Thothbots that Greg threw at the behemoth? Just one of those robots wiped the streets with the Utopian, probably the strongest hero in the city and one of the most powerful metas in the world. This monster apparently ate giant robots for breakfast, followed by a hot lunch of giant robots. This was no joke, and if our little group did not get a break then we were going to die very soon.

The passage narrowed to single file, and we had to stoop as we ran. It emptied into a round chamber. There were no other exits. We were trapped.

This was it. Game over.

———

"Tara," said Greg, "you've got a teleporter, right? You can teleport us out of here!"

Tara looked a bit abashed. "Sorry, Greg. We are just too deep underground. The signal cannot lock onto us this far down in the bedrock."

Greg turned to me. "Victoria, can you blast us an exit? Can your staff do that?"

"I am sorry, Greg. I'm on backup power here. We're too deep to access my primary power source in my satellite. I've got an internet connection, but that's it."

"Greg, what about your perspective bending knife?" I said. "With its power to let you jump from one corner to another corner somewhere else, we could escape here."

"I don't have it on me," said Greg. "I left it with the Tailor to study."

"Great," I said.

Greg's shoulders slumped, and suddenly he did not look much like a metahero anymore. He looked tired, like a man who had been through too much, seen too much. He appeared defeated, and even fragile. Suddenly my heart swelled for him, and I loved him more than I had ever loved anyone.

"Victoria," he said, "we need a miracle. I know you can make that happen because you're just that smart. Get Tara, Eustace, and yourself out of here."

"Greg?" I said.

"I am going back down that hall, and I am going to buy you time."

I was getting angry. I did not need a man playing hero to save me.

I was the hero!

Greg grabbed me and kissed me hard on the mouth, cutting off my angry retort.

"Metaheroes don't get retirement plans," Greg said to me quietly, and our eyes locked together.

Good lord, what a man.

A rumble reverberated through the rock beneath our feet; the leviathan prime was working itself free. Our time had just about run out.

Greg turned and faced the door we had used to enter this chamber, and he pulled back his coat sleeve and exposed his left bracer with the thothtech script etched on it.

"Stay back," he said. "I'm going to try something. The last time I tried this I blew myself out the window, so there is just no way of knowing what will happen when I try this again." His right hand swiped across the machine's letters as if he was paging through a smart phone's options.

A heavy suit of armor popped up from nothingness and clamped around Greg, piece by piece. If you blinked, you would have missed the transformation. There was a thick, metallic Saturn symbol on his chest plate. Greg had been replaced with an eight-foot-tall, steel-plated knight with cannons mounted on his shoulders and forearms.

"Yes!" yelled Greg, clearly elated by what he had done. His voice sounded a little muffled from inside the huge helmet he now wore.

"I knew it was possible. Now I'm wearing a version of the Thothbot. It's a wearable robot or power suit! I can fight a hell of a lot better than that stupid robot can on its own."

Greg turned to go down the hall and make his final stand when Tara stepped next to him.

"You're not getting your 'Butch Cassidy and the Sundance Kid' moment alone, you imbecile," said Tara. Her plasma guns whined as they powered up, and her eyes were backlighted by intense blue light. From what I had seen, her eyes only did this when she booted up and drew upon the crystal skull computer in her head.

Greg and Tara looked each other in the eye for a moment, and then both nodded to each other in solidarity. Greg marched down the hall, away from our chamber, and Tara followed behind. Somewhere in the distance there was an explosion, and we knew the leviathan prime was free and ready to end this.

———

"Victoria!" cried Eustace. "This isn't just any chamber. It is the heart of the stargate!" He seemed delighted by this discovery.

I will admit I did not know what the heart of a stargate looked like; I did not know stargates even had hearts. There was not much time to wonder about it because the rumbling cacophony of earth being moved was growing closer. The leviathan prime could not fit down the passage we had passed through, so he was gouging his own tunnel from the rock. The room shuddered with percussive waves from below, and I somehow knew Greg and Tara had met the monster head on.

"Victoria, can you see electromagnetic waves?"

"Just a moment," I said. Using the advanced retina-read screen I had installed in my goggles a while back, I activated my multispectral vision enhancements application.

"Oh my," I said.

As I mentioned, the chamber was originally round. At each of the four cardinal points stood a yard-high stone box or altar each mounted with a small crystal pyramid. The boxes themselves were three-sided, being open and hollow on their fourth sides. Modern Egyptologists classified these three-sided boxes as shrines, but some non-mainstream schools of thought claimed these were housings for unknown power sources or perhaps capacitors in their own right. The crystal pyramids that capped the boxes were something else entirely.

Now the chamber's floor and curved walls were cracked, and two of the shrines had fallen over, toppling their crystal capstones to the ground. My best guess was a prehistoric earthquake had done this. On an electromagnetic level, all four points in the wall radiated powerful signals, but all the emanations clashed badly with each other, making an ugly, disharmonious pattern. Every few seconds, one of the fallen pyramids arced with otherwise invisible power, and the broken currents erupted into a fractured web of energy.

It took a moment, but I finally understood what I was seeing.

We had discovered the mega-stargate's power source, and it was the earth itself. The geomantic forces that fed the gate used to be called ley lines, but now we understood them as energy leaking through seismic fault lines deep in the ground. The ancients understood ley lines and how to tap them for energy, but that technology was lost along with most other antediluvian knowledge. Well into known history, though, people had a habit of locating churches and temples along these lines, choosing their locations more by primordial instinct than knowledge of ley lines and their use.

Spire City, it seemed, was located on a major ley line junction. The earth energies that should have fed the city, its peoples, and its very history was shorting out and malfunctioning. What we had here was the most cataclysmically bad feng shui ever. Now I knew why this city was a trouble magnet. This is why misery upon disaster upon cataclysm had visited our hapless town. Ours truly was the city of the broken gate.

Down the hall, we heard Tara's amplified voice yelling in a forgotten language. I believe she was ordering the leviathan to back down, to trick it into compliance with Atlantean orders. A succession of thundering booms and a blast of hot, dusty air down the passage indicated this tactic had failed.

"Showtime," I said.

I knew how to fix our problem.

Spire City's psychic pipes were clogged, and I had been chosen as the plumber. Using my staff's tractor beam, I set about moving the chamber's cardinal shrines back into place, and then more gently the crystal pyramids that mounted each. This was a delicate operation because I did not dare break any of the crystal pyramid capstones. It was a miracle they had survived down through the ages as it was.

Greg stumbled back into the power chamber. He was filthy, his power armor gone, and he dragged Tara with him. Tara had several broken limbs, a missing foot, and some gashes to her skin that extended from her face to her ribs. Little broken doll. I almost felt sorry for her, but I knew she could be repaired later if she survived.

"The Thothbot armor pissed the monster off," said Greg. "I think we insulted him."

Tara wriggled free of Greg's grip, and she began a sort of hopping-hobbling combination move. "I thought the Atlantean commands would have an effect," said Tara.

"They did," said Greg.

"Yes," said Tara. "The creature thought we were disrespecting its original masters, blaspheming or something."

The chamber violently shook for a moment, and dust and small pebbles broke free of the walls and ceiling and rained down on us.

When I moved the last crystal capstone back into place, the room erupted into beautiful, magnetic harmony. The four electromagnetic waves wove together to make a mesmerizing pattern. It reminded me of a Buddhist sand mandala I had seen. With a last little bit of tuning, the whole magnetic pattern resolved into an elegant recursive shape, a fractal configuration that would repeat through every scale up and down the spectrum forever.

I believe Greg was the only member of our dysfunctional quartet who could not see magnetic waves, but even he was awed by flashes of color and the crystal capstone's flickering power bleeds that reminded me of Saint Elmo's fire.

The chamber walls above the exit cracked open, and a huge, black, clawed hand reached into the new fissure to leverage the stone walls apart.

"Victoria, my dear," said Eustice. "I don't want to tell you your business, me not being a metahero like you are, but..."

"But what, Eustice?"

"Could you perhaps tap into this newfound energy and use it?"

"Of course, Dr. Freemantle," I said, dialing into the magnetic pattern with my staff, letting the power build as the staff's batteries absorbed it.

"Now would be a good time, dear," said Eustace."Not yet," I said. The energy was intense, and my staff began to shake in my hand.

Rocks rained down around us, and an opaque eye peered at us through a giant hole in the wall.

"Pathetic humans!" bellowed the impossibly loud leviathan prime. "You have blasphemed against the elder peoples repeatedly, and now you will pay for your crime!"

Honestly, the monster was so loud I was surprised I could still hear anything."Victoria," said Greg. "If you intend to do something, now would be a good time."

"Hold on!" I yelled.

The staff had grown painfully hot in my hands, and it flashed with an alarming series of multicolored electric discharges. Sparks flew, and electricity danced up and down its shaft as I held my ground. I had not built it to function so far beyond its intended tolerances, so we were just about to find out just how good of an engineer I was.

"Wait for it... wait," I yelled above screaming electric buzzing.

The wall crumbled, and the leviathan prime raised its fists to smash us.

It never got the chance. My opening had come, and I cut loose with a massive torrent of raw power.

Have you ever seen lightning hit a transformer, with its burst of blinding white light and cascades of sparks flying everywhere? Or a pipeline explode, with flames reaching so high into the sky people in nearby states could see the fire's glow against the clouds? It was like that, only much more intense.

A dozen simultaneous bolts of lightning all woven together into a megabolt ripped into the leviathan, and it lurched back.

This time when it was hit, the monster's wounds did not instantly close again. I blew off huge chunks of the monster's anatomy, and he was not going to grow these parts back anytime soon.

The leviathan prime was stunned into inaction for a moment, then he began to shake it off and realize the severity of his injuries."

"But—but," he said, clearly flummoxed. Somehow, with only one leg and one partial arm left intact, the leviathan prime made a speedy retreat. It drug its burning, lacerated body along the ground, part crawling, part squirming as it fled. Rocks melted into smoking slag wherever its midnight black blood splashed.

———

A long moment passed, and I realized I had lost consciousness for a short while. Our little group was still in the heart of the stargate, and Greg and Eustice were busy bandaging my arms. The feedback from my blast had knocked me out, and I had burns on my hands where I had grasped my staff and on my feet where I had been grounded. My boots were insulated, but they weren't made for this kind of punishment.

"I don't think the damage is permanent," said Greg with a smile, "but you do need to see a doctor."

"Oh," I said groggily, trying to get my bearings.

"Don't worry, dear," said Eustace. "Your eyebrows should grow back in time."

"Eyebrows?" I asked. Where was my staff?

The staff was ruined. It was too damaged to dematerialize, and its circuitry was smoking. I was okay with this. I could always build a new staff, and I already had a laundry list of tweaks and improvements I was planning to make to it in its next version.

Tara slumped against one of the chamber's remaining round walls. Her repair protocols had already activated, and her burned and slashed chassis was being reconstructed, as well as her broken limbs. It was strangely fascinating because she was in no apparent distress, and she was content for the moment to wait for her damaged systems to be repaired. There was not much she could do for her missing foot until she got access to the right raw materials.

"Do you realize what you have done?" asked Dr. Eustace Freemantle. "You fixed the city above. Spire City's days of being a disaster magnet are over. It will no longer be a hub in the wheels of terrorist attacks, natural disasters, giant invisible robots, Nazi war criminals, or whatever. Bad things can still happen, but no more than would happen to any other major city."

"We may have put ourselves out of the metahero job," said Greg, followed by a rueful laugh.

"Not our luck, I'm afraid," I said. "No one gets out alive from being a metahero."

———

Life in Spire City took an upswing after this. The city still struggled with the standard Midwestern urban issues, such as the high cost of living, crime, and graft, but gone were the days when primordial goddesses tried to re-write the city, giant zeppelins rained down death from above, or colossal demons left long trails of total destruction. Crime wars became more uncommon; cyborgs stopped hunting mole people beneath the streets; and rogue metahumans stopped knocking down skyscrapers for mega-rituals.

Greg and I finished deciphering the thothtech alphabet, and the possibilities seemed limitless. For whatever reason, Tara decided against tying us up in court over the so-called proprietary knowledge we had collected. I am not sure why she changed her mind because she could have made our lives hell and cost us a fortune in attorney fees. I think she would have come down on us hard if we had attempted to take the thothtech public, but, as it was, we reserved it for our private use.

I built a new power staff to replace my old one, and this time I worked quite a bit of the thothtech into its design. I also included a few new automated features, as well as a low-level artificial intelligence with a tactical simulator to help me optimize the staff in combat. In the meantime, I recovered from my burns and bruises quite well, and my eyebrows slowly grew back.

The new Dr. Eustace Freemantle did not come to the surface world with us. He was, after all, not the same Eustace I had known, and our world was not his. Rather, he opted to stay with the megastargate's heart, and when the stars lined up again in another five-and-a-half months he intended to use the local stargate to leave the planet and explore the galaxy.

"I've never been off Earth," said Eustace. "My asvin was built here, and I only knew about the greater wonders of the universe through her memory banks. Now, by a weird quirk of fate, my asvin is gone, but I persist. There's nothing to keep me here any longer, and I yearn for the stars."

When Eustace and I said our goodbyes, I hugged him hard, and I might have shed a few tears. He may have been a holographic simulation of my mentor, but to me he was Dr. Eustace Freemantle in all the ways that truly mattered.

―――――

This is the part of the narrative where I am supposed to explain how this experience changed me. You have heard all that "heroes' journey" coming–of-age stuff before, so I will not insult your intelligence with that. Truthfully, my life went on pretty much as it had before—we are metaheroes, and lasting change comes to us with glacial slowness.

I did come away from the journey with a newfound respect for Dr. Eustace Freemantle and his scholarship. I already had known he was a great man, but his more outré ideas now impressed me more than ever. He had discovered marvelous things, and now I wondered if the next stage of human evolution might be jump started by rediscovering the wisdom and technologies of the ancients, much as Europe had been vaulted from the Middle Ages into the Renaissance by the rediscovery of the works of the classical Greek thinkers. Maybe now, it was time for mankind to rejoin the intergalactic Pangea that had once existed. The future is a land of shadows and fear, and yet I could not help but hope for a brighter day on the horizon.

Our beginnings are always with us, guiding us for good or ill, and maybe it was high time for humanity to shake off our collective denial, cast aside our communal amnesia, and take our rightful place among the stars.

―――――

Out in Sorrow Bay, the leviathan prime bided its time, regenerating all the damage it had suffered. It took years to reform, but that was no surprise. The humans had effectively hit it with the raw power of Planet Earth. The creature would not underestimate them again.

Leviathan prime floated to the surface of the lake, and it looked around at the night time sky and horizon. To the north stood Spire City, gaudily glowing until its light pollution blotted out the stars. The creature's beady black eyes narrowed in hate, then it slowly settled back into its healing sleep. Someday, no matter how many eons it took, he would make the humans and the city pay for their blasphemy.

LE BEAU MONDE

In Spire City's Ashley Park District at Willow Street, there was a lovely little combination tea shop and sidewalk café called the Le Beau Monde. None of its furniture or fixtures matched, granting it a lived-in ambiance, and patrons loved to gather there for its salon-like atmosphere of good-natured conversations and friendly debates. It was also a place where hipsters gathered for private, after-hours parties to drink dangerously excessive quantities of the rarest and most expensive teas they could afford, and their caffeine highs became so intense that the imbibers sometimes had out-of-body experiences or otherworldly visions. Those teas were not on the regular menu, but even the usual stuff came in a wide variety that ranged from the affordable to the outlandishly expensive. The pastries were tasty too, and everyone was welcome at the Le Beau Monde.

Mark Cassaday sat alone at one of the curbside tables, enjoying his tea. He was tall, devilishly handsome, with an athletic build and a stalking panther's grace. His long, dark hair was swept to one side, giving him more than a hint of the Byronesque. Mark wore military-grade combat boots, black cargo pants, and a black shirt to match. He had left his trench coat and hat on a nearby hat stand. The afternoon air was chilly, but it had been a long time since Mark had felt cold.

Mark was enjoying some Irish Breakfast tea. It was not expensive, but it was what his father used to drink, and now Mark did too. It had been almost 80 years since he had seen his father in life, but Mark felt closer to his dad now than he had in a long time.

It was May 5 of 2019, and spring was unfolding in northern Illinois. The Le Beau Monde was quiet at the moment, but any time now the lunch crowd would begin arriving. Street noise was intermittent at worst, and Mark enjoyed his moment of peace and reflection.

Mark was waiting for his date, and soon his patience was rewarded.

———

Leonora "Lea" Bonds arrived with two bodyguards in tow. She actually did not need them for protection so much as for crowd control, should the need present itself. One guard stayed in the cafe at another table, and the other man took up a position on the sidewalk beyond.

Ms. Bonds wore long gloves, a broad-brimmed summer hat, and overly large sunglasses. It was a poor disguise, thought Mark because anyone who got a good look at her fiery-hued skin immediately would recognize who she was. Her complexion was orange—not like someone who used too much bottle tanning lotion, but a vibrant orange, like no natural human skin. Her face and figure would have been beautiful on most women, but on Leanora, they oozed heart-thumping sex appeal. She seemed less real than a guilty pleasure on the eyes.

She's like a Vargas or Elvgrin painting made real, mused Mark to himself.

Leanora was a true double-trouble celebrity. On one side, she was a famous metahero called Torchsong, a flame-throwing, jet-powered heroine and a prominent member of the Squadron Premiere. Among her many powers, she could fly and toss fireballs, and her bright red hair flickered into living flame whenever she fired up. Her service record was exemplary, and her metahero pedigree ran deep, for she had followed in her father's and grandfather's fiery legacy.

Lea was not just a superhero, she was also an iconic and well-known recording artist self-named I-Kandi. She regularly sold-out arenas and her face on magazine covers boosted circulation by tens of thousands of copies. For the last twenty years, Lea had promoted her personal brand with provocation and shock, using nudity, profanity, and sexual antics to stay relevant and to question consensus views on morality. She may have been a singer with over twelve top ten songs on the pop charts, but she knew how to stir the pot by kissing women onstage, posing for coffee table books of aggressive nude photos, and mixing sacred symbols with bondage-themed costumes onstage and in music videos. She had long ago mastered the game of self-promotion and market penetration.

"Mr. Cassaday, it's such a pleasure to meet you, finally," Lea said as Mark rose and pulled out a chair for her. It was not Mark's nature to be so gallant, but this time was different. He was indifferent to pop culture, but even he had heard of Torchsong and I-Kandi.

"It's my pleasure," Mark said. "Your grandfather was a buddy of mine, back in my first life."

They sat, and the waiter brought Lea her tea of choice, the fabulously pricey Silver Tips Imperial, as well as more hot water for Mark.

"Grandfather died before I was born," said Lea, "so I take every chance I can to learn more about him."

"Disappeared," said Mark. "He disappeared. You can never count out a wily old bastard like him till you see the body. And, even then…"

"Disappeared," said Lea with a smile.

"I never saw him age. He may have, but I knew him for years and he never appreciably changed. Plus, dead metaheroes have a disturbing habit of not taking death seriously and reappearing. It seems to happen all the time, as though it were a publicity stunt or something."

"Like you did, Mr. Cassaday?"

"Sort of," said Mark. He did not want to discuss it and was eager to close this line of conversation down. "I'm an unusual case. But please call me Mark."

"Fair enough," she said.

"Tell me, Mark, how did you first meet my grandfather? What kind of partnership did you have? I've read so much about the Golden Age of Metaheroes, and most of it doesn't make sense. Most of the accounts were written second-hand, and the comic book versions were dreadful. The movies and television shows are just as bad."

"What do the history books say about the so-called Golden Age?" asked Mark.

"You know, the usual stuff. It was made up of lots of laconic, lantern-jawed, broad-shouldered white men parading around in tights. All these vanilla heroes had the same bland personality, and they were all cut from good moral fiber. Good always defeated evil. Metaheroes never fought each other, and their adventures were tidy, short, and ended decisively. The villains were robots, evil scientists, spies, crooks, and pretty much anything but metavillians. You know the stories, right?"

Mark chuckled, then he took a sip of his tea.

"I assume you know that none of that is true. The comic books were written as dumbed-down morality tales for twelve-year-old boys as the target audience. Your own metahero career should clue you in about all the wildly untrue crap they write about us."

Lea smiled impishly. "If the press only knew what actually goes on. Or what my hobbies are." As she spoke, her knee touched Mark's leg, and he didn't recoil or move it. Mark did not acknowledge the touch, but an unmistakable charge zapped between the two of them. He had heard rumors about Lea, and the antics she entertained herself with when she stayed at the infamous Archimedes Club.

"My mystery man career got going in 1947 after I recovered from some serious injuries I suffered in the last days of World War II. I arguably was the first mystery man."

"There was Elect," said Lea. "He already had been active back East since the late thirties."

Mark made a dismissive harrumphing sound, then said, "I always try to forget that self-important dumbshit. He certainly was no rough-and-tumble, street-level mystery man. He was more like a culturally insensitive god taking a working holiday among the unwashed masses."

"I've met him," said Lea. "He's bigger than life, and a little arrogant, but he impressed me as an okay sort."

CANDLEMAN

"'Bigger than life.' Bah." Mark collected himself then and took his story back up.

––––––––

"Your grandfather, Candle Man, entered the mystery man scene here in Spire City soon after I did, but I did not encounter him until 1949. His powers and flashy, orange costume made a big impression on people, and he battled monsters, demons, giant robots, you name it. I maybe was the first mystery man, but the only people who knew about me were the ones I saved and criminals I thwarted. Oh, and all corrupt judges, slum lords, counterfeiters, Soviet spies, assorted criminals, and crooked cops. Those were very different times, and without social media, cameras in every phone and street, or DNA evidence, it was possible to keep a low profile."

"Did you know much about Candle Man at that point?" asked Lea.

"Sure. I was a newsman. When Candle Man made his debut, he was all we wrote about for months. He was flamboyant, photogenic, and all his deeds were big and showy."

The waiter brought them more hot water, and they made fresh tea. Mark had had enough caffeine by this point that he believed he might imitate an incandescent bulb and begin to glow spontaneously. He felt as if he were trying to vibrate into a higher dimension.

"Were you called Hexagon back then?" asked Lea.

"No, dear. Hexagon became my working name in my second life. Back then, I was Saturnas, the Man of Saturn. I appeared pretty much the same as Hexagon does now, with the trench coat, fedora, mask, and knuckle dusters. Nowadays I've got Kevlar, and ballistic plates worked into my clothes, and a battle engine installed in my brain, but I'm not much different now than then.

"Spire City's crime lord in those days was Mr. Osiris. During the war, he had been one of the Nazi's leading operators in Cairo, and our first encounter cost him his right eye. Then he had made his way to America, and he had built a criminal empire based on stolen antiquities. I'm not sure if you've ever heard of Mr. Osiris before, but back then he was still a mortal man. Later, he took up sorcery, and our rivalry became the stuff of nightmares.

"But, back to the story. I had been gathering information on Mr. Osiris' gang for a while, and setting up the rival crime lords to oust him. It was not hard to arrange. As a reporter, I wrote articles that fed the fires of tension in the criminal community, and as Saturnus I preyed on street thugs and made it look like rival gangs were making moves on each other. I had plans to bring down the whole organized crime establishment at one time because stopping them and their money would end a lot of the crazy corruption that was tearing the city to pieces. It was an audacious move, I will admit. I believed I was the only one with the vision and cunning to make it happen."

"You must be a master at chess," said Lea.

"Ha," said Mark with a self-satisfied smirk. He loved to talk about his favorite subject—himself!

"If you don't have powers, you have to be smarter than your powered opponents. For example, do you know how to beat a metaspeedster? You might think it impossible because they can move so quickly! They can counter your every move, and an eye blink to us is minutes to them. But, you can defeat them. If you plan the fight, pick the location, and think out all the contingencies, you can beat a speedster to every punch. You cannot do it faster, but you can do it first. It's the same principle here. I was just a normal, non-powered guy, so I had to plan five or six moves ahead."

"I'm pretty sure you've never been normal a day in your life," said Lea, rubbing her knee against Mark's thigh.

Mark continued.

"That's when your grandfather showed up and threatened to derail my plans.

"Back in the forties, most criminal business took place on the docks, as well as the train yards southwest of the city. Spire City was still America's primary railway hub, or at least it was in the years before Chicago took that prize for itself. Hundreds of railroad lines converged here, as well as scores of railway roundhouses with their turntables, warehouses, and ramshackle offices. The railyards were ugly even then, covered in ash, and only weeds grew there. Cats, and the rats they fed on made up most of its ecosystem, and it was inhabited by bums, hobos, never-do-wells, and working-class lugs. It was hot, and it smelled atrocious.

"I felt right at home there.

"On the night in question, I was there searching for Mr. Osiris' henchmen, but what I found in an old, grimy roundhouse was your grandfather standing over Mr. Osiris himself. Your grandfather had separated the crime boss from his men, knocked him out, cuffed him, and tied him at the ankles. Candle Man was about to kick over all the dominoes I had set up over the last months!

"Candle Man was a real show stopper. He was a stirring figure to behold, tall, broad-shouldered, resolute, and all that. He also floated about a foot above the floor, as if physics were just too mean and inconsequential to worry an important guy like him. His uniform was similar to an aviator's, but all orange and brown, with goggles and a lighted candle emblem on his chest. That was a classy get-up, and your grandfather made it look great. It made me feel pretty shabby, in my beat-up fedora, trench coat, leather gloves, and mask.

"Nearby Candle Man, floating on its own, was a lighted candle nestled in the type of candlestick holder you could easily carry with the finger ring on one side. The candle flame somehow was bright enough to illuminate the whole roundhouse, yet not too bright to look at directly. Magic, I assume."

"Wow, just wow!" said Lea. She was fascinated, and she had moved her chair closer to Mark's. "My powers are different from Dad's, and his powers were different from Grandfather's. This is great stuff to know!"

"Candle Man's eyes fastened on me right away. I think he saw everything in the candle's spectral radiance. That was my impression, anyway.

"'Stop right there, citizen,' Candle Man commanded. His delivery was without irony or a self-conscious wink, so he probably did not know just how over the top and silly he sounded.

"'Listen up, you flaming fat-head,' I said, as I approached Candle Man and his prisoner. 'You need to haul ass out of here because you are messing with an operation I've been working on for a long time now. If you take that man into custody, then you'll ruin everything.' From what I could tell, Mr. Osiris was out cold, and there was a huge, purple welt rising on the side of his bald head. I knew the bastard was still alive because dead men do not bruise.

"'Hold up,' said Candle Man, turning away from me and addressing his floating candle. 'Candle, can you identify this newcomer?'

"Things had just taken a left turn into weirdsville! This guy talked to candles!"

"'Certainly,' said the floating candle in a ghostly, hollow voice that seemed to project from everywhere and nowhere at once. I was used to some pretty strange stuff, but a talking inanimate object was a new one for me. I cannot explain it, but this really creeped me out."

"Creeped out?" asked Lea. "You don't strike me as scared of anything."

"You would be wrong, my dear. I was scared all the time. Paranoia was the only thing that kept me alive through the war. Well, that and a whole lot of stubbornness and a twitchy trigger finger.

"'This subject,' continued the floating candle in its spectral voice, 'is the mystery man known as Saturnus. He fights organized crime here in Spire City. He should be considered resourceful and very dangerous.'

"'Ah, thank you, Candle,' said Candle Man. He did not seem impressed with me.

"'I'm sorry that I've wandered into your turf, Saturnus. But, this man is a dangerous, wanted felon, and it is my job to clean up Spire City. I got to him first. Better luck next time, eh?'

"By now, I had moved close enough to Candle Man and his captive that I could speak without raising my voice.

"'You don't understand what's at stake, Candle Man. If you turn Mr. Osiris in, you really will spoil everything. I've got the dominoes lined up to knock down organized crime, but it all hinges on this particular game piece. The only thing you would accomplish by taking him off the street is to create a power vacuum for the other crime bosses to fight over, and this city would burn in the crime war that followed. Leave now, and leave Mr. Osiris behind, before it is too late.'"

Candle Man shot me the same glare he otherwise might have reserved for a babbling simpleton.

"'Pretty words,' said the floating hero, 'but I'm not buying.'"

I whipped out my Luger pistols and aimed them at Candle Man. I was not in the mood to argue, and I sure was not going to compromise.

"'Time to reconsider, glow boy!' I said. 'Fly away now, or I'm starting with your kneecaps and working my way up. There are too many innocent lives at stake for me to back down.'

"The floating candle popped off a little spit of fire, and that bloomed into a fireball that roasted the floor where I had just been standing. I had rolled clear and simultaneously fired both guns as I vaulted through the air.

"My bullets got within a few yards of Candle Man before they flamed out and vaporized.

"I was severely outgunned. It was as if I were a rowboat trying to take out a destroyer!

"I finished my roll with a vault forward—it was time to see if Candle Man also was shielded from my fists!

"As it turns out, he was.

"I was blown back by a superheated wall of pressure that was a reasonable facsimile of a small bomb detonation. If I had not been wearing my mask, then I am sure my eyebrows would have been singed off! Attitude will only get you so far, the same then as now.

"I landed flat on my back, hard. The air had been knocked out of me, and I knew I was going to be feeling that one for days. I rolled onto my side, got my legs beneath me, and managed to climb back to my feet as I painfully gasped for breath.

"'Enough,' said Candle Man. 'I don't need my powers to take down a punk like you!'

"'What?' I said, almost disbelieving my luck. Candle Man had raised his fists and assumed a boxer's stance. Could he possibly believe that he was going to take me out mano a mano? As an Irish-Italian lad I had grown up as a hard-scrabble street fighter on the dangerously violent streets of Spire City, then I had trained with the United States Army, then the French Foreign Legion, and then finally with the Office of Strategic Services. I almost felt a little guilty for the punishment this metahero had coming. Almost.

"I was still wobbly from the body blow I'd just taken, but even then it was not too hard to bob and weave out of the way of Candle Man's flying fists. I blocked his well-telegraphed blows with my arms and open palms, but I barely used the fancy footwork I was known for, and I had not yet bothered to strike back.

"'Are you sure you don't want to rethink this?' I asked.

"'You puffed up sonovabitch!' said Candle Man.

"Great. Now Candle Man was red-faced with anger as if I had insulted his manhood or something. Maybe he knew he was outclassed, or he thought I was not taking his attacks seriously. The hero redoubled his efforts, and I knew then that I had no choice. I was going to have to drop him. I did not want to hurt him—not too much, anyway—but he was going down. The only thing that could save him now was a freak of fate or a deus ex machina.

"The freak of fate won out.

"Mr. Osiris had regained consciousness during the struggle. I had not seen him wake up, but, even though he was bound hand and foot, he had jammed his heels against the floor, triggering a secret razor in his boots. Then the crafty bastard kicked me in the leg."

"Nasty!" said Lea.

"It was one of those old-school spy tricks, stuff Mr. Osiris had learned while working for the Nazis. Secret weapons like that could mean the difference between life and death. I took a gash to my right calf, and, while it was not a severe wound, it certainly caught my attention.

"'Dammit!' I cursed, then jumped out of Mr. Osiris' range and swung my now divided attention back to Candle Man.

"'Too late.

"Candle Man was a naive fighter, but his jab to the side of my head was very . . . earnest. The sonovagun knew how to throw a punch like he meant it!

"I collapsed into a nearby pile of scrap metal, and only kept from falling all the way to the ground by grabbing a convenient welding table with both hands. Flukes like this were the reason even the best fighters cannot take for granted the seemingly inevitable outcome of a battle. I had been full of myself and my skill, and I had my ass handed to me for it. The old 'fog of war' cliché may seem hackneyed, but it is true.

"'Get up, Saturnus!' said Candle Man. 'I'm not done with you yet! I am going to teach you a lesson you won't soon forget!' It seemed Candle Man had learned his dialogue from the Saturday Matinee serials—what a cornball!"

"Cornball?" asked Lea

"Ah, you know. Someone that has a high opinion of themselves and who doesn't realize when they sound silly."

"So, you are telling me that my grandfather kicked your butt?" Lea sounded amazed, but also as if she was having a silent laugh at Mark's expense.

"Yeah," he said.

"I was mad now. I stumbled to my feet, and I raised my fists. I was still wobbly, but I paid that no mind. I was more pissed that I was bleeding into my boot from Mr. Osiris' sneak attack. It had been a stupid, avoidable wound, and I was lucky the blade had not been poisoned. I also was embarrassed by my comeuppance from Candle Man.

"Candle Man's punches came pounding down like a hail storm with anger management issues, but I blocked them all. I could see his blows coming from a mile off, and I did not need any of my patent combination strikes to finish this. My right fist shot through Candle Man's guard and exploded on his chin like a cannonball. His head snapped back, and his knees buckled. I had not hit him all that hard, at least not by my standards, but Candle Man hit the floor like a sack of wet concrete. His magic candle disappeared instantly."

"Heroes are not supposed to fight heroes," said Lea with playfulness in her eyes. "Anyone who watches cartoons knows that."

"Right," Mark said, but he dragged it out into a long, doubting "riii-iiight."

"I cannot believe you punched out my grandfather!" said Lea. "You two were supposed to be best friends, crime-fighting partners, and two of the founding members of the Vigilante Association, the first metahero group in the world."

"That all came later," Mark said, after which he downed another cup of tea.

"So, did you leave my grandfather there, in the train house?" asked Lea.

"No, he would not have been safe there. I really did not wish him harm, you know. Instead, I threw him over my shoulder, found a train car I could stash him on, and hid him there. I let the yard bull know that Candle Man was there, and tipped the fellow a twenty to keep an eye on him."

"Yard bull?"

"The old train yards had security guys to keep hobos off the trains. Yard bulls."

"Wow," said Lea.

"I imagine Candle Man came to his senses about the time his train rolled into St. Louis."

"What about his floating candle?"

"It had faded out the moment knocked out Candle Man."

"Weird," said Lea. "And what about Mr. Osiris?"

"I knocked him back out with a right jab, then picked his cuffs and left him in the train shed. He was in his own territory, so it was unlikely that anything would happen to him. Leaving him with a dislocated jaw was my payback for the cut he had given me."

"Crazy," said Lea. "Did your plan work? Did you knock out Spire City's crime network?" Lea's face had drawn close to Mark's so that by now they were both shaded by her hat's wide brim. Her perfume, he decided, was rather... compelling.

"It did work. The peace lasted for several years. It took a long time for organized crime to rebuild here."

"And my grandfather?"

"Later, he and I ended up working together. We became friends. I was best man at his wedding, and he was at mine. I even taught him how to really fight, although that took a while."

Lea leaned in for a kiss, and a jolt of lightning shot through Mark's abdomen as her hand moved up his leg and onto his crotch. She knew what she wanted, and Mark could respect that.

"Let's get out of here," Lea whispered in Mark's ear. "I've got an apartment a few blocks away."

As the two rose to leave, Mark Cassaday figured he would have to visit the Le Beau Monde more often. That was some damn tasty tea!

A QUICK FAVOR PLEASE

Before you go can I ask you for a quick review?

Would you please leave this book a review on Amazon?

Reviews are very important for authors, as they help us sell more books. This will in turn enable me to write more books for you.

So, please do me a great favor and leave a review today using whatever platform you are reading on. It's quick and painless and will only take a second.

Thank you so much for reading, and thank you for being part of this adventure.

Scott A. Story and Benita G. Story

AUTHORS

Scott A. Story is a freelance illustrator and cartoonist who lives in the Midwestern USA. You can find more about him at www.scottastory.com and www.johnnysaturn.com. A good place to keep up with his publishing ventures is his Amazon author page.

Benita G. Story is a writer, educator, and expert in all thing's wool in the Midwestern USA. See more about her at www.thefiberpusher.com.

Story Studios is an umbrella for Scott and Benita's writing and art. To date they have published multiple graphic novels, numerous comic books, as well as posters, calendars, and more.